Love in the time of Britpop

Tim Woods

Set list

– Happy Again –

Rain slants my face as I head towards Sheffield station, adding new notes to the bouquet of wet tarmac. Streetlights illuminate each icy droplet hurtling towards me but the city looks better in this gloom, more like its natural self. It could almost double for Gotham – if Batman had a pot belly and a Blades shirt. Cold, windswept urbanity becomes the perfect backdrop for this significant step towards manhood.

My first proper affair.

If it counts as an affair. I'm single, after all. What does that make me: the affairee? I make a mental note to check with Rob when I get back; he's a philosophy student, he knows about these things.

Yet my excitement is overwhelmed by the gnawing awareness that what I am doing is wrong. Breaking up a relationship is not something to be proud of. Another thought that refuses to disappear is the distinct possibility that I'll be back in Sheffield before the evening is through. It's two days since she invited me to stay. Maybe she's changed her mind. Will she even remember? I've brought enough cash for two single train tickets, just in case. Buying a return seems like admitting defeat before I've set off.

This lack of certainty made packing tricky. Do I bring enough clothes for one night? One week? One hour? After much deliberation, I stuffed my battered old rucksack with two changes of underpants, a pair of socks, a toothbrush, a stick of deodorant and a spare T-shirt (the one with the cover from *All Change* on it; the first album I bought on CD, I'm hoping this might bring me some much-needed good karma).

The hardest decision was how many condoms to bring. Packing more than ten might look ambitious; bringing one might look cheap, or could be a disastrous miscalculation. I don't know if Grindleford has a shop where I can restock. Do village shops even sell condoms? It's in a National Park, after all. As a compromise, I've brought two packs of three with me. Five are in the rucksack and one is tucked in my wallet in case she pounces on me at the station. Which is unlikely, admittedly, but I'm a long way out of my comfort zone here.

'A single to Grindleford, please,' I say to the woman in the ticket office, handing over my student railcard.

'Grindleford is it, luv? Very nice, very nice,' she chuckles knowingly while pressing the buttons on her machine. A fresh tsunami of fear engulfs me: does she know what I'm up to? Is Grindleford the destination of choice for young philanderers? Maybe she's from Grindleford and will be ringing ahead to let them know there's another one heading their way.

I throw a handful of change at her and grab my ticket. She's still chortling as I scarper away. I scan the platform for anyone I know, desperate to avoid their inevitable scorn and disapproval. Only as the sodium glare of the platform lights fades from view do I manage to breathe normally. We trundle through the backstreets of Sheffield, and paranoia is finally nudged aside by a warm glow of satisfaction.

I'm off to meet the girl of a sizeable number of my dreams.

I'm going to her house, hopefully to get up to no good.

Seven weeks ago, we'd barely spoken. This is progress. Considerable progress.

I'm growing up.

Female Of The Species

There are times when I regret choosing geography. Now is one of those times. I'm stuck in an airless lecture theatre, hidden deep in the bowels of a vast concrete tower block, trying to make sense of the latest pointless subject to fly over my head. And Quaternary Paleoenvironments are a new low. I can't even work out what they are; the first lecture of term is half an hour old, and all I've written is the title, underlined three times. Below that, nothing; I haven't understood anything in enough detail to take notes. On the flip side, my sketch of a plate of baked beans is coming along nicely. The subtle shading gives the beans texture, and the bite mark on one corner of the toast is pleasingly realistic.

From my unforgiving wooden bench near the back, I check to see who else has turned up. Most faces I know; some from tutorials, others from six-a-side matches or after-lecture drinks. And, in the centre of the second row – same place as always – is Louise Banks. A sheet of black hair sweeps down her back, shimmering in the flickering strip lights. The slender gold bracelets on her wrist tap out a rhythm as she writes. And her tight-fitting cream sweater perfectly outlines her– no, no, don't stare, remember what your sister told you, girls don't like that.

She tucks a lock of hair behind one ear, then continues to scribble away, nodding occasionally as she absorbs every word spoken, every complex diagram beamed up from the overhead projector. Not only is she stunning, she's intelligent, witty, kind-hearted …

She might be, anyway. I don't actually know. Because despite spending two years on the same course, we've never spoken, for one reason or another. One reason being that I've never summoned up the courage to approach her, another being that she's never given the slightest indication of knowing who I am. Or caring.

The main reason, though, is sat next to her. Jonathan. According to department gossip, they share a flat off Ecclesall Road. Which he owns. Flash wanker; how many students have their own flat? Or move in with their girlfriend before they're twenty?

But it's time to rectify that. I set myself targets at the start of each year. Having a conversation with Louise Banks is one for this year. Talking to a girl my age could be described as a modest ambition – but she's no ordinary girl. She's the best-looking and most lusted-after one in the department. This will take courage, skill and luck. None of which I possess in huge quantities.

I return biro to notepad and draw glasses on one of the baked beans. Instantly, it's Graham Coxon. As I add a Gallagher-esque monobrow to another, Louise tucks her hair behind her ear again. Even this small act is a thing of grace and beauty. My twice-weekly opportunities to admire Louise Banks are a good reason for studying geography.

The only one, in fact.

* * *

One lecture ends and I head towards the geography department for the next: geographic information systems. Otherwise known as GIS. Otherwise known as drawing maps on computers. It sounds easy, which is how I prefer my courses. The campus overflows with student life, mostly first-years gathered in excitable clusters to chatter loudly about how many people they've slept with so far, or how pissed they got last night. But I'm a third year, such juvenile trivialities no longer matter. I saunter past, casually kicking a pebble as I go. After skilfully dribbling around a discarded crisp packet and befuddling a dandelion with a smart Cruyff turn, I hit a fierce pile-driver towards a dustbin – and it pings millimetres in front of the advancing Louise Banks.

'Shit, I'm really sorry.'

She glares at the offending pebble, now cowering behind a bin, before turning to me. From beneath two immaculately groomed eyebrows, the left of which is arching steeply, she fixes me with a look which, based on my limited understanding of females, I estimate as two percent surprise, five percent amusement and ninety-three percent contempt.

'Honestly, I'm really, really sorry.'

'You've already said that. Luckily it didn't hit me. If it had, you'd know about it, these boots are brand new.'

I stare at her boots, which look expensive, then back at her. Her gaze now rests on my battered old trainers, which I didn't get around to replacing during the holidays. The first trickles of sweat escape from beneath my fringe.

'Heading to the geography department?' she asks eventually, eyebrow slowly returning to its usual position.

I nod dumbly, unable to form actual words.

She sets off and, a couple of paces behind, I am faced once again with the paradox that has frustrated me since I first noticed girls. I desperately want to meet them – especially ones like her – and yet it is what I dread more than anything. Once past that initial encounter, I can usually bumble through, but those early moments still fill me with panic. It's the pressure of all the things they expect you to be – amusing but not infantile, interesting but not domineering, confident without straying into arrogance – but there's also the time

5

factor. You have to be all those things instantly. First impressions count and mine are pitiful.

The silence hangs between us: I need to think of something to say, and fast. Technically I've already ticked off my ambition of speaking to her, but it doesn't count; I only said eight words and three of them were 'really'. My eyes dart over the surrounding noticeboards, scouring them desperately for inspiration. But there's nothing useful, just brightly coloured posters promoting upcoming student nights. Written across them in huge purple letters is crude graffitied advice about what Sheffield Wednesday fans can do to themselves; a similar suggestion for the city's students covers the opposite side. Those won't work, either.

Up ahead, a group of students are holding up handmade signs with Coca-Cola logos on them, but it isn't clear if they're in favour of it or against. I decide to make an insightful comment about this, but before I've managed to think of one, she speaks.

'And, did you score?'

Score? In what sense? Drugs? Sex? It's unlikely that she has me down as a major player in either field.

'Your little game of pebble football back there. I assume you weren't actually aiming for me.'

'Oh, that. I guess so.'

'Congratulations.'

Silence. The onus back on me to break it.

'Do you, er, like football?'

'No. I went to an all-girls school, we played tennis and hockey.'

Silence again.

'I'm Chris, by the way.'

'I know.'

It's not a vast improvement, but I've got through a few sentences without apologising for anything. And she knows my name. This has to be a good sign.

We reach the geography department, a vulgar design of glass and pebble-dashed hexagons. I weigh up whether commenting on its ugliness will qualify as witty or astute, but she's already halfway up the steps. I follow her to the computer lab, still a few paces behind.

Professor Stafford perches cross-legged on a table. An intimidating tangle of grey hair encased in a sprawling green jumper, his eyes narrow as we enter. His expression is simple to read: one hundred percent scorn.

'Work in pairs,' he growls, 'two to a computer.'

Clearly, he doesn't trust us to grasp the concept of a pair. But this slight on my intelligence is swiftly forgotten, as Louise is already surveying the room. I know what she's doing: checking to see if there are better options than me. Normally there would be several, but my luck's in. Of the ten students present, eight are already in pairs, and of the other two, one is a creep and the other a weirdo.

'Do you want to work together, Chris?' she asks, not looking at me.

'Um, sure, thanks.'

'I'll get a handout.'

'Great, thanks.'

'Stop thanking me.'

'Sorry.'

'And stop apologising.'

We squeeze in next to each other and our machine whirrs lethargically to life, a white flash followed by a dark grey-green screen. As I type, Louise flicks through our worksheet. Her reflection is sharp in the convex screen, and I take advantage of a rare opportunity to admire the front, rather than the back,

7

of her head. It's even better up close; GIS is already proving an excellent choice.

Even our first exercise is mildly engaging, making maps to show the growth of New York over time. But as the minutes tick by, familiar anxieties resurface. The other pairs chat easily, but we work in silence. The clock ticks over to 11:40: I've got only ten minutes left to make a better impression than pebble-kicking mute.

'I've never been to New York,' I mutter. As chat-up lines go, it has limitations: short, uninteresting and pointing out something I haven't done. Still, it's one of my better efforts.

'Jonathan and I went in the summer,' she replies. 'We're thinking about moving there next year. He's planning on a political career in London in the long term, obviously, he's already got lots of useful contacts in the Labour Party.'

There's a lot to digest here.

First, she feels no need to explain who Jonathan is. She hasn't introduced herself, now I think about it. It must be great, the confidence that comes with being half of the department's alpha couple. And their expectations for post-university life differ wildly from mine. Their options are London or New York, presumably with high-flying, well-paid jobs in either; mine are Safeway in Tavistock or a few shifts in the village pub. We move in different worlds, and theirs sounds loads better.

'You should go,' she continues. 'The shops, the restaurants, the museums; everything actually, it's all fantastic.'

'Did you go anywhere else?'

'We were supposed to travel around New England, but Jonathan had to come back for some fucking Labour event,' she says, bitterly. 'I still haven't forgiven him.'

I'm shocked. Not by her anger – although it's intriguing to hear that not everything is rosy – but by the swearing. She seems far too graceful to curse, and certainly not one of the big ones. 'Fucking' sounds so much dirtier in her clipped tones, with all seven letters fully enunciated. It's how I imagine the Queen might pronounce it, should she opt to liven up her Christmas speech.

'Where have you travelled?' she asks.

I pause before answering. My only overseas experiences are the French Exchange at school, which doesn't count as it's only France, and a trip to Goa with Matt, my best friend in Devon. They were three weeks of utter hell.

'I spent the summer exploring India. It was awesome.'

'I'd love to go there,' she says, turning to me and, for the first time, smiling. I smile back, or at least try to; it's not easy to balance smiling with gawping. Her face is even more magnificent this close: flawless skin, the merest hint of makeup, thick eyelashes, a wispy grey beard and coffee-stained teeth ...

'Neither of you will be going anywhere if you don't get some work done. This assignment must be completed and handed in by Friday – *this* Friday – or it gets a zero. Two zeros and you fail the module, which means you'll resit it next summer. In Sheffield, not New York, India or anywhere else. So get on with it.'

Professor Stafford slips away as quickly as he arrived, and we share sheepish grins in the computer screen.

'Tut tut, Christopher. I've only known you for an hour and you're already getting me into trouble.'

'Sorry Louise.'

'It's Lou. Louise is for when I've been *really* naughty.'

She winks as she says this, which instantly turns 'naughty' into 'filthy' and conjures up all kinds of delicious mental images. Which was clearly her intention as, ever so gently, she nudges her leg against mine.

Then leaves it there.

We're touching at the knee. There's a full square centimetre of physical contact between us. Through incremental movements so tiny they can be denied if necessary, I reposition my foot so it touches hers. She doesn't move hers away.

This is unexpected, scary and hugely exciting. But the clock is ticking and I know, from every slushy film I've seen that this is it. The Moment. Carpe diem, as the Latins say. Fortune favours the brave, said someone else. (Winston Churchill, I think. Possibly Stuart Pearce.) Only the strongest will survive, according to Hurricane #1, Oxford's third-finest band after Radiohead and Supergrass. OK, I'll probably survive either way, but the point stands: I need to act, and it's now or never. She's already putting away her neatly labelled folder of notes. This is my last chance to seize the diem.

'Er, do you, um, fancy getting a coffee somewhere?'

'I can't, I'm meeting Jonathan for lunch.'

'No, of course not. Sorry.'

'Maybe next week?' she says, pulling on her jacket.

'Sounds great.'

'See you, Chris.'

'Bye, Louise. I mean Lou.'

And, like that ... she's gone.

As I head up the hill to Crookesmoore, I review our first hour together. It wasn't an unqualified success. Given the chance to do it again, I wouldn't start by kicking a stone at her; perhaps she could find me browsing a heavyweight novel. Balzac, something like that. There would be fewer awkward pauses. And I'd definitely sweat less. But on the plus side, I've spoken to Louise Banks. One ambition for the year ticked off, and it's only the first morning of term.

2

Fine Time

'What the fuck are you eating?'

I look at my plate of chicken nuggets, scrambled eggs, baked beans and oven chips, trying to work out what has offended Rob.

'What's wrong with it?'

'Chicken? On the same plate as eggs? That's taboo, my friend, the Mother and Child Reunion. Ask Paul Simon; moody bastard, but at least he knew right from wrong. In fact, ask your mum, she's a big Simon and Garfunkel fan, isn't she?'

'You don't want any, then? Ah, of course, you're a vegetarian now, I keep forgetting.' I spear an especially succulent nugget and wave it at him. 'Remind me, why are you a vegetarian?'

'Because of my profound love and respect for all animal life,' he replies. I suspect it's more a cunning line to spin when he's trying to pull. He gave up smoking last year just so he can pass himself off as a troubled ex-addict struggling with his demons. 'Except for wasps,' Rob continues. 'I got stung by one of those stripy little bastards halfway up a route today. Almost fell off.'

While notionally a student, Rob spends almost every day climbing rocks. And while I come up with new ambitions at the start of each year, his have been the same since day one: to become president of the university climbing club. Equipment officer in his first year, treasurer in the second, his sights are now set firmly on the biggest prize. Music might be my first love, but it comes a distant second for Rob O'Neill.

'Well, this is chicken, not wasp, but I'll chuck it in the bin if it offends you,' I shrug, adding my plate to the pile in the sink.

'No, I'll eat it, there's no point wasting it if it's dead already. But as separate courses, like any right-thinking person. At least that way one of us will have shown some respect to this poor unfortunate creature, which gave its life to be nuggeted and breadcrumbed so that we may eat.'

I knew he'd crack; Rob has an appetite like a landfill site. He rinses a plate under the hot tap, then picks out a cleanish saucer for the nuggets to emphasise his moral superiority. It's a downside of living with a philosopher, they're forever starting pointless arguments to show how clever they are. I'm eager to tell him about my hour with Lou, but there's little point in starting until he's recounted every last detail of every single climb he's completed.

'... and at that point we decided to call it a day,' he says, scooping up the last of the beans. 'Don't worry, I've finished, there's no need to keep nodding, I know you're not listening. Anyway, we'd best get going, I don't want to be late for Wales' second-finest troubadours.'

'After the Super Furries?'

'Nope, Ether. A superb band from Caerphilly. You won't know them.'

We've got tickets to see Gorky's Zygotic Mynci, one of the quirkier bands around. But first we have to meet Andy Salisbury, housemate number three. A fan of Ben Sherman shirts and expensive lager, he's as close as we get to a New Lad in our house and, being a typical medical student, he works hard and drinks harder, meaning he's always late for everything.

We've arranged to meet in the Washington, our favourite pub in the city. There's little extraordinary about it, inside or out: a black-and-white cube on the corner of Devonshire

Green with an unremarkable beer selection. But during our early days in Sheffield, Rob discovered that it was owned by someone in Pulp. He didn't know which one, nor did he have any evidence to support the claim, but even this limp association with such Sheffield legends was sufficient to elevate its status. As we sit in our usual corner, I seek his opinion on progress with Lou.

'Leg touching? On the first day?' he says when I've finished. 'That's a notable achievement, especially for you. It's fair to say you've made some sort of impression.'

'I thought so.' His enthusiasm is encouraging; he's even stroking his rapidly expanding ginger-brown beard in a thoughtful manner.

'The question, of course, is *what* sort of impression. Because another reading of today's events is that you kicked a stone at her, ignored her for the best part of an hour, and then she turned you down when you asked her out.'

'That is another perspective. I preferred your first one, though.'

Rob takes a long pull on his pint. 'And it's a week before you'll talk to her again?'

'Most likely. We only have one tutorial a week.'

'You don't know her address? Or her phone number?'

'No to both.'

'And she's got a boyfriend, who owns their flat?'

'I don't know for certain, but that's the rumour.'

'Hmm … then we know he's rich, as well as better looking than you.'

'I didn't say that.'

'I assumed. Anyway, I would just ask her out again the next time you see her. What's the worst that could happen?'

'She could stop sitting with me. She could tell her boyfriend, who's also bigger than me. In fact, she'd probably tell everyone on our course. That's three things, off the top of my head.'

'If she takes offence, you can claim you meant as friends. But if you don't ask, you'll never know. Shy kiddies get no sweeties.'

'I'll think about it,' I mutter.

'Well, go to the bar while you're thinking,' he says, draining his glass. 'Mine's another Guinness. And some Scampi Fries.'

'I thought you were a vegetarian?'

'It doesn't apply in pubs. Get some pork scratchings as well.'

* * *

It's one of those joyful occasions when a gig dramatically exceeds expectations. I haven't listened to much Gorky's, largely because half their songs are in Welsh, a language that sounds like it's being made up on the spot. But live, they are something a little different: mellow, and more experimental than most bands. Their sound veers towards medieval at times, all slow rhythms and harmonic singing. I leave with the buzz that a glorious night of music always provides, already looking forward to reliving it through the reviews in next week's *NME*.

Rob insists on chips on the way home, and we debate their performance in the queue. He claims they were much better in the tiny club he saw them play three years earlier. Before they were famous, which is when he claims to have seen most bands. Andy missed most of their set and doesn't offer any opinion, preoccupied instead with the age-old curry sauce versus battered sausage debate. He eventually opts for both and, packets in hand, cans in pocket, we perch on the nearest garden wall.

'This is good,' I say, picking out the fattest, greasiest chips to devour first.

'You get better chips in Manchester,' says Rob. Everything's better in Manchester.

'Not the chips, I mean the three of us going out together,' I insist. 'It's our last year in Sheffield, we should make the most of it.'

'Not mine,' says Andy, biting off half a sauce-soaked sausage. 'I've got three more years after this, and that's assuming I pass them all.'

'I might stay and do a master's,' adds Rob. 'It depends if I finally get to claim my rightful crown as club president.'

'What about you, Chris?' Andy asks. 'Any plans for next year, or are you heading back to the countryside to milk cows and chase foxes, or whatever it is you do down there?'

'I haven't really thought about it,' I shrug. This is mostly true; my mind has been too full of music, football and how to approach unapproachable girls. But Lou's mention of New York made me realise I need to start thinking, otherwise I'll end up back in Devon. The mere thought of which makes me shiver. 'But it won't be another degree, judging by my grades. So this is *my* last year as a student, and we should celebrate it. Here's to us,' I say, raising my can of Vimto. 'The Three Musketeers.'

'There were four of them,' says Andy.

'And they were French,' notes Rob.

'The Three Degrees, then,' I suggest, scraping out my packet. I'm down to the crispy bits already; how do chips disappear so quickly?

'They were black,' says Andy. 'And American. And women.'

'Alright, here's to the three housemates from Sheffield. Two of which are pedantic wankers.'

'Two of *whom*,' corrects Rob.

'I can only concur, Chris,' says Andy, screwing up his empty wrapper and chucking it towards the nearby bin. He misses by three feet. 'So cheers all round, it's been a top night and I am going to conclude it by getting plastered in one of this city's dancing emporiums, hopefully in the company of a young lady. Who's with me?'

'No thanks,' I mutter. Watching Andy chase girls is nauseating. His self-belief comes from looking and sounding like Hugh Grant's younger brother, and his thirst for women is matched only by his thirst for alcohol. It's the reason I haven't asked his advice about Lou; the last thing I need is him sniffing around.

'Me neither,' says Rob, picking up Andy's chip paper and placing it in the bin. 'I'm out climbing tomorrow.'

'Your loss, gents, your loss,' grins Andy, lighting a cigarette. He heads for the city centre while Rob and I head home. The streets are deserted and we walk in a silence that is only comfortable when you are with your closest friend and have a stomach full of beer and chips. After running through the evening's highlights once more, my thoughts return to Lou. Am I reading too much into things? She has a boyfriend, one who could annihilate me in any kind of contest, whether brain- or brawn-based. Before today, she ignored me for two years. She's the longest of long shots.

And yet she definitely nudged my leg. On purpose, I'm certain of it.

'Chris, can I give you some advice?' Rob says, interrupting my thoughts. 'Don't worry too much about this girl. It's taken you two years to speak to her; if you overthink it, you'll get all worked up and won't even manage to do that again.'

'I'll try. Thanks, mate.'

It's good advice. And pointless. There's absolutely no chance of me not overthinking this, because it's too important. If, by some miracle, something happens with Lou, it will be a major achievement. And there have been far too few of those in my life, major or otherwise. I've never done anything of note: never starred in a play, never come top in a maths test. I've even failed to capitalise on the few things I'm good at. I can play the guitar, but I play it on my own, at home. I haven't formed a chart-wrecking band like so many others; I don't know any drummers. Or bassists. And if I've got further hidden talents, then they're positively hermit-like in their commitment to being left in peace.

Nor have there been many incidents in my twenty years and nine months; my parents never divorced, I wasn't fiddled with by a weird uncle; I never even had a fight at school. I've not had any life-altering tragedies, either. Gran died last winter, but she was eighty-one and had a sixty-a-day habit. Sad, naturally, but none of us could claim it was a surprise. So I need something to mark me out, to get me noticed. Getting somewhere, anywhere, with Louise Banks would be just the trick. I'm not remarkable but she is and, if I'm lucky, some of her star quality might rub off on me.

Rob heads straight to bed and I go to my ground-floor room. Taking the crumpled ticket out of my pocket, I smooth it out, ready to be placed on the pin board above my desk. Mum gave it to me at the start of university for lecture timetables and revision schedules. But it quickly assumed a far more significant role: a record of all the bands I've seen.

The tickets originally went up randomly but, as the board filled, it developed its own hierarchy. The biggest bands and most memorable nights gravitated towards the centre: Oasis at Sheffield Arena; Suede in Doncaster; Cast in Manchester, when we stayed with Rob's brother. Small but impressive bands are confined to the outer rim, such as Salad, Menswear, Reef at the Foundry. There are still a few spaces left, to be filled in the coming weeks. I've already bought several tickets, despite promising Mum I'd budget this year. Some outgoings are non-negotiable.

Taking pride of place in the middle is my '97 Glastonbury ticket, but there's a space next to it. That's reserved for Blur, when I finally get to see them. That's my second ambition for the year. They're the one big band I haven't seen live and I need them for that sense of completeness. Hours have been spent on extortionately priced ticket hotlines, but without success: dial, hold, hang up, redial. I almost saw them at the V Festival, but Rob insisted we watch Ash instead. I followed dutifully and Ash were superb, but it was a missed opportunity. Hopefully this year I can make up for it. I'll keep checking the music magazines for news of a tour.

On top of that, it's time to find a proper girlfriend, by which I mean one who lets me hang around for more than a few weeks. Talk to Louise Banks, see Blur, find a girlfriend. Even with the first one accomplished, it sounds like more than enough to keep me busy for a year.

I pin the ticket on the right-hand side of the board, halfway between the centre and the edge. Once in place, I pull off my sweat-soaked T-shirt and make a mental note to clean my teeth extra thoroughly in the morning.

3

Play It Cool

My stomach works through a punishing gymnastic routine on route to campus. Despite Rob's advice, I've spent the week fretting over my next encounter with Lou and still haven't come up with a plan. The most pressing issue is what to do when the lecture finishes. Last time I met her on the way to the tutorial, but I can't rely on lightning striking for a second time. Somehow, I need to make sure that we sit together.

Option one is to stride over at the end of the lecture and start chatting away like we're old friends. That's the boldest approach, but also the one most likely to fail – especially with Jonathan nearby.

Option two: leave quickly and loiter outside, then 'casually' bump into her again. I'll need a better opening gambit than kicking stones at her, though. And I don't have one. Not yet.

The third – and safest – option is to sprint to the computer lab, sit in the same seat, act aloof and hope for the best. This is the act of a pathetic coward, but it's the one with the lowest likelihood of public humiliation. And there is an exceptionally small chance that she'll interpret it as the act of someone so supercool and self-assured that he isn't fussed who sits with him. That could be pushing things, though. I've been practising aloofness all week and still resemble a goldfish with a head trauma.

Yet that's just the first problem. Lurking behind it is a far greater concern: that nothing is going to happen, ever. And that comes with a side helping of frustration. Things could have been so, so different …

1996, the geography department's meet-and-greet event for first years. The promised cheese and wine turned out to be warm Chardonnay and diced-up Babybels, but it was sufficiently sophisticated to impress this eighteen-year-old freshly arrived from darkest Devon. I went to refill my plastic cup and she walked over. Confident, composed; she tucked her hair behind her ear as I stole a glance across at her; in response, I blushed and fixed my gaze on the stack of napkins at the back of the table.

As I scoured the pit of my stomach for the willpower needed to speak, a mysterious figure appeared on her other side.

'Hi. I'm Jonathan.'

And with that, the chance was gone. She turned to him, leaving me holding a plate of dissected lunchbox fillers. The two of them got together soon afterwards.

That could have been me.

Hi.

Why didn't I think of that?

Let's be clear at this point: I'm not a total novice. I've made *some* progress with girls since then, including a fling in the second year with an older woman (only eight months older, but that counts, it definitely counts). But I'm realistic about my place in the romantic running order. Not bottom of the bill, but certainly not one of the headline acts. In my happier moments, I see myself as third or fourth on the line-up: Mansun, maybe, perhaps even a Placebo on my better days. But Louise Banks is a different prospect: she's Radiohead on the Pyramid Stage, all flashing lights and soaring guitar solos, with thousands of worshipping fans fighting for a closer look. She's out of my league and I know it. So does she.

Joe Everitt, commonly known as Chemical Joe due to his phenomenal capacity to consume drugs, is lurking outside the lecture theatre. We've sat together since the first year, on the rare occasions that we both turn up. He's in his usual outfit of black jeans, black puffa jacket and black beanie hat. With a neatly trimmed goatee and suspiciously fat rollup, he looks like the fourth Fun Lovin' Criminal.

'Hey man,' he mumbles, inhaling deeply.

'Hey Joe. Good weekend?'

'Still comin' down from it,' he says, stubbing out his joint on the wall and returning the unsmoked half to his jacket pocket. 'You?'

'Went to the football. Sheffield United v Portsmouth. Two-one to the Blades. Shall we go in?'

I understand even less of the lecture this time around, but that could be because I'm not listening. With every passing minute, the moment of truth – or more likely disappointment – draws closer.

'What's up, man?' Joe whispers. 'You're staring at her even more than usual.'

'I sat next to her in the GIS tutorial last week,' I confess. 'I'm hoping I can do the same this week, but not sure how to make it happen.'

'You sat with Lou? Nice one, man, nice one. No reason why Jonathan should get all the fun,' he says, sitting up. 'Want me to distract him at the end? I've been meanin' to ask when his mate Blair is gonna legalise cannabis. 'Bout fuckin' time, I reckon.'

'Thanks, but he doesn't do that course. I just need to make sure I'm in the right place at the end of the lecture.'

'Cool, man, cool. Let me know how it goes.' He shuts his eyes and settles back into his seat for a snooze.

But when the lecture ends, I still haven't decided what to do. Having narrowed my options down to two and three –

one is beyond me – I squeeze past the sleeping Joe and trot out of the lecture hall.

Once outside, I realise I've forgotten my rucksack and sneak back in. Lou's still there.

'Forgotten something?'

'My bag,' I mumble, tripping on the steps as I go to retrieve it.

'You can walk with me to the geography department if you like,' she says as I walk down them carefully, and sets off before I can reply.

I smile to myself as I follow. Through luck more than planning, I've got what I wanted. Almost; there's one more hurdle …

'And yes, we can sit together again,' she says. 'I'm assuming that's what you were working yourself up to ask. Come on, we'll be late.'

* * *

Professor Stafford races us through our latest GIS exercise: plotting the changing voting patterns of Sheffield's electoral wards. It seems as good a starter as anything.

'Did you vote at the last election?' I ask Lou as we click our way through the exercise.

'Of course. It's our democratic duty, as our teachers drummed into us at least a million times at school. Besides, Jonathan would have killed me if I hadn't. Well, he wouldn't have killed me, but he's mad about politics. Did you know that he volunteers for the Labour Party? The department agreed to let him skip some lectures for it. He's planning to run for union president later this year, that sort of experience is extremely useful if you want to pursue a career in politics, actually. Which he does, of course. It takes up most of his time these days, weekends, evenings, and this term it's during the week as well. He says it's vital for his career but we rarely have any time together these days and when we do, he's busy preparing stuff for the next New Labour event. He reads three or four newspapers a day, can you believe it? It's important to understand the views on all sides, he says. It drives me mad, they're always cluttering up the flat, but it's his passion, I know that ...'

Never have I received such a long response to a yes–no question. I let her continue, though. It means I don't have to think of anything to say.

'... it all kicked off in the run up to the last election, he got so involved, and then on the night itself, he'd just put so much time and effort into getting Labour elected, he was swept away with it all as the results came in, the excitement, that sense of something truly incredible happening, he said it was the greatest night of his life. Do you remember it? Wasn't it amazing?'

I do remember that night. The dining room in my halls of residence was converted into a giant TV room and overtaken by huddles of students, eyes fixed on the big screen. Everyone cheered as each constituency went red on the BBC map. This was the most monumental political event of our lifetimes, we were repeatedly told, and the first one in which we'd had the opportunity to make our voices count. I remember looking around me – at friends, drinking buddies, those with whom I was on nodding terms in the breakfast queue – and thinking: you didn't vote, because you were playing football all day. And you didn't vote because you were asleep until four pm and then went straight to the bar. And you didn't vote because you're an idle bastard and I've rarely seen you out of your dressing gown all year. And you, if you did vote, voted Tory, seeing as you once drunkenly let slip that your family has been blue through and through for generations. Yet here you are, playing Billy Bragg songs on your guitar and acting like you can't wait to join the workers' struggle.

I doubt a quarter of the people in that room voted. Living away from your parent's home meant registering with the local electoral office, which meant a trip into the city centre and digging up an acceptable form of ID – all of which is far too much effort for the average first-year student. Yet they all clapped and whooped and acted like Blair had scored a last-minute winner in the FA Cup final, rather than getting more votes than that other idiot who everyone hated anyway. I only voted myself because Dad threatened to withdraw car-use privileges all summer if I didn't swear I'd put a cross down for someone. Since then, I hadn't given it a second thought.

Until now.

'Of course I remember. Wasn't it incredible? Who did you vote for?'

'Labour, of course. Who do you think I voted for?'

'Well, I just wondered because … did you not vote Tory?'

'Of course I didn't. Why would you think that?'

'You said you went to a private school.'

'When did I say that?'

'Last week. You know, playing tennis and hockey.'

'I went to an all-girls school, not a private school. You shouldn't make such sweeping assumptions, Christopher.'

'You're right. Sorry.'

'Apology accepted,' she replies, although it's begrudgingly, judging by her scowl.

I try to focus on the exercise, cursing myself for screwing things up so quickly. A few minutes pass before I dare to steal a screen-reflected glance to gauge how annoyed she is, but she catches me and skewers me with a glare. Fortunately, a half-smile is forming beneath it.

'I can't believe you think I'd vote Tory,' she whispers. 'I'm not *that* posh.'

'Ignore me, I'm from Devon. We're suspicious of anyone who uses more consonants than vowels.'

She snorts loudly and we both spin around to check we aren't going to get into trouble again. Fortunately, Professor Stafford is reading a book in the corner, completely oblivious to the twelve other humans in the room.

'OK, enough about me,' Lou says. 'Tell me something about yourself.'

'Like what?'

'What are your hobbies?'

I briefly consider whether I can get away with saying jungle exploration or lion taming. But it's evident already that Lou is much smarter than me. 'Music, mostly. Listening to music.'

She frowns; whatever the right answer was, this isn't it. 'That's not a hobby, though, is it? Everyone listens to music.'

'No, I don't mean at home. I go to loads of gigs, keep an eye out for the latest bands, read the music magazines, y'know, follow the whole scene.'

'That still doesn't count. Everyone does that when they're at uni.'

'OK ... I play football every week,' I say, willing this to meet with her approval. 'Twice, some weeks.'

'All boys play football. You can't help yourselves, like you with that pebble last week. Don't you do any proper sports?'

'I quite like snooker.' I'm not holding out much hope for a better response.

'Oh God, really? Snooker?'

The disappointment in her voice is clear; she makes very little attempt to hide it. I'm annoyed, though. Surely being part of Sheffield's thriving music scene is a worthwhile use of my time? Doesn't football count as a "proper" sport? Yet amid my resentment, fresh doubts bubble up. Hearing them out loud, my interests *are* unimaginative. Rob has his climbing, while my sister Cecilia was an active member of the debating society at Oxford, as well as watching loads of bands. Even Andy finds time to play rugby amid his medical studies. Everyone I know does something more interesting than me: martial arts, yoga, wargaming, orienteering …

'What do you do, then?' I snap back. 'I mean proper hobbies, obviously, not just two of the world's most popular pastimes.'

'I played hockey at school, I told you that. I was captain of the school team actually, but I haven't found the time here. I still play tennis in the summer, and I do a fitness class once a week. I played the cello in the university orchestra in the first year, but I gave it up last year, it took up far too much time. And I help Jonathan with his Labour Party stuff when he needs it.'

'Wow, that's a lot. And all proper ones, very impressive.'

I mean it. I'm envious. Everyone else is getting much more out of university life than me. As I chew the end of my biro, deep in thought, Lou nudges me under the desk.

'My turn to apologise, I didn't mean to be dismissive. Football is a proper sport, of course it is. I'm sure you're very good at it.'

'I really am not,' I reply. A little too quickly; I could have sifted out a few highlights from over the years. The lucky-but-impressive-nonetheless goal from the halfway line last year; my diving/flopping header the year before; and, of course, my famous hat-trick for the school team. They were all tap-ins from no more than three yards out, but they earned us a 3-2 win and I got a round of applause from my teammates afterwards. I even got a pat on the back from the opposition coach. I'll have to slip it into the conversation somehow, omitting the fact that I was eight at the time. And that the opposition captain called me a goal-hanging twat.

And I'll have to do it quickly, as Lou is already packing up her things.

'Do you still want to go for that drink?' she says suddenly, flicking her hair behind her ear.

'Erm … sure.'

'Let's go to Bar One. Hurry up, it always gets crowded at lunchtime.'

* * *

With music and football, my two areas of expertise, already dismissed, I need to pull a rabbit – preferably a cultured, fascinating one – out from somewhere. But despite searching in the deepest burrows of my brain, I fail to flush one out.

'Try families,' suggests Lou as we walk across the campus.

'Eh?'

'You're trying to think of something to talk to me about. I can hear the little cogs whirring in your mind.'

'Is it that obvious?'

'All boys are the same when they're talking to beautiful women.'

She doesn't lack self-confidence, but why would she? If everyone else can see it, she's bound to as well. And it gets me out of a hole. 'OK, tell me about your family.'

As her earlier speech about Jonathan's political ambitions hinted, Lou Banks can talk for a very long time if you get her on the right subject. She's off again, providing me with a detailed history of the lives of three people I've never met.

'… so after that, Daddy decided to set up on his own as an architect, and Mummy ran the business for him, pretty much. She was a school teacher originally – and yes, if you must know, it was a private school – but stopped to have me and Bex and never went back to it, so it made sense for her to help out, she could fit that around looking after us. We still live there, in the same farmhouse. Well, Mummy, Bex and I do. *He* now lives in Hertfordshire with his new wife – who is a gold-digging bitch, by the way – and her two vile children. He left when I was thirteen. I still hate him for it.'

I don't know how to respond. Instinct urges me to ask about the step-mum – I have a vivid picture of a foxy Home Counties temptress with a delicious smile that seduces weak-minded architects – but it seems too soon; I've only known Lou for a week. I need to pick up on something different. Come on, think, what else did she just tell me?

'So, er, what kind of farm is it?'

'I beg your pardon?' She looks perplexed; should I have gone with the step-mum?

'You said you live in a farmhouse, I just wondered what kind of farm it is.'

'It's not a farm any more. Daddy sold most of the land. He renovated two of the barns as well, we rented them out for a while, but he sold them after the divorce. It would have been too much work for Mummy on her own, and–'

'It's not a farmhouse, then.'

'What are you on about?'

'If it's not a working farm, then technically you don't live in a farmhouse. It'll have been reclassified as a residential property.'

This is lamentable, even for me. It's hard to imagine that anyone has ever tried to impress a girl by outlining the finer points of rural building administration. 'You usually get twelve months to process the paperwork,' I say, accepting that it's already far too late to salvage this. 'My dad's a planning advisor for Devon council, that's how I know about this stuff,' I continue, feeling miserable and utterly lost. 'My mum was a veterinary nurse. But she's retired. She keeps bees now.'

Lou has stopped walking and is staring at me, the left eyebrow so high it's lost behind her fringe. 'She's got over ten thousand bees.'

An image from my childhood flashes before my eyes. On a wet winter's day, one of the local farmers got his tractor stuck in his quagmire of a bottom field. He spent two hours revving the engine while I sat on the gate, watching the wheels splatter a neat arc of mud behind him. When I asked, years later, why he persisted for so long, he admitted that he didn't know what else to do.

I'm beginning to understand how he felt.

Incredibly, Lou hasn't walked off, nor is she searching for a blunt instrument with which to put me out of my misery. Instead, she puts her arm through mine.

'OK, Christopher, seeing as you're such a stickler for accuracy: I live in a house in a village in the Peak District, which used to be part of a working farm – a sheep farm, I think, but I'll have to check for you – before it was bought and renovated by a thirtysomething couple, my parents, who moved up from Hampshire and lived there happily with their two lovely daughters until the husband buggered off to marry a slapper much younger than himself and live in fucking Watford.'

'You should get that put on a sign for the gate.'

She slaps me playfully on the back (I think it's playful; it hurts like hell) and I let out a silent sigh of relief. Situation redeemed, and in much less time than it took Wurzel to get his tractor out of that field.

4

She Makes My Nose Bleed

Bar One. The main drinking den on campus. It's rammed, even though it's not yet midday. Students are nothing if not predictable. But as I search for a way through to the bar, Lou strides confidently into the crowd, which parts before her like the Red Sea. Students of all shapes, sizes and genders stare as she goes. I catch up and revel in what might be my only chance to pretend we're a couple.

'What do you want to drink, Christopher?'

'Did you say your dad was loaded? I'll have a rum n' Coke, then,' I reply, grinning broadly at the witticism; after dabbling unsuccessfully with farm classification, it's good to be back on the surer footing of music.

'Rum and Coke? At midday? Have you got a drink problem?'

'No, it was a joke. Like the Pulp song, "Common People".'

This world-famous anthem obviously fails to register. The raised eyebrow of contempt is back up, touching at least eighty percent.

'Never mind,' I say quickly. 'Look, why don't I get the drinks and you find us somewhere to sit? What do you want, an alcopop or something?'

The eyebrow stretches up towards the nineties.

'No, I'll have a beer, please. A lager.'

'Pint or half?'

'Do you ask your male friends that question?'

'A pint it is.'

I squeeze through to the bar, chastened but happy. She's elevated me from geography acquaintance to friend in little more than a week. This is progress. The awkwardness of last week is behind us – behind me, she was fine from the start – and we've been chatting easily for nearly half an hour. I collect my bitter and her lager from a surly barmaid and consider which topic to plump for next. There should be plenty of options: I just need to avoid anything to do with paternal infidelity, Jonathan, politics, jokes based around song lyrics, beverage-based sexism, snooker and football. I opt to play it safe with that other getting-to-know-someone-at-university staple, one I haven't used since the first year.

'How come you ended up at Sheffield?' I ask, squeezing in next to her and placing the drinks on the quarter of table free from discarded glasses. 'Didn't you fancy going somewhere further away?'

She sips her pint, grimaces at its flatness and puts it back down. 'The official answer is that I was attracted by the high standard of teaching and the wide range of modules on offer in the geography faculty at the University of Sheffield. The honest answer is that I didn't get into Oxford. I don't know why, I got three As at A-level and both Oxford and Cambridge were happy to accept all of my friends. But not me.'

'I wouldn't worry about it,' I reassure her. 'Sheffield's loads better than Oxford.'

'You must be the only person in the entire world who thinks that.'

'No, I don't mean for studying and all that bollocks, I mean as a place. I've been to Oxford, my sister went there. It's full of toffy knobs wearing pastel shirts with the top buttons undone, and girls wearing long flowery skirts, sitting about on these square lawns and talking about poetry from hundreds of years ago. Sheffield's got much more character. It's loads better living here, trust me.'

She fixes me with another stare from her extensive repertoire; sceptical, this time. I start on my own pint, slowly, I need a moment here. This is a controversial statement and I'll need to back it up.

'Radiohead and Supergrass are from Oxford, of course. Near enough, anyway. But then we've got Pulp and Longpigs, so I'd call that one a draw.' Oxford possibly shades that battle, on reflection, but I don't want to contradict myself too quickly; this is my area of expertise.

Hmmm. Hurricane #1 are also from Oxford. Does that count for or against?

'I don't know why you like all that Britpoppy stuff,' Lou sniffs. 'It all sounds the same to me.'

'Right, first of all, you're only permitted to say that about any sort of music once you've got grandchildren. And secondly, you're wrong, totally and utterly wrong. The music scene in this country right now is absolutely phenomenal. Quite literally, it's a phenomenon. I mean, there are so many incredible bands at the moment. Just think about all the classic albums of recent years. *All Change. 1977. I Should Coco. Definitely Maybe. The Sun Is Often Out. Fuzzy Logic.* And that's just the bands who hit top gear with their debuts. Blur's back catalogue is a collective masterpiece. And here, in Sheffield, we're right at the heart of it, there's someone fantastic playing every week. You have to see these bands live to really appreciate them. Have you ever seen Suede live? No, of course you haven't, but it's like music and theatre all rolled into one.'

I pause to take a breath and she's smiling at me. Not laughing at me, but smiling with … what's this one, affection?

'What's so funny?'

'You are,' she replies. 'I've never seen you so animated. You and Joe usually look like you're hibernating in lectures.'

'Well, music's my passion,' I reply, stifling a whoop of joy on learning that she's noticed me in lectures. 'Anyway, what music do you like? Violin concertos? Chamber music?'

'Piss off. I listen to dance music mostly.'

'I mean proper music. With words.'

'Anything, really,' she shrugs. 'Whatever's on the radio.'

'But you must like some of it more than the rest. Come on, who's your favourite band? Don't worry, I won't judge you.'

She lifts her pint to her lips, thinks better of it and puts it down again. 'Robbie Williams.'

'He's not technically a band.'

'Michael Jackson?'

'Jeez, and you really have no idea why Oxford rejected you? Try and think of someone who has other people playing instruments near them when they're singing.'

'Why does it have to be a band?' she huffs. 'Oh, I've got one, the Beautiful South!'

'No, I'm not having that. It's fine to *like* the Beautiful South, everyone *likes* them, but they're not anyone's favourite band. Not anyone under forty. Although *Miaow* was a fine album, credit where it's due.'

'So because I don't like the same bands as you, you dismiss my opinion as invalid? And you call me a snob?'

'I said you were posh, not a snob. And you were dismissive of my hobbies, remember? OK, I'll give you an easier one. Who do you like more, Blur and Oasis? They're both on the radio a lot.'

'Blur.'

'Why?'

'Oasis are too hairy.' She starts giggling. I shake my head in despair. Still, she has a point. Having spent many, many hours considering this matter, I'm now firmly in the Blur camp. At first, I sided with Oasis, especially when 'Roll With It' and 'Country House' battled for the coveted number one spot. I preferred their uncomplicated rock anthems to Blur's artier pretentions. But not long after arriving at university, Rob explained, in painstaking detail, how utterly misguided I was. By then, I felt ready to switch allegiances. It's a bit like graduating from lager to bitter. Oasis – lager – are fizzy and exciting and much more palatable at first, and perfect for your teenage years. But as you get older, you realise how much more depth, variety and interest there is in bitter. Like Blur. Yet I don't know any bitter drinker who didn't go through the lager stage first. Although in Devon we all started off on cider, which scuppers the analogy somewhat. Maybe The Levellers are the cider; I'll have to refine this theory further before sharing it with anyone.

'Maybe you and I should go to a gig together,' I say, as casually as I can, although annoyingly my voice has risen by about an octave. 'As long as Jonathan doesn't mind.'

'He's not really into all that stuff,' she replies absently.

'Who does he listen to, then?' I'm not even slightly interested in which bands Jonathan likes, or anything else about him, but her attention is drifting; she's looking around the bar to see who else is around.

'He likes James. They did that song about sitting down,' she adds helpfully, in case I'm struggling to place one of the great early Nineties bands. Although not that great, of course; Madchester, Baggy, Shoegaze, whatever you want to call it, was nothing more than a warm-up to the far superior Britpop. Even Rob, a defiantly proud Mancunian, admits this. But it might be tricky to explain to Lou, given her limited knowledge and interest.

'Isn't he a bit young for all that?' I say, happy to get a dig in.

'He's two years older than us. He spent a year working in London after his A-levels, then a year volunteering in Africa.'

Of course he did. He couldn't just work in Safeway for a summer like normal eighteen-year-olds. 'Even so, it's all a bit dated now, isn't it? Does he listen to the Carpenters as well?'

'No I don't,' comes a deep voice from behind us, 'but I do like Leonard Cohen, and he's old, so the charge stands. Hi babe. Hi … Chris, isn't it? Jonathan Gilbert, nice to meet you. We've played football against each other.'

How long has he been there? How much did he hear? As he places his broad shoulders squarely between Lou and me, I notice he's wearing a crisply ironed pastel-blue shirt, with neat creases down each sleeve and the top two buttons undone. Exactly the sort of look I was mocking a few minutes ago, but now I feel underdressed. I'm confident that my frayed jeans are a lot less expensive than his, and my old football top has ripped shoulders, courtesy of the university's unforgiving AstroTurf pitches. For the first time in my life, I wish I owned a pastel shirt. I also wish that Plymouth Argyle didn't play in lurid green and white stripes.

'I thought you had Labour meetings all day?' Lou says, turning her whole body away from me. He casually takes her hand, their fingers locking right in front of my face.

'We're pausing for lunch. I popped into the library and Maria said you were here.'

He's taking the discovery of his girlfriend drinking with another man extremely calmly. It's either due to his supreme self-confidence, or he's instantly dismissed me as no competition. I need to say something, not least to remind them that I'm still here.

'How's your football team, Jonathan? I think we're playing each other in a few weeks.'

'Not bad, thanks. We won our first match eight-nil. How about yours?'

'Lost nine-one. I scored the one, though.'

'Still, early days.'

What's the etiquette when someone catches you in a pub with their girlfriend? Offering them a drink is surely the least that's expected.

'Can I get you a drink?'

'No thanks. Babe' – he's talking to Lou again at this point, obviously – 'I came to tell you I'm busy this afternoon. They've asked me to help with a house-to-house in Woodseats. Meet the voters, that sort of thing. I'll be finished around five.'

I'm not the only one who wilts under Lou's eyebrows of contempt. His face drops as she stares at him.

And their fingers unlock.

'That's fine, I'm sure Chris will keep me company. He asked me out for this drink, after all.'

And finally, there it is: the tiniest flicker of recognition on Jonathan's face. It's barely noticeable – a brief narrowing of the eyes as he glances at me, the look held for half a second longer than that first, dismissive one – but my status as a rival male has at last registered.

'I'll meet you outside the library at five. *If* you're free. I'm going for a drink with the chaps over there. See you around, Chris.'

I raise a hand in acknowledgment but don't get one in return. Lou and I are alone again. Just the two of us. And a hundred or so other students.

'So, Christopher,' she says, putting her arm around my shoulders and tousling my hair. 'What do you want to do?'

Is this really happening? I know we've been flirting, but it's all been very gentle up to now. And Jonathan is still around – or is that the attraction? It must be. She wants us to fight over her, right here in Bar One, pool cues for weapons. But who will she be supporting? Maybe my lust for her *is* reciprocated; maybe she's been obsessing about me ever since last week's tutorial. Maybe …

'Come on, fuckwit, do you want to finish our GIS exercise, or do some reading in the library? I want to get ahead before next week's lecture.'

Or maybe not.

5

Connection

If the flickering embers of sexual tension need fanning, geography text books are not the weapon of choice. When Lou seeks my view on the most significant types of biostratigraphical data, I make my excuses and leave.

There's no sign of anyone about at home, so I sneak into Rob's room and steal *Between 10th and 11th*, an early Charlatans album that he's insisted I listen to. It's much better than their recent stuff, apparently.

* * *

It was through our shared love of music that Rob and I met. I passed those first days at university, empty of lectures and devoid of friends, by getting to know the city that would become my new home.

Day 1: explore new room (which took until early afternoon – no mean feat considering it was little more than a dozen cubic feet) then lie on bed to ponder why everyone else has already made friends.

Day 2: systematically check out the pubs between halls and campus. Conscious to not eat into my student grant too early – as Mum reminded me, it was for books and food not booze and CDs – I drank a half-pint in each, making mental notes about which best met a young student's needs. (Except on my way back, I discovered Record Collector, the music shop of my dreams, and blew three weeks' budget in ten minutes.)

Day 3: visit the main campus. While wandering the labyrinthine corridors of the Students' Union, I spotted him reading the A4 posters taped across one wall. His long ginger hair was tied back in a ponytail and he had a ring in one ear. As I sneaked closer, I saw he was wearing a Longpigs T-shirt. Perfect; this would give us something to talk about, thanks to Cecilia, who had sat me down for a pep talk about the stuff that really mattered at uni.

'Right, little brother, if you want to impress people, you'll need more than Oasis, Pulp, Suede and Blur. You need to know about up and coming bands.'

'Like who?'

'Try Longpigs – it's not *the* Longpigs, by the way, the same as Pet Shop Boys. That sort of detail is important, it shows that you know your stuff. They're from Sheffield, too, which is worth mentioning to anyone you meet early on. Look,' she said, passing over the latest *Melody Maker*, 'they've got a gig coming up. See if they are any tickets left.'

'Right, will do. Are they any good?'.

'They produced the best debut by any British band since *Generation Terrorists*.'

'And will this impress girls as well?'

She scrutinised me, mouth twisted down at one corner. 'Maybe get a haircut before you go. And try using deodorant a bit more regularly.'

It was time to test Cecilia's theory out.

'You like *Long*pigs, then?' I asked the ginger ponytail, stressing the first syllable to make it clear I knew there was no 'the'.

'Yeah, going to see them next week,' he replied, still reading the posters. 'You?'

'I've already got my ticket. I reckon *The Sun Is Often Out* is the best debut album since *Generation Terrorists*.'

'I hate the Manics.'

'Me too. I only like that album.'

'Fancy a beer beforehand?'

'Sound great. I'm Chris.'

'Rob'.

Hands were shaken and details arranged. It was so much easier than talking to girls.

Few bands pass through rural Devon, so Longpigs were my first proper gig. At least that's what I told Rob. I'd seen Bon Jovi at Wembley with Dad in '95, his early eighteenth birthday present to me. It was phenomenal: Van Halen as the support act, and then the boys from New Jersey played hit after rocktastic hit, many embellished with ten-minute guitar solos and jaw-dropping fireworks. There was more leather on show than at a tanners' convention, and when eighty thousand fans held eighty thousand lighters in the air for 'Bed Of Roses', I nearly wept. They did two encores and even dragged Bob Geldof up on stage. It was, by any criteria, a fantastic night. But I knew, even as the throbbing bassline to 'Livin' On A Prayer' filled the stadium, that Eighties poodle rock would cut very little mustard at university.

Especially with people like Rob. In those early days, as he talked me through his likes and dislikes, who was a must-listen and who was atrocious, it became evident that he was several steps further along his own musical odyssey. I had inherited a substantial legacy from my parents – tapes of Flower Power classics from Mum, and Dad's expansive rock trivia – but Rob had something else: experience. Not only had he heard of every band around, he'd seen them live. I'd tell him about nights spent listening to Northern Uproar at a friend's house, and he'd counter with stories about driving through the night to watch Geneva in a tiny venue in Scotland, or the time he got drunk with the lead singer of Jocasta at a festival in Sweden (that festival must have lasted at least a fortnight, given how many bands he claims to have seen there).

And he knew everything about every Britpop band: every unreleased album, every obscure B-side, every past member who had left to form a smaller, better band that no one had heard of. It was exhausting yet inspiring; Rob impressed on me the need to be ahead of the curve by knowing about Curve reforming, and having the solo stuff they'd released in between to prove it. I'd come to university to learn, and Rob was an excellent teacher.

As we waited for Longpigs to come on stage, he outlined his defining music theory: the three stages of Britpop, to be used at any gig. If the band were touring with their first album, you needed an anecdote or obscure fact to prove you were listening to them long before anyone else; quoting from the recent *NME* review was unacceptable. Bands touring their second album were simple: it wasn't as good as the first one, and you'd only come in the hope they would play the B-side from an early single, which didn't chart but was your favourite. If they made it as far as the third album, which was far from certain in the cutthroat world of music, then they had lost it/sold out/become overproduced. I quickly stole this argument for myself to use with every other music fan.

The Longpigs gig couldn't have been more different to Bon Jovi. There was little of the Wembley bombast to mark their arrival; they simply shuffled on stage, clad in a uniform of plain black T-shirts and jeans, their heads drooped, looking like this was absolutely the last thing that they wanted to be doing on a Tuesday night. The venue was small and suffocating, a miserable six lights rather than six thousand. But I loved it from the first shimmering chord. Their songs were brooding, melancholic, almost petulant at times, yet each came with an intensity only heightened by the confined space. They played just eleven songs – no encores here – but each one was a maudlin gem, delivered with angry, frustrated energy.

Still buzzing afterwards, we headed to the nearest pub to round the evening off with a beer. It was there Rob told me he was gay.

'I thought it was better to get it out in the open. You know, if we're going to be friends. Is that cool?'

It was. It was very cool. I'd never met a gay person before; they were thin on the ground in rural Devon. Rob was an urbane, rock-climbing homosexual with a ponytail and an earring, whose older brother knew someone who went to school with one of the Happy Mondays. He was exactly the kind of person I'd been hoping to make friends with.

'Yeah, of course,' I replied, as casually as I could.

'Excellent. I'm going to see These Animal Men in a couple of weeks. Fancy it?'

'Definitely. Their latest album's brilliant.'

'They've only released one album.'

'I mean that one. Love it.'

We toasted the new friendship being forged in the Steel City.

* * *

I settle back, eyes closed, to appreciate the Charlatans album properly. Rob's right; it's better than their current stuff. But halfway through the second play-through, the doorbell strangely rings. I look at my bedside clock; five-thirty. Who calls round at five-thirty? It soon rings again and I get up to chastise this unwelcome visitor for their impatience.

'Oh. Hi Lou. Alright?'

'Fine, thank you, Christopher. Nothing too dramatic happened in the library during the two hours since you left.'

'Er, how did you know where I lived?'

'I asked Janet on the reception desk. She's not supposed to give out other students' details, but she likes me and I promised I wasn't going to murder you. Which I'm not.'

'That's good.'

'Can I come in?'

I'm reluctant to allow this. No female has entered our house since ... when? Not this term, certainly. Rob never brings them back, obviously, and Andy is rarely at home himself. There are good reasons why I seldom bring them here. For one I don't know many, but mostly it's because the place is unfit for them. The hessian mat in the hallway is more hole than mat, and what little remains kicks up thick clouds of dust when you step on it, the legacy of the hundreds of unwiped boots that have left their detritus upon it. Has it ever been Hoovered? Not by me. There's woodchip on the wall in most rooms, and I'm not sure if its dull yellow-brown tinge is the original shade or the colour to which it has faded. I make an immediate vow to tidy up a bit more in future. Or see if one of the others can be talked into it.

'Er, yeah, come in,' I reply hesitantly, stepping aside to let her in. 'What do you want?'

'A cup of tea would be nice. And after that, I've got a question about our GIS assignment.'

'I thought you were meeting Jonathan?'

'He's been held up, so I decided to come and see you instead. Nice place.'

'It's really not. I live with two other lads, so it's a bit, you know ...'

'Don't worry, I won't judge. Or touch anything.' She hangs her jacket on a hook and stands by the three rarely used bikes that clog up the hallway.

'Do you want a biscuit? With the tea?' I ask.

'What sort have you got?'

'Well ... none. I'll have to go to the shop and get some. We don't have any biscuits in the house.'

'Why don't you have biscuits in the house?'

'Because we eat them.' What else would you do with biscuits?

'Don't worry,' Lou says. 'Tea will be fine. I assume you have milk and teabags?'

'I'll check.'

She's acting very oddly. There's a glint in her eye and she's looking at me far more than she usually does. And there's no hint of disdain behind the looks either. It's very unsettling.

'Should I come to the kitchen with you?' she asks. 'Or wait in another room?'

Panic strikes: where to send her? The living room is straight out of a Tolkien novel, a damp, dingy den in which the curtains are rarely opened, the windows never. The sofa and armchair are apparently a matching set, but their floral pattern has worn so thin it's impossible to verify. There's a small wooden cupboard with a broken door in one corner – I have no idea what's in it – and while some might consider the huge beer-can sculpture in the fireplace a form of contemporary art, I doubt if Lou is one of them.

No, the living room isn't a good option. Yet the kitchen is little better, its surfaces submerged under piles of unwashed mugs and plates, its shelves overflowing with out-of-date bottles of condiments, most of which pre-date my time here. The spreading patch of mould above the door was certainly there when I moved in.

The only other option is my bedroom and sending her there would be a good move tactically. Most sex takes place in the bedroom, according to a late-night documentary I accidentally stumbled across on Channel 5. Therefore, if a girl is in your bedroom, the likelihood of you having sex with them is increased. It's basic probability; we did it in GCSE maths. OK, the exercise focused on rolling six sixes in a row, but the principle is the same. (And if maths teachers want

44

teenage boys to take more interest in probability, they should plan their lessons around the likelihood of having sex rather than dice.) Unfortunately, my bedroom's distinctive and unshakeable odour – somewhere between damp trainers and a guinea pig cage – might act as a counterbalance to any mathematical advantage it gives me. You get used to it after a while, but it comes as a shock to first-time visitors. It remains, however, the best option.

'You can wait in my room if you like.'

'This one?'

I nod and she goes in. But alone in the kitchen, I realise my mistake. My room may contain slightly fewer nasty surprises, but they are all mine. Elsewhere I could blame Rob or Andy, but my room is my room, and all that is in it. Like the Plymouth Argyle poster, seven years out of date because I'm too mean to buy a new one. Will this be seen as a touching tribute to my hometown, or the mark of an overgrown child? The print of the *Definitely Maybe* album cover is reliable, if unimaginative, but is a 'Wisdom of Pooh' poster really going to impress a girl like Lou? It seems unlikely; I can't imagine Jonathan has one in his bedroom. Their bedroom.

My guitar is a plus point, of course. I rarely play it but it still looks cool. The scattered CDs are a cause for concern, though. She's revealed her own taste in music to be pitiful, but that doesn't mean she can't pick fault in mine. It's mostly good stuff, of course, but a few of Dad's poodle rock classics are hidden among them. Most of these guilty pleasures are safely hidden in a drawer (so Rob won't spot them) but I can't shake the nagging feeling that *Money For Nothing* is lurking out in the open.

Nervously, I enter my room carrying two teas plus a packet of sugar lumps pilfered from Andy. Lou is perched on my bed, flicking through one of my books. The rest of which she's tidied up, along with my magazines. My CDs are now stacked in neat piles. Odd behaviour, but at least there's no sign of Knopfler's luminous pink headband anywhere. I set the mugs on the floor then sit down next to them, carefully scanning the duvet for any giveaway stains.

All clear.

So far, so good. I check which book she's picked up. *High Fidelity,* Nick Hornby. That's OK, surely? I don't need to tell her it belongs to Rob, or that I haven't got very far. Except she isn't reading the book, she's reading the bookmark.

Oh shit, the bookmark …

'Ignore that,' I splutter. 'I'm not even sure where I got it from.'

'*More* magazine, July 1992, according to the small print at the bottom of the page,' Lou replies.

'Ha, yeah, I guess so. It makes a handy bookmark, that's all.'

'Do you still read teenage girls' magazines?'

* * *

Cecilia's magazines were a revelation when I discovered them, overflowing with features fascinating to the young adolescent male: fashion pages full of models in bikinis, agony aunt pages crammed with sexual dilemmas, and of course *More*'s highly detailed 'Position of the Fortnight' line drawings; all items that were missing from my weekly copy of *Shoot!*. On one occasion, flicking through the pages in search of inspiration, a headline caught my eye: '10 ways to tell that boy you *like* him!!!'. I read it slowly, soaking up every word and hardly believing my luck.

'Make eye contact with him!'
'Flick your hair oh so casually!!'
'Move your hand slowly up his thigh!!!'

This was it: the forbidden knowledge that all male teenagers yearned for, a field guide to the mysterious creatures that sat on the opposite side of the classroom and only ever talked to boys three years older. With my penknife, I carefully scored a neat incision along the crease to ensure its absence would not be noticed. I then folded it up and kept it hidden in the book by my bed, where no one would find it.

* * *

But the karma police have finally turned up to deliver their punishment for this larceny. There's no dignified way out. I'll have to come clean.

'I got it from one of my sister's magazines. You know, confused teenage boy, girls are a mystery, that sort of thing.'

'*More* was always my favourite. Especially 'Position of the Fortnight'. I was never brave enough to try them out, though.'

There's no way I'm touching that one.

'And? Did it help?' she continues.

'What, with girls? Not as much as I'd have liked. It tells you when they're flirting with you, but doesn't explain how to get them to do it. But at least I know the signs for when that day finally comes.'

'Let's see how well you know them.' She puts the clipping on the floor and sits cross-legged across from me. Then rests her knees softly against mine.

'That's number three,' I say, trying to prevent my voice from squeaking. '"Touch his leg with yours". Although that's my knee, not my leg.'

'It's part of your leg. What about this one?' She reaches over and brushes the fingers of her right hand against my left one.

'Number six'

'Very good. What about this?'

She takes both of my hands in hers and looks deep into my eyes.

'Number nine. Although it says you're supposed to be subtle about it.'

'I'm never subtle.'

She leans over. I give up trying to hide my erection and shuffle my legs so that she can move even closer.

'Do you like me, Chris?'

'Very much.'

I can't lean in any closer without our lips meeting, yet I don't dare, not yet. We sit, hands holding, legs intertwined, lips half open, breathing the same air …

'Go on, then, kiss her, you won't get a better chance. Then you can introduce me.'

Lou snaps away from me with the speed of a mousetrap. I swing round to see Rob leaning in the doorway, a gleam of white teeth splitting his ginger beard. Standing by the bed, Lou tucks her hair behind her ears, but in a nervous, embarrassed manner, not a seductive number-four-play-with-your-hair way.

'I thought you were out?' I growl.

'You thought wrong. I'm Rob, Chris's housemate. You must be Lou,' he says, holding out a hand.

'Hello, yes, I'm Lou. I'm on Chris's course, we do the same course.'

'Yes, he's mentioned you a few times. A few times each hour, in fact.'

'That's nice. Well, I'd better be off. I only came around for a cup of tea. Bye, Chris. Nice to meet you, Rob.'

She grabs her bag and scurries towards the door. Rob steps to one side to let her past and we both listen as the front door slams shut.

'She's forgotten her notes,' says Rob, nodding to the folder on my bed.

'She has.'

'And she didn't drink her tea.'

'You can have it if you like.'

He's ruined the moment I've been waiting two years for, but I'm not angry. Getting this close to kissing Lou Banks is enough to keep me in a good mood for weeks. Months, probably.

'So, what do you think?'

He drains the still-steaming mug in one go.

'You were right, Chris. She's a stunner. Far too good-looking for you. But that, my friend, was flirting. She must like you. God alone knows why. So, what's your next move?'

'Not sure yet. I might try talking to her again, see how that goes.'

'Talking to her? Wow. Lucky girl,' Rob says, heading to the kitchen to make another brew. 'And if that goes well, you can invite her for one of your legendary picnics.'

'Fuck off.'

* * *

I haven't always been this bad with girls. For roughly three weeks during my first term, I galloped about the campus like a pony, giddy with my new sense of freedom. Freedom from my parents, freedom from being perpetually skint (thanks to a generous loan from Devon Local Education Authority) and freedom from the tedium of rural life.

But mostly freedom from being myself. Growing up in a nondescript village outside a small town in the arse end of Devon, I'd known all the girls at school since we were at playgroup. More importantly, they knew me, which severely hampered attempts to sleep with them. It's hard to cultivate the image of a smouldering sex god when they can remember the day you had to carry your wet shorts home in a carrier bag.

But at university, I had a clean slate: no one knew me or my past. On top of this came a wave of confidence-fuelling hormones, unleashed by the overwhelming number of girls around campus. They came from up north, down south, out east and far west; from Leeds, London, Liverpool and Leicester. Others were from further afield: Germany, Sweden, China, Scunthorpe. There were shy and studious girls and loud and drunk girls; there were goths, druggies, rock chicks, hippies. There were sporty ones, posh ones, ginger ones … no baby ones, and all of them scary, but a little less so than usual.

During these heady days I fell for Debbie, a law student living three blocks away from me. We met through Andy, who had slept with someone on Debbie's corridor and felt obliged to meet her again. He brought me along for moral support and she brought Debbie. Naturally, she intimidated me at first – she spoke three languages, went horse-riding and loved French cinema, all habits I associated with grown-ups – but as the alcohol flowed, I overcame my nerves and started nodding along while she chatted. Then came the actual words. By the end of the evening, I was drunk enough to ask her out on a proper date. Another night in the hall bar wasn't going to impress someone like Debbie. Instead, I suggested a picnic in the Peak District. She agreed, and the next morning we met at the main entrance.

Things went downhill from there.

The rain – cold and persistent, pretty much the Sheffield standard – intensified as we ran to the bus stop, and a quick study of the timetable revealed that I'd got the times wrong. An hour's wait with little shelter, the faint whiff of piss and not much to talk about; I'd run out of questions about French cinema the previous night.

When we finally reached Castleton, it got really bad. Standing side by side in the rain, I withdrew the packed lunch

I'd carefully prepared: a round of peanut butter sandwiches each, two bags of McCoys – one cheese and onion, one grilled steak – and a bottle of Buck's Fizz (she'd mentioned that she liked wine). Debbie looked on solemnly as I poured it out into the two cups I'd nicked from the canteen, but when I leaned in for a kiss as I handed hers over, she nearly choked on her sandwich with laughter.

She was very nice about the whole thing, agreeing that a picnic was a lovely idea, and she liked peanut butter, and the rain wasn't my fault, nor the infrequency of the buses – the lack of an umbrella was perhaps an oversight, but anyone could forget a thing like that. I pleaded with her not to tell everyone in our halls and she was as good as her word.

She only told one person. Who then told everyone else. By breakfast the next day, the entire population of my halls knew. People I'd never met came over to ask if I had any peanut butter. One or two even bought jars of it to put in front of me, cackling as they left. It continued for over a week and I had little option but to laugh it off, while making a mental list of all who mocked me.

If/when I'm king, they will be first against the wall.

6

Do You Remember The First Time?

Time flies when you're brooding. For two weeks, I don't see Lou outside of lectures and tutorials, and while we still sit together, there are always at least seventeen centimetres between our chairs. Conversation is muted and she scarpers immediately afterwards. It isn't a total rejection, but it is evident that I've missed my chance.

On top of this, I have another problem. The autumn semester is halfway through and I haven't started my extended essay, which has to be submitted in four weeks. I haven't even come up with any ideas for what to write about, as I confess to Professor Pryce during our meeting one Friday morning. He isn't overly helpful or sympathetic.

'Choose an area of geography that interests you – any will do, it doesn't matter which – then think of a question about it. Examine the evidence for and against to build an argument. Conclude by repeating what you've written, but in fewer words. That's it.'

The first point is the tricky one. Nothing I've been taught at university so far has interested me. But seeing as Professor Pryce led several of those courses, I don't feel I can say this. He sighs loudly and, for the first time in the fifteen minutes I've been there, looks away from his computer screen.

'Look Henderson, just pick a subject. If you can hand in six thousand words on something, anything, related to geography then I guarantee that I'll pass it. I have little interest in reading one of your essays, so there is absolutely no way I am going to fail it, as that will mean I have to read two of them. Now bugger off to the library, try to find some inspiration there.'

Six thousand words sounds like an awful lot. Hasn't all the geography been studied? The theory of longshore drift, for example; that's pretty much agreed on. I'm not sure what I can add to the debate. But he's back to his computer screen. I leave his office and walk past the library – in two years, I've never found inspiration in there – and head for Devonshire Green. The pubs will be opening soon, and unlike libraries, you can drink beer in them while thinking.

The Washington is empty except for the landlord, who grins cheerfully as I walk in, pouring me a pint of Wards without being asked. This pleases me no end: it means I'm a regular, even though I'm certain he doesn't know my name. Settling down at our usual table in the corner, I remove the notepad from my rucksack then scrabble around for a pen.

Riverine systems? Too dull.

Glaciers? Same drawback.

I chew my pen, well and truly stumped. The landlord turns the sound system on, now he has a customer to entertain. *Sense* by The Lightning Seeds. A cheerful choice, if somewhat lacking in geographical stimulation.

Professor Pryce's words play over in my mind: think of a question that interests you. The major question right now, of course, is: will anything further happen between Lou and me? I've obsessed about her for two years – no, obsession is too strong a word; it makes it sound like I'm stalking her (and if you don't know where someone lives, your stalking options are limited). A crush sounds too childish for someone about to turn twenty-one. Infatuation? Yes, that'll do. I've been infatuated with her for two years now. Initially, it was based on her looks – which are incredible, have I mentioned that? – and it stayed there for most of those two years. But having got to know her, the infatuation has intensified. I like being with her. OK, she's rude to me a lot of the time, nor does she seem overly impressed with me. But she came round to see me.

She came round to see *me*.

There must have been a reason. There's a sliver of hope – if I can just work out what to do next. I decide to follow the learned professor's advice and examine the evidence. An obvious place to start with any methodological investigation is to observe historical patterns. To that end, I list all the women I've slept with to look for any trends that might show me how to move things forward.

I turn over a fresh page and write the first name: Martina.

* * *

Last week of my first term. Halls of residence Christmas party. Everyone is going and everyone will be drunk. The wounds of Debbie's rejection are still raw and I have thirty quid left of my grant for the term. More than enough for an evening of alcoholic excess that will blot out my failure to get even close to getting laid.

Everyone in halls knows Martina. Her distinctive appearance – black dress, black hair, black stockings and knee-high black leather boots, all offset by a constantly changing rainbow of lipstick and eye shadow – marks her out from the crowd, which is clearly the point. She's pointedly detached, carrying about her a superior air that makes me suspect she's from London. But on that overcrowded dancefloor, I find myself jiving drunkenly near her. Then next to her. Then with her. Then kissing her. Before I've worked out exactly what's happening, she's leading me across the courtyard to a block far, far away from my own.

The chilly night air clears my sozzled head slightly, but nothing sobers you up like the realisation you are about to have sex for the first time. As Martina opens the door to her room, I panic: a real girl is about to see my pale, scrawny body (a 'pigeon-chested bastard', as Rob bluntly put it). More urgently, I'm not sure what I'm supposed to do. I know the biological basics, thanks largely to the collection of porno videos owned by Matt's dad, but the order in which the different steps should be taken is still unclear. As is how you kick the whole thing off, given that I haven't called round to clean her windows or fix her photocopier.

Thankfully, Martina takes the lead. She removes my clothes, then hers. And, a few minutes later, in a tiny room in a hall of residence in Sheffield, I lose my virginity. Martina seems to know enough for the both of us and her insistence on keeping the lights on means I can satisfy the final few queries about female anatomy that Matt's dad's pornos left unanswered. She kicks me out in the early hours, and I stagger, happy and freezing, through a dusting of mushy snow back to my room. I've finally managed it. Sheffield: Sex City. Pulp were right all along.

I'm still glowing the next day when I see her walking towards me in the lunch queue.

'Hey, Martina!'

Nothing.

She continues to the back of the queue without so much as a glance sideways. I'm stunned. I was prepared for lies and pain and sorrow, maybe even a few germs and pneumonia. But not this: this is brutal. How can someone go from being eye-level with your genitals to refusing, a few hours later, to acknowledge your existence? It doesn't seem right. It's bad manners at the very least.

* * *

I couldn't have sex for over a year after Martina. Not through choice; I simply failed to find anyone else willing to take part. Fortunately, Sheffield offers plenty of distractions for a young man with a student grant in his bank account. The pubs along Ecclesall Road; the record shops tucked away in side streets; student discounts for both Wednesday and United; the parks, the cinemas, clubs and curry houses; and, of course, the non-stop gig circuit. I was so busy that, by the end of my second year, I began to wonder if I even needed it.

Then I met Suzanne.

One muggy Friday evening, I headed to the geography library to return a book about meteorology. I'd forgotten ever taking it out, but after discovering a stack of terse notes with escalating fines in my pigeon hole, the only sensible course of action was to sneak it back into the library and swear I'd never borrowed it in the first place. After successfully negotiating the electronic sensors at the door – a double-wrapping of tin foil always does the trick – I was hunting for its correct shelf when a girl with a tangle of blonde hair marched over.

'Have you finished with that?' she snapped.

'Er, yes. Do you want it?'

'Yes.' She snatched it from me and headed for a table by the window. I felt things stirring that hadn't stirred for a while and, despite not knowing anything about her except which textbook she was reading, I followed as far as a shelf of journals from where I could study her more closely. Her long bare legs stretched out from tight denim shorts, and her skimpy top didn't even bother trying to contain her cleavage. But on my fifth peek, she caught me.

'Do you want your book back?'

'Er … no. I didn't understand it, if I'm honest.'

'No, nor do I', she sighed. 'Fancy a drink instead?'

We headed to the Star & Garter, a cosy pub directly opposite the department, in which she told me she was studying for her final exams. I settled quickly into my usual role of nodding along and letting the girl talk, but after one drink she said she wanted to go home. There was no invitation to go with her, yet it was somehow implied. I followed obediently. She asked if I wanted a cup of tea while unlocking the door, but then headed straight to her room. My year-and-a-half-long famine came to a swift end.

The next morning, we even remembered to exchange names.

I returned to the library on Monday, hoping to see her again. There she was, same seat, same book. She told me to give her ten minutes to finish. We didn't bother with the pub this time. This pattern was repeated the next day, and the next. By the following Friday, she told me she needed to cram in more studying and that I needn't bother coming up to the library, we could meet outside at six-thirty each evening. After a couple more days, she told me to go straight to her house at eight each evening.

This was the perfect summer romance: energetic sex every night and the days free to spend as I pleased. We didn't see each other outside of her bedroom for a whole fortnight, until the need to revise for one of my own exams forced me back to the library. I headed over to find her.

'Hi Suzanne, how's it going?'

'Awful. My last exam is tomorrow: fluvial geomorphology, and I don't understand any of it.'

'Should I come round tonight?' I asked, worried that our routine might be interrupted.

'Sorry, I'm planning an all-nighter.'

'Maybe tomorrow?'

Without replying, Suzanne peeked past the shelf that hid us from the rest of the library. Next, she undid the top button of her shorts, took my left hand and slid it inside. Holding it firmly in place, she moved herself back and forth while I stared at the shelf. Glaciology journals. Twenty-four volumes.

Three short squeaks later – which, rather disturbingly, brought back memories of Ozzy and Geezer, the guinea pigs we had when I was little – she removed my hand.

'Did you just have an orgasm?' I whispered.

'I did. Thank you very much.'

'Wow.'

'Wow indeed.'

We shared an awkward silence. I wasn't sure how to respond. Or where to put my hand.

'What happens now?' I asked eventually.

'I need to do some work.'

'Are you not going to … y'know?' I nodded in the general direction of my groin, in case the meaning wasn't clear.

'Not now, no. Later, though.'

'What time? What time should I come round, I mean, not what time for the actual … act.'

'I understood. Come round at the usual time.'

'Cool. See you later.'

'Chris?'

'Hmm?'

'Don't tell anyone about this. Seriously.'

'OK.'

'And Chris?'

'Hmm?'

'Wash your hands before you go.'

One week later, it was over.

She rang and asked to meet. I hoped, now that her exams were finished, we could spend a whole day together. Do something romantic: a walk in the park, or perhaps the new Godzilla film. Followed by sex, naturally. But as soon as I arrived, she told me she was leaving.

'My parents are coming to pick me up this afternoon. I wanted to say goodbye before I left.'

'When will I see you again?'

'Never, I expect. I won't be coming back. I'm moving to Swansea and I need to find a place to live.'

'Swansea?'

'I've been offered a job.' She didn't say what it was, and I didn't care; I was too busy trying to calculate how much train tickets to Wales might cost.

'I could come and see you there.'

'There's no need. It's been fun, Chris, and you've really helped me these last few weeks. I needed something simple and uncomplicated to distract me.'

'Simple and uncomplicated?'

'Meant in the nicest possible way, I promise.'

We stood there, holding hands. Two hearts under the twenty-storey Arts Tower.

'I'll miss you.'

'No, you won't. You're a twenty-year-old male. You'll be over me in a couple of weeks, and you'll have forgotten about me completely by autumn.'

She was half right. I did get over her, about twice as quickly as she predicted, but I certainly didn't forget. Even now, I make a point of remembering our time together regularly. Always with a box of tissues to hand.

* * *

I drain my pint and study the list. Two girls in two years, to add to the none in eighteen years before that. It's distinctly unimpressive for someone approaching their twenty-first birthday. It only just qualifies as a list.

Average, middle of the road, nothing special.

Me all over.

Still, using the analytical skills nurtured under Professor Pryce's diligent stewardship, I identify some encouraging trends (while acknowledging the statistically insignificant sample size).

One: both were prepared, for periods varying from three hours to three weeks, to spend their time with a scruffy, music-obsessed Plymouth Argyle fan. Lou has also done this, albeit without bucketloads of enthusiasm.

Two: both chose to study in Sheffield – again, the same as Lou.

Three: Suzanne was a geographer. So is Lou. Does this indicate a progression towards partners with similar academic interests? I certainly hope so.

Four: Martina and Suzanne were both more attractive than I should reasonably be aiming for. This recent upward curve is most encouraging, although it's going to have to rise even more sharply to reach Lou's level.

The major negative conclusion is that I still have no idea what to do next. In both instances, I was the passive beneficiary of someone else's actions. What little sex there's been happened *to* me, rather than being instigated *by* me. The closest I've got to affirmative action is following someone in the library and staring at them. It's not a fool-proof strategy on which to base all future liaisons and fails to outline a clear pattern to follow with Lou, other than tempt her into the glaciology section and hope for the best.

No, I'm going to need to think of a Plan B. And C. Probably D as well.

I order another pint; this could be a long afternoon.

7

Lucky Man

The twenty-four-hour computer room on Glossop Road is a grim place. Inhabited solely by students looking one or more of suicidal, bored or asleep, it reeks of body odour and Wotsits, an unwelcome combination that is magnified by the stifling heat coming from the rows of clunky cream computers. Their incessant buzzing is compounded by the unending whoosh-whoosh-clack of the huge printers stationed behind the reception desk.

It is these machines that I hate more than anything. Printing costs a staggering five pence per sheet and the university insists that all coursework is double-spaced and printed twice, meaning four times the cost for each piece submitted. However succinct I make them – and they rarely get close to the target word count – the final sum charged by the sour-faced receptionists is invariably outrageous, especially when converted into the number of pints it would have bought. I wrote a letter of complaint to the university's finance officer in my first year, my sole venture into student activism. She replied to explain that student grants were there to cover exactly this kind of study-based cost. I wrote again to tell her that I pissed my grant up the wall halfway through the first term and was living off my overdraft and cheques from Grandpa. She didn't reply to that one.

My first piece of GIS coursework is even more of an injustice. With several colour maps needed, the costs escalate further, as colour print-outs cost fifteen pence a sheet. I reluctantly withdraw a fiver on my way there.

It's Friday. Deadline day and therefore packed. I am forced to walk along the rows in search of a free terminal. Just as I'm about to give up and spend the fiver in Bar One, I spot a familiar sweep of dark hair in the far corner.

'Hi, Lou.'

In less than a second, she manages to look surprised, almost pleased, then anxious as she checks who's within earshot.

'Hello, Christopher. What brings you here?' she says, tucking her hair behind her ears. She has exquisite ears.

'Printing out my GIS coursework.'

'You've already finished it? It's not due for another week.' She nods at the chair next to hers, inviting me to sit. I slide the floppy disk into its slot, shaking my head at the imminent outlay. Two copies, twenty pages each, and ten in colour. I hope a fiver will be enough. Lou leans over to see what I've written. Time to put Plan B into action: be mysterious and unavailable.

'I might go for a coffee later,' I say, scrutinising one of my maps.

'Might you indeed,' she replies, still reading over my shoulder. 'And who *might* you be going with?'

'Ah, that's for me to know.'

'Yes, I suppose it is. Were there that many people living in Brooklyn in 1900? Shit, I'll have to recheck mine now.'

This isn't going to plan; James Bond never gets side-lined by geography questions. 'Anyway, about that coffee ...'

'Chris, I'm not sure if you're trying to ask me for another drink, but if you are, then I can't, I'm meeting Jonathan for lunch.'

Bugger. Plan B doesn't extend as far as what to do if she says no. Which, with hindsight, is a bit of a flaw. And Plan C is not an option right now, as I don't know where the nearest florist is.

'How about next week?'

'It's reading week, we don't have any classes. You knew that, surely?'

'Yeah, of course,' I lie. 'We could meet anyway, if you like?'

'I can't. Jonathan's hired a cottage in Scotland. Somewhere on Skye. We're leaving tomorrow.'

'Oh. Sounds great.'

I have no idea if Skye is great or not, but know I could never afford to hire a cottage there. It wouldn't occur to me; it wasn't even Plan D. The differences between myself and Jonathan are, once again, all too evident. How did someone roughly my age get to be so much more grown up?

'Things are still serious between you two, then?'

'Do you mean between me and my boyfriend of two years, who I live with? Yes Chris, they are.'

'It's just the other week, at my house, I thought ...'

She swivels in her chair to look right at me, but the half-smile has been replaced with a knitted brow. Her eyes bore into me. I've never seen her properly angry, but suspect this is merely the warm-up.

'You thought what, exactly? I have a boyfriend, Chris. Nothing could happen between us. And you really shouldn't have tried it on last week, that was completely out of order.'

'But you came round to my house–'

'Only to get some notes.'

'–and you were flirting with me.'

'It was just a bit of fun, I thought you knew that.'

'But you were the one who rubbed my legs, and took my hands, and ...'

This is all wrong. I didn't even invite her round; how is this my fault? I turn off my computer and remove my floppy disk.

63

'Sometimes girls flirt with boys because they want a bit of attention,' Lou says, fractionally more gently. 'I guess your little cut-out-and-keep guide to women didn't explain that.'

'I guess not. It won't happen again.'

'Good.'

I wait a couple of minutes before departing to make sure it doesn't look like I'm storming off. But there's only so long you can stare at a switched-off computer before you start to look a bit stupid.

'Chris?' she whispers as I stand up. 'I'm sorry if I led you on, but nothing is going to happen between us. We're just friends.'

'It's OK. I get it. See you around.' I sling my rucksack over my shoulder and head for the door in what I hope is a wounded, brooding manner.

'You need to collect your print-outs from the desk.'

'Good point. Thanks.'

So, this is where I stand. Second place, if that. Who knows how many others she's stringing along? It's been a bit of a waste of time, all things considered. I collect my print-outs; four pounds exactly. One pound change. Not even enough for a pint to cheer myself up.

Instead, I set off home to dissect, in depth and alone, yet another failed attempt at seduction. At least it gives me something to fill the hours until *TFI Friday* starts.

* * *

I manage to stretch out the post-mortem until Final Score on Saturday, and a rare win for Argyle perks me up somewhat. Even better, the next gig on the calendar has also come around. I suggested to Rob that we see Silver Sun. They are that rarest of things – a band I knew about before him – and, even better, it's at the Leadmill.

I've been there over twenty times and every last one has been a hypnotic experience. It was love at first sight, first sound, first smell, first taste. The club is big enough to feel significant – the fact that it was the setting for Pulp's first gig adds considerable indie kudos – yet it's still small enough to feel intimate: you can count the beads of sweat on the drummer's forehead if you're prepared to brave the mosh pit. A sooty, red-brick building near the station, it has that air of scruffy, unpolished dishevelment that all great venues have, but not so much that you felt the need to get a tetanus jab the next day. The darkly painted walls quickly become slick with condensation, while the flypaper-like floor grabs at your shoes with its claws of spilt beer, chewing gum and other unidentifiable grime. The stacked speakers pulse basslines through you like electric shocks, while the bottles of beer begin each evening chilled, getting progressively warmer as the bar staff stop bothering to stack them in fridges.

But it isn't just the venue; I love being part of a scene, a crowd. They wear the same T-shirts – always one colour, with a band logo on the front – and dance with the same slow, awkward swaying movements, which build up to whatever you want as the alcohol loosens your joints. They talk about the same bands and adore the same songs, from the instant classics to the obscure and plain odd. If Britpop is our religion, then the Leadmill is its high temple in Sheffield.

But for once, possibly the first time, I'm struggling to tune in. Silver Sun are vigorous enough, all energetic guitars and a lead singer who's clearly been studying Jarvis's repertoire of mic-swinging and wobbly limbs. But it feels like Britpop by numbers, all knowing lyrics and over-zealous guitars. Perhaps I've heard too much of this stuff; I'll have to sneak in a bit of Bon Jovi when I get home, try to balance things out a bit. But it's not the band's fault, not really. My mind is elsewhere.

Back in the computer room and the latest conversation with Lou.

Another disappointment. Another rejection. The latest in an increasingly long line.

The band finishes and I'm about to leave – I lost Rob to the throng at the front a long time ago – but as I head for the door, live music segues into club night. 'Bug Powder Dust', the perfect start to any night of head-nodding and shoe-shuffling. Maybe I'll stay, just for this one. I buy a beer – still chilled, thankfully – and search for a relatively moisture-free patch of wall to slump against.

'Thank God you're here, finally someone half-intelligent to talk to. Well, quarter-intelligent.'

'Lou! What are you doing here?' I say, startled. I didn't even notice her walk up, but now she's sharing my bit of wall.

'One of the girls from halls is celebrating her twenty-first tonight. I've not been here before, so thought, why not? It's alright,' she says, although her half-hearted shrug suggests that it's little more than.

'Aren't you supposed to be in Scotland?'

'We're not going to Scotland,' she snaps. 'New Fucking Labour need Jonathan more than I do, apparently. Or he needs them more than me, anyway. He's postponed it, the selfish bastard.'

A tiny crack in that small window of opportunity has re-opened, although I'll have to play this one extremely well to capitalise.

'So you'll be in Sheffield this week?'

'I'm going home to do some reading. That's what we're supposed to do during reading week, isn't it?'

'I suppose so.'

'Why don't you come with me?'

'What?' I'm convinced I've misheard her. It's easily done in the Leadmill; my ears usually ring for a good few hours afterwards.

'I said, why don't you come too? We do the same courses, we may as well study together.'

'You want me to come to your house?'

She leans into me. Shoulder to shoulder becomes arm to arm. Her fingers flick out in search of mine. I make them findable.

'Mummy's at my auntie's house, we'll have the place to ourselves.' Her fingers are now twisting around mine. 'What do you think?'

I'm not sure what I think. She's performed a complete, one-hundred-and-eighty-degree U-turn – without any explanation or justification – in little more than twenty-four hours. I've gone from being an annoying pest breaking up her relationship to being invited to her house for … what, exactly? Officially, it's only an invitation to read textbooks together, but her fingers are now stroking the back of my hand. This is hugely exciting – and yet also extremely unfair. It's hard enough trying to work out what's on girls' minds; it's near impossible when they constantly change them. I briefly consider turning her down, just to see what it feels like, but she's now got one hand on the small of my back. Debates about the fickleness of the female mind can be put on hold for another time.

'Yeah, OK. That'd be great. Should we meet at the department?'

'You'll have to meet me there, I'm not driving down with you. Someone might see us.'

'No, of course.'

'Be at Grindleford station, seven o'clock tomorrow. I'll pick you up.'

'OK.'

'I'd better go and find my friends. Don't try and kiss me.'

'No, of course not. Sorry.'

'And don't start saying sorry again. See you tomorrow. Seven pm. Don't be late.'

'I won't.'

Now would be a good time to play it cool, but I need to be sure. I keep hold of her fingers as she moves away.

'Lou, do you like me? Because sometimes you act like you do, but at other times you act like I get on your nerves. It's a bit confusing.'

'A little bit,' she replies, after some consideration. 'But I'm only telling you because I'm drunk.'

'How much?'

'I've already said, a little bit.'

'How much of a little bit?'

'On a scale of one to ten?' she asks, the right eyebrow lifting.

'Yep.'

She shakes her head. 'I'm not going to tell you. If I say a high number, you'll get all full of yourself. And if I give you a low number, you'll put on that sad puppyish look. Which is quite endearing, but I'm not in the mood for it right now.'

'I can take it.'

'OK. Between four and seven.'

'That's not very accurate.'

'It's all you're getting.'

'Well, for me it's a nine and a half,' I reply, taking a swig of beer. 'It has been since the first year.'

'I know. You've been staring at me in lectures since then.'

'How do you even know that? I always sit behind you.'

'Girls have their little tricks too,' she laughs. 'And how dare you only give me nine and a half.'

'It would be a ten, but your language is often quite unladylike, so I deducted half a mark.'

'I'm sure I can reclaim it, one way or another.'

She pulls her hand away and walks off without turning back.

That's how you play it cool.

My mouth is dry with fear and expectation: I need another beer. Searching in my pocket for cash, I find my ticket for the night. Even if Lou changes her mind, which is far from impossible, this is still a truly memorable night. The night she invited me to her house.

Silver Sun are going right in the centre of my pin board.

8

Country House

Her car is parked halfway up the hill that leads away from Grindleford station. I planned to amble over casually, jacket slung over my shoulder, but the rain has increased from an urban drizzle to a rural deluge. Instead, I run to the car, using my rucksack as a makeshift umbrella. It doesn't work very well.

'Did anyone see you?' Lou asks as I shut the car door.

'I'm fine thanks, how are you?' I reply gruffly, shoving an overflowing carrier bag of books from the passenger seat.

An ominous sign: it suggests she's planning to do a lot of studying this week.

'Sorry. How was the journey?'

'Short. And no, nobody saw me.' I decided during the fifteen-minute train ride that the woman in the ticket office was merely jolly, not suspicious. 'I wasn't sure if you'd be here.'

'I wasn't sure if you'd come.'

'Well, I did. You invited me.' Worth clarifying that now, in case there is any dispute later.

'You can shove my books in the back if you like. I drove straight here, so haven't been home yet.' She makes a cautious scan of the deserted road, then pecks me gently on the cheek before starting the engine. It doesn't look like the emergency condom in my wallet is going to be needed.

The journey proceeds in silence. I use the time to fine-tune my latest entry to the Guinness Book of Killer Seduction Lines.

'So, this is Grindleford.'

'It's Upper Padley, actually. Grindleford's across the river.'

'Why is it called Grindleford station?'

'I don't know.'

We sit in her car, outside a wooden gate, beyond which is a grey stone cottage.

The rain beats loudly on the roof.

'Can you open the gate? I know it's raining, but you're already wet.'

'No problem,' I reply but remain in my seat. I have to ask, even though I might hate myself if I don't get the answer I want. 'Lou, are you sure you want to do this?'

'Yes. I think so.'

'I don't want to mess things up with you and Jonathan, if you're planning to patch things up.'

'I'm not planning on him finding out. We're still together, I just need … a break.'

'OK.'

'Any more questions or shall we go inside?'

'Just one more. Did you say your mum is away?'

'Yes, she's in Bournemouth.'

'Then why are there so many lights on?'

* * *

'You should have rung ahead, darling, I'd have got some shopping in.'

Lou's mum is very like her youngest daughter. Well spoken, well dressed, with dark hair and minimal makeup. Just a bit wrinklier.

'Why aren't you in Bournemouth? We were expecting the place to ourselves,' Lou replies. 'To study, we do the same course,' she adds hurriedly.

'Your auntie's not well, I'm going next week instead. Have you both eaten? There's some soup left over if you're hungry,

Chris, I'll get you a bowl. Would you like some cheese with it? I've got a bit of Wensleydale somewhere, it's very good, it's got little pieces of apricot in it. Maybe some wine too? Or a tea first to warm up?'

She searches through various drawers and cupboards before bringing out a set of expensive-looking bowls and cutlery. Everything in the kitchen looks expensive, while also managing to appear old-fashioned. It's not unlike the National Trust houses I was dragged around as a kid; a few stuffed animal heads wouldn't look out of place.

It's the biggest kitchen I've been in. The oven has eight hobs on it; who needs eight hobs? What kind of extravagant banquets are cooked up in here? One wall is covered by a gargantuan rack of herbs and spices, while another is hidden behind an array of pointy metal utensils that would service a medieval torture chamber. It's also drowning under a tsunami of food: a giant loaf of crusty bread takes up most of one counter, jockeying for space with the jars of pasta, rice, beans. There are two – two! – overflowing fruit bowls and, I notice as Lou's mum takes out the wine and cheese, the fridge is bursting at the seams. All this for one person; I wonder what it looks like when she *has* been shopping.

Lou's mum hands me a huge bowl of chunky vegetable soup and then passes over the bread, along with a small china dish containing real butter. She's right about the cheese, too, it's mouth-wateringly good.

'What about your week in Scotland?' she asks Lou, hunting in the cupboards for more delicacies.

'Jonathan's got Labour stuff on this week, so he cancelled it. He's more in love with Tony Blair than me.'

'Don't be so silly, dear, you know how seriously he takes his politics. I'm sure he couldn't avoid it. Are you and Jonathan friends, Chris?'

The tone remains friendly but the change, while subtle, is noticeable. She's testing me out, checking why I'm really here. Through a mouthful of fluffy white bread and crumbly, apricotty cheese, I play along.

'More acquaintances than friends. We've played football against each other a few times. I've only really got to know Lou this term, even though we've been on the same course for over two years now. Isn't that funny? Hopefully I'll get to know him better soon. Lovely soup, Mrs Banks. Is it homemade?'

Lou scowls at me across the table. I grin back, milking this rare turn with the upper hand.

'Thank you, yes it is. Perhaps Jonathan can come and join you both once he's finished whatever he's doing?'

'That sounds fun, doesn't it Lou?' I smirk. She flings more death stares across the table but, as I slice off some of the Cheddar with chives that has appeared, I no longer care. Sex is looking increasingly unlikely, but the kitchen's warmth and the Banks' cheese selection has already justified the train fare. Anyway, it seems that the inquisition is over, as their conversation quickly turns to people I don't know and have no interest in. I tune out and focus on polishing off as much food as I can. When Lou's mum refills my soup bowl without me even having to ask, I wonder if I can come and stay every weekend, regardless of whether Lou's here or not.

But after scraping out the second bowl, I'm exhausted. Whether it's a soup overdose, the two glasses of wine or the emotional drama of the last few days, I'm done. I make sure that my stifled yawn is noticeable.

'Chris, you look tired, dear. Let me show you where the spare room is.'

'Thank you, Mrs Banks.'

'I'll find you some fresh towels as well.'

'Lovely, Mrs Banks.'

Lou remains at the table, her face unreadable. Regret? Relief? Annoyance? I'll find out soon enough, but hopefully it can wait until morning.

* * *

'Chris? Are you awake?'

'I am now,' I grumble.

She slides under the silky-soft duvet and wraps her legs around mine. I decide I can let her off this once.

'God, that was so embarrassing.'

'What time is it?'

'One o'clock. Move over.'

'Have you been talking to your mum all this time?'

'If you call a rant about the evils of infidelity "talking".'

'Does she suspect something?'

'Of course she does, she lived with Daddy for twenty years. And keep your voice down, she might hear us.'

A sliver of moonlight creeps in through the curtains. She looks more beautiful than ever. I'm tangled up in bed with the most perfect girl I know. And I still don't know what I'm supposed to do next.

'Chris … I like you. Maybe more than a seven.'

'Is that higher or lower than Jonathan's number?'

'I like him, too. I love him. But not as much as I used to. And I don't think he feels the same way about me anymore.' A single tear slips down her cheek, jolting me fully awake. This is now serious. While for me the last few weeks have been exciting and confusing in equal measure, the situation is evidently upsetting for her. And I don't want to end up getting blamed for it.

'Listen, Lou, I don't need to do any reading this week. I never read any of the stuff on those lists we're given. How about you go to your room, and tomorrow we go for a walk or something, then I'll head back to Sheffield, give you some space to think about what you want. When you've decided, come and find me in Sheffield. If you decide you like me, then you already know how much I like you. If you decide you want to be with Jonathan, that's fine, we can still be friends. Does that sound OK?'

There are more tears now, and a few sniffles. 'Yes, that sounds OK.'

'Good.' I shuffle in the sheets, getting ready to spread out once more.

'Except for one thing. Can I stay here tonight?'

'Sure.'

'Thank you, Chris. You've been great about this.'

I know I'm doing the right thing. It feels grown up, it must be the right thing.

* * *

'Chris? Are you awake?'

'What time is it now?'

'Five-thirty.'

'Does everyone wake up at this time in the Peak District?'

'I haven't been to sleep. I've been thinking.'

'All night? Seriously?'

'I haven't made a decision yet. But I wanted to say thank you for being so understanding about everything.'

'That's fine. It probably could have waited until nine o'clock, though. Can I go back to sleep now?'

'If you like.'

I close my eyes, then open them as Lou slides her hand over my stomach.

The lower bit.

'What are you doing?'

'You're leaving today …'

'To give you space to think things over. I thought that's what you wanted?'

'I've done enough thinking for now. But we need to be quiet, she'll go mental if she hears us.'

My sleep-starved mind is all over the place. I tried to do the honourable thing, to respect her wishes. Is this a test to see if I meant it? Or my reward for being noble? And where the hell did I put those johnnies?

She's now on top of me, pulling off my T-shirt, but slaps my hand away when I try to do the same to hers. I give up trying to work out what the rules are and lie back. Briefly lifting her hips, she slips my boxer shorts off with one hand, then finishes me off quickly. It's something of a surprise when she wipes her hand on the duvet. I'm not offended – I've done the same thing myself, literally thousands of times – but despite the spice rack, the cheese selection and the great big country house, I'm beginning to suspect she isn't as posh as I thought all this time.

* * *

She's gone by the time I wake up.

Eight-thirty; no point going back to sleep. Not knowing where the shower is, I pull on my clothes and walk down the curved wooden staircase to the kitchen. Mrs Banks told me to make myself at home, and while that offer probably doesn't extend to watching *The Big Breakfast* in my boxer shorts with a bowl of Rice Krispies, I reason that a hot drink would be acceptable. Kettle on, I track down the teabags and select the largest mug I can find in a wooden cabinet that contained hundreds of the things, all with their handles pointed at precisely the same angle. There's a packet of Dunhills on the windowsill, so I take one along with the lighter and head outside. A huge tortoiseshell cat, which I missed last night, eyes me suspiciously from the top of the fridge, before leaping down and racing upstairs. No doubt to report on my cigarette theft; I dislike cats generally, but this one seems a particularly miserable specimen.

It's a stunning morning. The late autumn sun peeks above the horizon, illuminating the dew that rises then hangs in the fields. Sheep greet each other grumpily across the valley. A church clock chimes nine. It's soothing, serene; rural charm by the bucketload. I grew up in the countryside and wasn't all that impressed; why is this different? It must be the sheep. Sheep always look cosy and pastoral. Cows simply looked confused or annoyed.

I wonder how often Lou comes back here. I only see her on Tuesdays and Thursdays; I have no idea what she does during the rest of the week. I don't really know her at all; we first spoke seven weeks ago and there are still many unknowns. Yet it seems strange for someone so confident and self-assured to remain so close to home. I was desperate to get away after my A-levels. Not so far that the train fares became prohibitive, but far enough to prevent any impromptu visits from my parents. Somewhere bigger, certainly. I'm living the story of every American rock song: small-town boy hits the road, looking for bright lights, loose women and adventure. And I'm not from a small town; I'm from the last house on the outer street of a tiny village a few miles from the small and pointless town of Tavistock. I'd like to see Bruce Springsteen turn that into a song.

It wasn't just our village I was escaping; I was desperate to get away from Devon completely. When I tell people that's where home is, their response is always the same: 'Ooh, that must be lovely'. In their minds, Devon is all cream teas and country pubs, sandy beaches and summer holidays. But they're thinking of Lynmouth, Totnes, Dartmouth. They're not thinking about my bit: inland, near the Tamar. Some might say the countryside around us is scenic, but when it's the same scene every day for eighteen years, the novelty fades. And the stench of silage does little to help. Freshly cut meadows can give off a certain rustic pungency, but our village smells of slowly decomposing wet grass. It's very different, trust me.

Of course, when you explain this, they'll say: 'But it must be nice living so close to Dartmoor.' These words are spoken only by people who have never been to Dartmoor. Dartmoor is shit. It's windy, bleak and saturated, even when it hasn't rained for weeks. You can walk for miles and all you'll see is bogs. 'Oh, but it's so atmospheric.' For atmospheric, read cloudy. And don't get me started on the ponies. They're just small horses, not bloody unicorns. There was nothing to keep me in Devon at eighteen, and there will be nothing to bring me back at twenty-one, except the lack of alternatives.

The worst thing was the lack of gigs. Oasis never dreamed of playing Tavistock; if you want live music, the best you can hope for is a Showaddywaddy tribute act or the latest brother–sister folk act singing pitiful, self-penned ditties about how the moors are a bit spooky at night. Admittedly the scene picks up a bit in late October, when the Salvation Army band take up their residence outside Woolworths. Matt and I spent many happy hours trying to lob pick'n'mix into their instruments (five points for a tuba, ten for a euphonium). But proper music? Not a chance.

Yet my childhood was happy, if uneventful. Lou's, from the little I've learned, was much more traumatic – and yet she chose to remain close by. Maybe the more the cord to home is frayed, the tighter you needed to hold on to it. Yet another query for Rob; I'll have to start writing these down, so I don't forget them.

'Hello Chris, did you sleep well?'

Occupied by thoughts of home, I somehow missed Lou's mum coming outside. She's wrapped in a white silk dressing gown that barely reaches her knees. She has good legs for someone who must be in her fifties. I could easily develop a crush on her, if her daughter wasn't enough trouble.

'Very well, thank you Mrs Banks. I made myself some tea, I hope that's OK.'

'Of course, dear. Cigarette?' She holds the packet of Dunhills towards me.

'Thanks. I have to admit, I stole one already. Your cat caught me in the act. I don't think it approved.'

'Oh, don't worry about Stevens. She's always a bit jumpy around strange men.' The emphasis is on strange; subtle, but still noticeable.

'Stevens? Oh, right, I get it.'

'Louise's father was a big fan. We had to listen to him trying to master 'Morning Has Broken' every evening for months before he got bored and moved on to the next hobby. That was typical of him. He always loved music, though. He had over five hundred records. Lou tells me you're a music fan, too.'

The way she speaks about him in the past tense is disturbing, as if he's dead. Perhaps he is to her. It's hard to escape the feeling that her mistrust of him extends to all males, though; she's smiling, but it isn't especially warm. I get the distinct impression that I'm welcome in her house as long as I leave at the earliest opportunity.

'Did you and Louise have a chat last night? She told me things have got a little confused between the two of you.'

'We did. I'm going to head back to Sheffield today, give her some space.'

'That sounds very sensible.'

'It went a bit further than either of us expected, I suppose. I knew she was with Jonathan. They'll get through it, I'm sure.'

'And how about you? How are you feeling?'

Well, Mrs Banks, I'm not too sure. I've desperately wanted to have sex with your daughter for over two years now, but I never thought she liked me – didn't think she even knew who I was. But a few weeks ago she started flirting with me, led me on for a bit, came round to my house and nearly kissed me but changed her mind, then she got pissed and invited me here. Which I hoped would be a week of non-stop shagging, but you ruined that by not going to see your sister, even though she's sick – which is a little bit selfish of you, if I'm honest – but while initially frustrating, about an hour ago your daughter helped me to ejaculate onto your expensive-looking bedsheets, shortly after we agreed that nothing was going to happen. So all in all, I'm a little vexed.

'I'm fine, Mrs Banks, thanks for asking.'

'Louise has always been a heartbreaker. But she's had a very difficult time these last few years. She's not as tough as she seems.'

I find this hard to believe, but say nothing. Banks women are not to be crossed. At least she asked how I'm feeling; Lou never has.

'I expect Louise told you that her father left me for another woman,' she continues, lighting another cigarette and passing the packet to me.

'Um, yes, she did.'

'It's a terrible thing for anyone to go through, Chris. Even though you're all still young, it still hurts. For everyone involved.'

I suck on my Dunhill.

'I can give you a lift to the station if you like, there's a train to Sheffield shortly after ten. Would you like some breakfast first?'

'That would be lovely, but I said to Lou that we'd–'

'Are eggs and bacon OK?'

'Great. Thank you.'

Maybe an earlier train is a better idea. Lou will understand. Besides, it doesn't feel like I'm being given a choice. We go inside and before long I'm tucking into another hearty meal, the eggs and bacon accompanied by beans, a herby sausage and some toast and tea. As I mop up the bean juice with the last bit of toast, Mrs Banks, now smartly dressed in a matching pastel jacket and trousers, returns.

'We'd better get going, you'll miss the train.'

'I should say goodbye before I leave.'

'Oh, there's no need, I'm sure. You'll see each other back in Sheffield before long. I'll get you some paper, you can leave her a note.'

My pen hovers over the paper; what's the polite thing to write after you've almost slept with someone for the first time? And how do you phrase it so that her mother, who will no doubt read it, can't work it out? In the end, I scribble a quick note and swill down the last of the tea. Soup, wine, cheese, fags, a hand job and a full English breakfast; this little trip to the country hasn't been a complete write-off.

9

London, Can You Wait?

It feels too soon to go back, too anti-climactic after weeks of simmering tension that has yet to be resolved. And the smug note I left for Rob and Andy to explain my absence will dramatically lose its impact if I turn up again the next day.

Instead, I do something extremely rare: I act on impulse. I need space, a chance to clear my head. Normally that doesn't take long, but these latest events are deeply confusing and I need a female perspective on them. If anyone can tell me what's going on, it's Cecilia. So, back at the station, I withdraw forty pounds, buy some wine gums and the latest *Melody Maker* and, through gritted wallet, buy an open return to London.

I've never been to London, not properly. My sole experience was an ill-fated school trip. Despite leaving at four in the morning, our coach got stuck in a traffic jam on the A303, leaving us with only enough time to circle Trafalgar Square three times as Mr Greenwood, the head teacher, pointed out the various sites of national importance as they flew past. I have little interest in seeing them at a more leisurely pace, but I do want to see the spiritual home of Britpop. London more than pulls its weight in terms of bands – Suede, Sleeper, Placebo, Kula Shaker, Echobelly, Elastica, 3 Colours Red and Gene, among others – and most migrate there before long, with Camden their collective hangout.

But once I've made my way to Clapham Junction, I realise I don't know where Cecilia lives. I know her address – 61 Northcote Road – but have no idea which way it is from the station. A man roughly my age is sitting on the pavement outside the station; I go over to ask for directions.

'Excuse me, I'm looking for–'

'Fuck off.'

He doesn't even look up. I'm shocked; cockneys are never this unhelpful on *EastEnders*. Fortunately someone else is coming, an elderly man shuffling slowly towards me on his stick.

'I wonder if you can help me, I'm looking for Northcote Road. Hello? Hello?'

Nothing; not even a flick of the head. With the locals of little use, I duck back into the station, aiming for the small kiosk by the escalator which has a small selection of books. I thumb through a pocket A to Z, looking for the correct page.

'You buyin' that?' asks the overweight man squeezed into a tiny booth.

'No, I just wanted to check–'

'Either buy it or put it back. It's not a fuckin' library.'

'Alright, alright,' I reply. Why is everyone in London such a miserable bastard? Grandpa always warned me off this place: nothing good ever happens and everyone is an idiot, a criminal, or both. I should have listened. At least in that brief glimpse of map I worked out that I need to head left. It takes a bit of searching, but eventually I reach the right road and find Cecilia's house.

Except it's a café, not a house. I walk in, feeling confused and wishing I was back in Sheffield. London feels too big for me.

'I'm looking for number sixty-one,' I tell the huge balding man behind the counter. He looks vaguely Mediterranean, but I can't tell which country he's from. Nor does the menu behind the counter offer any clues; all it has on it is thirty variations on a full English.

'This sixty-one,' he replies. He doesn't look at me either, but at least he answered without swearing, instantly elevating him to the status of friendliest Londoner so far.

'OK, I must have got it wrong. My sister said she lives here.'

'Tall, nice tits?' The hand gesture is a little unnecessary.

'Erm, yeah, I suppose so.'

'Flat upstairs. She come back six, six thirty.'

The clock next to a picture of those old ruins in Athens says two-thirty. And it's freezing outside. 'Is it alright if I wait here?'

'You buy something?'

I read through the chalked-up menu; everything is nearly twice the price of Sheffield. 'I haven't got much money, actually. I'm a student.'

He starts muttering away to himself, a string of what I assume are Greek obscenities, and turns to the pans bubbling away on the cooker. Still with his back to me, he reverts to barked English. 'Sit at back. Not window.'

I shuffle miserably to the back of the café. Half an hour in London and I've been sworn at, ignored and twice made to feel cheap. Paddington had been offered free board and lodgings by this point in his visit to the capital; it doesn't seem fair. From an uncomfortable plastic chair with a crack in it, I eye the sticky pastries piled high behind a smeary glass screen. It's been hours since breakfast, but with the pre-journey wine gums and Tube ticket, I'm already eating into my budget for the trip far too rapidly.

A splodge of cream splurges from the side of one of the cakes, and two flies descend on it greedily.

Even the cakes are taunting me. This is going to be torture.

The café owner disappears through the door behind the counter, and a tiny woman with a scarf around her head takes his place. Is she his wife? Mother? She could even be his daughter; while he looks about fifty, it's harder to determine her age. When the only other customer leaves, she looks over and beams at me. I return the gesture with interest, grateful for this morsel of kindness in such a hard-nosed city. After poking her head quickly through the door to the back, she brings over a cup of tea and one of the cakes, tapping the side of her nose as she retreats. I think it was the one with the flies on it, but I'm grateful nonetheless.

The clock reluctantly ticks over to three o'clock.

There's a copy of the *Daily Mirror*, but little news to be scavenged from within. "When a man is tired of London, he is tired of life," Mr Greenwood repeatedly informed us during our anti-climactic school trip. I can't remember who said it, but they are the words of someone who hasn't spent the afternoon in a poky Greek café in Clapham. Still, he or she was right; there's little point sitting here. I must go and explore my capital city.

It only takes a few streets to realise that London isn't like the fairy tales paint it. The streets aren't paved with gold so much as fag ends, discarded newspapers and dog turds – but I like it. There's an energy to the place, a busyness that you don't find elsewhere. Everyone seems to be heading somewhere important, and I swiftly adopt their approach: long strides, head down, eyes forward, look serious. It's tiring at first, but you quickly cover a good distance. When I stumble on a large park – Battersea, according to the sign on the gate – I finally see what all the fuss is about. There, beyond the leafless bushes, is the River Thames and, fifteen minutes further along, I'm presented by that famous skyline: Big Ben, the Houses of Parliament, one of the bridges, lots of other smart-looking buildings. Further along, the Millennium Wheel is slowly taking shape.

I find a bench to take it all in, but the sun is dropping and the temperature with it, so ten minutes of soaking up is enough. After several wrong turns, a bit of luck and thankfully no need to ask anyone for directions, I'm at the café once more.

'Your sister, she back,' mutters the owner gruffly, eyeing me as if he can detect the scent of unpaid-for pastries on my breath. I hurry out, following his pointed directions to the side of the building. Cecilia is picking up her post in the doorway when I walk up.

'Chrissy! What are you doing here?' she asks, leaning over to give me a one-handed hug, a handful of letters in the other.

'Came to see you. And Camden.'

'How long have you been here?'

'Since two. I've been for a walk along the river, and spent an hour in the café downstairs. I got a free cake from the woman who works there. Is that his wife?'

'Yes, she's a dear. Much nicer than him, the old perv. You should have let me know you were coming, I've got plans tonight. Anyway, come on up.'

I follow her up a steep, narrow set of stairs to her flat. 'I thought you lived in a house?'

'Do you know how much rent is in London? It's a bit cramped, but it's all I can afford. Charities don't pay that much, sadly.'

'Which one is it that you work for?'

'Help the Aged.'

'Like the Pulp song.'

'I think Pulp took their song title from us, but yes, like the Pulp song.'

I sit on the cracked red leather sofa, which is far too garish to be Cecilia's. In fact, most of the furniture looks shabby. Not that my house in Sheffield is any better, but I expected more from London. Once she's finished with the messages on her answerphone, she sits next to me.

'How's London life?'

'Hectic. Expensive. Tiring. Sometimes fun, but draining more often than not. Still, you timed your visit well. I've got a spare ticket to see the Bluetones tonight. Fancy it?'

'Definitely. How come it's going spare?'

'Tom can't make it. Let me get changed, then we'll have to leave, it's the other side of town.'

I have no idea who Tom is but I'm ecstatic that he's busy. A proper gig in London, and a decent band to boot; that goes a long way towards justifying the train fare.

The crowd at The Forum is different to the Leadmill. A little older, more diverse and, I hate to admit, quite a lot cooler. Rather than a strict uniform of band T-shirts and jeans, people are wearing all manner of clothes: hoodies, shirts, rugby tops, jumpers both woolly and V-necked; one dandy even has a waistcoat on. Nor is everyone drinking beer. Some have shots and there are even people drinking wine. At a gig. Incredible. Everyone oozes confidence, they can be themselves, no need to fit in. I eye them with a mix of envy and suspicion, trying to work out what from their mannerisms and dress code I can take back up north. The man stood next to us notes my *Mother Nature Calls* T-shirt and nods in recognition. I consider launching into Rob's second-album theory, but I'm not confident I'll hit it off with someone wearing canvas shoes and bright red trousers.

The warm-up act are called Jack. They slink off stage almost as soon as they've arrived. They're rubbish, frankly, but I note the name so that I can tell Rob I like them. Minutes later the Bluetones trot on in their place, launching straight into the big hits. We stand at the side – although a dedicated music lover, Cecilia has never been a mosher – but by the third tune, we're both bouncing away. I've always pegged the Bluetones towards the mellower end of Britpop, but they're an energetic prospect live. They slow things down mid-set as they work through the more reflective numbers, but before long it's a raucous singalong, each tune delivered with wit and charisma by Mark Morriss, who bounds around the stage with gusto aplenty. They round the night off with a rousing performance of 'If…', the signature tune from their second album. So rousing that I blow ten quid's worth of budget on a T-shirt on the way out, justifying the splurge by the fact that I didn't pay for the ticket. I've kept it, though: this is my first London gig, so the Bluetones are going very, very close to the centre of the pin board.

* * *

Cecilia hasn't surfaced by midday so I flick through the football news on Ceefax, searching for a snippet on Plymouth Argyle while half-heartedly polishing off a second bowl of cornflakes. She's always favoured dull, sugarless cereals, but with nothing else to eat in the flat, I've little alternative. She appears just as *Football Focus* is starting.

'So, little brother, tell me all about Sheffield. How are things going?'

'Pretty good. I've already ticked off one of my ambitions for the year.'

'What was that?'

'I talked to this girl I like, she's called Louise. Lou.'

'That was your ambition? For the whole year?'

I could tell her about the stuff that went beyond talking, the stuff in Grindleford/Upper Padley, but she's my sister and is halfway through her breakfast. It wouldn't be fair.

'Well, she's very pretty and popular. Not everyone's talked to her.'

'I dread to think what the other ambitions were.'

'Find a proper girlfriend and get tickets to see Blur. I've not managed either of those yet, though.'

'And apart from those earth-shattering dreams, how are things generally?'

'Alright, I suppose. The weather's been a bit grizzly.'

'Grizzly? Goodness me, you're even starting to sound northern. And I meant with your course.'

'Oh, that. Fine. Should get a 2-2.'

'Mum and Dad won't be happy.'

'They'll get over it. Anyway, they're still too busy boasting about your master's from Oxford to notice. Forget about that, though, I've got something else I need to ask you about.' I want to get her guidance on the Lou situation, but she ignores me.

'What about next year, though? What are your plans?'

'I've not really thought about it yet,' I shrug.

'And when are you going to start thinking about it? You're over halfway through your penultimate term. Time is ticking, little brother.'

'Maybe I'll do a master's like you did.'

'In what?'

'Geography, obviously.'

'It doesn't work like that. You have to specialise. And how are you planning to fund it?'

'Don't the council pay for it?'

'No, not postgraduate courses. You have to find funding, which takes ages.'

'Really? OK, I'll do something else then. Why are you so bothered, anyway? Did Mum put you up to this?'

'She didn't know you were coming' she says, putting her bowl in the sink. 'Nor did I, remember? I'm just trying to nudge you into action. Life's tough out in the real world. Trust me.'

I came to London for a Britpop road trip, not a lecture about my academic failings, so pointedly resume my odyssey through the pages of Ceefax. After twenty years of being my sister, Cecilia is quick to spot that I'm close to a full-on sulk.

'Sorry, I didn't mean to have a go. Come on, let's go and explore Camden. Who knows, maybe we'll see someone famous.'

We don't. Nor any fucked-up blokes selling tickets to raves, despite Pulp's promise that they can reliably be found here. But we do find stalls selling daft clothes and overpriced food. Cecilia treats me to tea and a bagel, which goes some way towards compensating for the meagre nourishment on offer in her flat. After exhausting the market's limited possibilities – can there really be that much demand for incense sticks and beads in London? – we walk to the Good Mixer, where I offer to buy us both a pint. It makes a significant dent in my budget – I'm well into my second twenty-pound note by now – but according to the *NME* it's the best place to spot Britpop's movers and shakers. Hopefully it'll be a big name like Graham Coxon or Justine Frischmann, but I'll settle for someone out of Menswear. (I like Menswear, but rarely listen to them anymore. Rob has banned them from being played in the house.)

'Seen anyone famous?' I ask, sitting down with our drinks.

'Not today, but I did see a musician in here once.'

'Who? Damon? Brett?'

'Nick Berry.'

'Fair play, he had a number one hit.' We both laugh and clink glasses; she had a crush on him back in the Eighties.

'Who's this Tom, then?' I continue, recalling the free ticket from last night.

'A friend. We're sort of seeing each other.'

'I knew it. That's why you looked so pissed off when he cancelled. I trust he had a good reason? Or is he about to be on the thick end of one of your week-long moods?'

'One of his kids is sick.'

'He's got kids? Wow. How old is he?'

'Thirty-two.' She pauses. 'He's also got a wife. They live in Reading. We work together. Promise you won't tell Mum and Dad.'

'Of course not.' I take a long pull on my pint, hoping I look as thoughtful as Rob when he does it. 'What are you going to do?'

'Keep seeing him. Wish things were different. Eventually get hurt when he refuses to leave his family, even though I know that he shouldn't. He says he'll do it, but I know he never will. And I don't want him to. Not really.'

'I'm sorry.'

'Don't be. It's my fault, I knew he was married before we got together,' she sighs.

I hate seeing her like this. She's helped me out with sibling advice, many many times over the years, and now I need to repay her. Yet this is a delicate situation; I need to find exactly the right thing to say.

'Is Tom a big Bluetones fan?

'He is,' she laughs. 'Although he prefers the Wonder Stuff. He's always telling me how great they are.'

'They're alright. Definitely not great.'

She laughs again. 'Thanks, Chris. As always, you've managed to zoom in on the most important issue. Anyway, what did you want to ask me about earlier?'

My own romance, however tangled, seems insignificant now. There are no kids or wives involved, just three geography students who should all know better. 'Nothing important, I was just hoping for some tips about up and coming London bands to impress my mates up north.'

'Let's head back home and I'll have a look through my CDs. There's bound to be some of Tom's you can borrow. He listens to Chapterhouse a lot, you might like them.' She drains her pint; two pounds twenty, gone in one gulp. 'After that we can go to the Ethiopian restaurant around the corner. I'll treat you as a thank you for cheering me up.'

'What sort of food is that?'

'Meat stews, beans in spicy sauces, all served with a kind of sour, spongy bread. It's tastier than it sounds.'

'That can't be hard,' I say, hesitantly. 'I wonder what they did with all those tins of corned beef and spaghetti hoops our school sent them during that famine they had?'

'I'm sure they were very grateful. Come on, let's go.'

At my insistence, we take the bus back to Clapham instead of the Tube. I've already decided to head back north tomorrow and want to soak up as much of the city as I can.

'Oh, did you hear the rumour about Blur?' Cecilia asks as I stare out at the traffic-clogged streets.

'The new album? Out next year, I think.'

'No, about them splitting up. Graham's fallen out with Damon, apparently. They don't even talk to each other anymore.'

I swing round. 'What? Where did you read that?'

'Tom told me. A friend of his knows someone who knows someone who knows the band, that sort of thing. This album will be their last, he reckons. Graham wants to go solo.'

I don't ask for further details. I don't dare. This is devastating news which, if true, means I'll never get to see them live. My pin board will never be complete. More famous buildings whizz past, but I no longer care. Grandpa was right all along; London is to be avoided at all costs.

10

You've Gotta Look Up

The one downside of the current deluge of music is that there's too much of it. Before I've had time to scrutinise the music press to verify the rumour of Blur's demise, the next big event is upon me: Pulp's latest tour. We were too slow to get tickets for Sheffield, but Rob's brother managed to get some for the Manchester gig. The journey there is a chance to ask Rob about the Blur situation, and after that the Lou situation, but before that I have to sit through the latest tedious news from the climbing club. He beats me to the punch on the train back too, telling me about some guy he's met through the LGB society. Only when we are back in Sheffield does he pause, but before I seek his wisdom on either issue, I demand his thoughts on the phenomenal gig we've just seen.

'Come on then, what's your verdict?' I ask, still buzzing.

'Five out of ten. And I'm being generous because we managed to catch the last train back.'

'Don't talk bollocks, you can't give Pulp a five. They get at least an eight just for being Pulp.'

'So essentially, Chris, you're saying I can only give them an eight, nine or ten, based on your pre-determined validation of their music. Which defeats the point of asking for my opinion.'

'No, I'm not saying that, I'm saying five's too low for *that* gig. They were awesome, and *This Is Hardcore* will go down as one of the great albums of the decade. If not all time.'

'Possibly, but only among those who don't know any better. *Separations* is a vastly superior piece of work in almost all respects.'

'Come on, be honest: when "Common People" kicked in at the end, did you not feel even the slightest sense that you'd witnessed something truly special?'

'No, I did not. Anyway, that was on *Different Class*, which was alright but hugely overhyped, and is already suffering from overexposure due to–'

'What's going on over there?' I ask, pointing across the street.

'Police, an ambulance, lots of distressed-looking ravers outside a nightclub ... I can only surmise that some sort of incident has taken place. Probably a drugs overdose, given that's what those poor unfortunates are forced to imbibe to get through a night of their interminable dance music.'

'Do you think we should go and help?'

'Help how, exactly? Watch over the paramedics and check that they're doing everything correctly?'

'Shit, they're wheeling someone out on a stretcher. Must be a bad one, they've got one of those tubes attached to their face.'

'So? It's got fuck all to do with us. Come on, let's head to the Washington, see if they're doing a lock-in. If they are, I'm prepared to upgrade Pulp to five and a half.'

'They were a seven, minimum. And you're showing a disgraceful lack of loyalty to your adopted city.'

'They're not all from Sheffield. Candida Doyle comes from Northern Ireland.'

'Whatever,' I growl, cross at his lack of appreciation for Pulp but also in awe of such indifference in the face of genius. 'Is *Separations* really better than *Different Class*? I've never heard it.'

'Undoubtedly. I've got a copy somewhere, I'll dig it out for you when we get home. Come on, it's freezing out here. And once we're there, you can fill me in on your dirty weekend in the country.'

Part of me wants to tell him, but I'm still annoyed with his rejection of Pulp. Besides, there's only so much advice about women I'm prepared to take from a homosexual rock-climber with a ginger ponytail.

It's time for an older, worldlier perspective.

It's time to go and see Mike.

* * *

Mike Moore is in the third year of his PhD in something related to glaciology, and is nowhere near completing it. I met him in the first year, when he led some of my tutorials. I was struggling with an essay, he offered to take a look at it and I gratefully bought him two pints afterwards. It got a good mark, so when the next essay was due I knew exactly where to turn for help, and how many pints it would cost me. This mutually beneficial arrangement only altered when Mike realised it would take him less time to draft the essays from scratch, rather than sift through my incoherent rubbish. And credit where it's due: for two years, the price has remained fixed at two pints, no inflation. His academic integrity means that he makes me read each one through before I hand it in, and he usually asks me a few questions to ensure I've understood the basics. I don't mind, though; I'm always happy to spend time in his company.

To me, Mike is the epitome of how to be an adult. He listens to Radio 4. He knows every James Bond film off by heart: the girls, the villains, the director, writer, locations – everything. He looks cool, too. He wears an exotic-looking wooden bead necklace and often walks around barefoot, a habit he picked up on a gap year in Thailand and which shows off the tattoo of a lizard just above his left ankle. Best of all, he has a dark brown fedora which goes everywhere with him, whether it's the height of summer in the UK, or if he's in the Arctic on his latest round of field research.

And he lives a cool life. On one of my early visits, I was captivated by his photos: colourful tents pitched high on glaciers, sleds laden with supplies, and especially the one in which Mike leans casually on a rifle in the snow. He explained that all the scientists in the Arctic have to carry one in case they're attacked by polar bears. There's even a picture of a polar bear next to it, and it was many months into our friendship before he confessed to cutting it out of the *National Geographic*. He's never actually seen a polar bear, but it doesn't matter. Mike is my hero.

I knock on his office door and walk in without waiting for a reply. Mike is tending to his treasured chilli plants, which take over both windowsills and which he is constantly fussing over, even checking their soil moisture levels with a sensor that he "borrowed" from the departmental store.

'Chris, old boy, how's tricks? Come in, make yourself at home.'

'Hi Mike, how are you?'

'Mustn't grumble, Christopher, mustn't grumble. Coffee?' He turns and imitates the pouring of a pot of coffee, one of his many gestures. He can never stop fidgeting; he's always biting his fingers, tapping pencils on the desk or fiddling with the beads around his neck. The only thing I never see him do with his hands is typing, which might explain why his PhD is going so slowly.

'From Guatemala this one, quite earthy, very moreish,' he continues, scooping out the grains from a foil packet. This is another of his qualities: highly advanced coffee-making skills. Before meeting him, my only experience of the drink was the freeze-dried granules Mum brought out whenever her beekeeping friends came. By contrast, Mike has a glass device in his office – a French Press, he calls it – into which he carefully spoons finely ground beans imported from the farthest corners of the world. Once happy with the amount, he pours over the hot water – never boiled, that brings out too much bitterness – then waits exactly four minutes before plunging and pouring. I always time my visits for mid-morning or mid-afternoon, knowing that he is religious about making a fresh pot at these times. I'm not entirely sure I like coffee – it's very bitter, even with sugar – but I definitely like the idea of it. It's exactly the kind of thing you should drink in the office of a PhD student.

'Guatemala's in South America, right?'

'Central America technically, but close enough. Although possibly not for a third-year geography student. What can I do for you today? Another essay that needs my input?'

'Extended essay this time. I need a subject to write about. Any ideas?'

'What about something glaciological? Fascinating subject, although I'm biased of course, and I can offer you my postgraduate expertise at discounted rates. Or you can copy my essay from four years ago, it's unlikely any of our esteemed professors will remember it.'

'No thanks. Glaciers leave me cold.'

'Very droll, old boy, very droll. How about climate change? Very controversial subject, several experts saying it's going to become *the* defining issue over the coming years.'

'Never heard of it. Anyway, forget about essays for a moment, first I need your advice about a girl. Or a woman, I suppose, now we're in our twenties. What age do you switch from one to the other?'

'Depends very much on the girl, or indeed woman, in question. This wouldn't be Louise Banks, would it?'

'Er, yeah. How do you know that?'

'I've seen the two of you together in the computer lab. Doesn't she have a boyfriend, though? Gilbert, the tall fellow who's into politics?'

'That's the one. I can't stop thinking about her. She – this is a secret, OK, you can't tell anyone – she invited me to her house during reading week.'

'Go on, go on,' Mike enthuses. He's perched on his desk, fingers clasped beneath his nose, totally focused. Far more so than he ever is when talking about glaciers.

'I don't know what I should do next,' I sigh. 'Or if I should do anything about it, seeing as she's got a boyfriend. You know, morally and stuff.'

'Why her?' Mike asks suddenly, leaping up and snapping his fingers at me.

'What?'

'Why her? There are plenty of fine-looking specimens in the department, and many more across the campus. Why not chase someone who doesn't have a boyfriend?'

'She's *really* pretty.'

'There's nothing else? Nothing a bit deeper?'

'She's funny, too. And clever. But it's also her ... unattainableness. Is that a word?'

'I'm not sure, but it'll do for now.'

'What I mean is, she's much more attractive and popular than me. I guess I'm enjoying the challenge.'

Mike flicks the kettle switch off before it reaches a rolling boil. 'Except the odds *are* stacked against you, and pretty heavily. Not least with the boyfriend to consider. He's got that aura of self-confidence. Overly confident, some might say.'

'He's better-looking than me,' I admit bitterly.

'And much cleverer; I've marked some of his papers. Very impressive. Several factors in the "against" column, old boy. And I'm struggling to think of many in the "for". No offence.'

'None taken. Doesn't seem fair, does it?'

'Life's not fair, better to accept that now and get on with it. And yet, let's just hang on a minute ...' – Mike's pacing around the office now – '... you're a cheerful, fresh-faced young chap yourself, and seem to get acceptable marks with the absolute minimum of effort, even for the essays I don't write. And you've proved in the past that you have an uncanny ability to punch several levels above your weight. The delightful Suzanne Harrison being a case in point.'

'You knew about that?'

'Everyone did, at least up here on the top floor. None of us could believe it, but we all knew about it. I used to watch you from my window; for a whole week, you turned up at six-thirty sharp and stood there, staring at the library. I could have set my watch by you. As neither of you carried badminton racquets, one could only surmise that you were up to some other business. "When the impossible has been eliminated, Watson, whatever is left, however improbable, must be the truth."'

'Is that Shakespeare?'

'Conan Doyle. Here's your coffee, now remember to breathe in the aroma first, it prepares the palate.'

I kept my fling with Suzanne secret from everyone except Rob, so it's mildly disappointing to learn I'm not the master of disguise I imagined. Only mildly, though; it's far more pleasing to discover people know I slept with her. That kind of gossip can do wonders for your reputation. I make a mental note to find out whether Lou knows and, if not, to make sure that she finds out.

'Don't add too much, old boy,' Mike scolds as I pour milk into my coffee. He drinks his black, but, ever the host, keeps a small carton of semi-skimmed for guests not ready to go all-in. 'Now, let's recap,' he continues, whisking the carton away from me. 'She lives with this Jonathan chap, who's an impressive young fellow, no doubting that, and they've been together, what, two years? The chances are that flirting with you a bit of harmless fun. But, on the other hand, she's living with her boyfriend while everyone else is living the life of Riley in a student house. So it's possible, just possible, that she's decided she's a bit young for all that. And all that political nonsense must get damn tedious after a while.'

'Very perceptive.'

'You're too kind. So my advice is to ask her out for another drink. But confidently, like you mean it. Boldness is the key here. Show her you think you're good enough for her. Even if it doesn't lead anywhere, you've not lost much, as you never really had a chance in the first place. If it does, then you'll be riding out with the best-looking filly in the whole damn stable. Albeit with a heap of emotional nonsense to deal with afterwards, but well worth it on balance, I'd say.'

'Sound advice. Thanks, Mike.'

'You're welcome, old boy. Let me know how things go. And while you're finishing your coffee, you have a look at this atlas. On reflection, it's absolutely disgraceful that you don't know where Guatemala is, and I simply can't let it go.'

11

You've Got A Lot To Answer For

Mike's right: I have to talk to Lou. The only problem is, I can't find her.

She's not in the lecture on Tuesday and she doesn't turn up for the GIS tutorial either. Nor is she there for the Thursday lecture. I hang around the geography department in the hope of bumping into her, but to no avail, and with our circles of friends barely touching, let alone overlapping, there is no one I can tap for information.

I find her on the following Monday afternoon. She's in the library, sitting at the same table where I first met Suzanne. But her expression as she glances up at me quickly dispels any notion that this is a good omen. It's too late to turn and flee, so I perch gingerly on the chair opposite, angling it towards the door so I have a head start should a quick exit be necessary.

'Hi, Lou,' I whisper. 'I wasn't sure if you'd come back yet.'

'I came back two weeks ago.' Her attention is now back on her books.

'Oh. You weren't in the tutorials or lectures last week.'

'I've been busy.'

'I got you a copy of the handouts,' I say, reaching for my rucksack.

'I've already got them.'

'OK.'

She doesn't look good. Her eyes are bloodshot and her hair isn't shimmering in the way it usually does. Fortunately, I know better than to point any of this out. 'Is everything OK?'

'Not really.' She still won't look at me, but at least puts down her pen. 'I was planning to call you, once I'd stopped being quite so furious. But I haven't. Not yet.'

What have I done? I thought we left on good terms? She told me how great and understanding I was. I remember those two clearly, as they are compliments I rarely receive. I haven't spoken to her in between times; how have I managed to annoy her?

'Well, I would have called you, but I don't have your number. Is that why you're cross?'

Silently, she reaches into her bag, lifting out a small piece of folded paper and sliding it across the desk. The note I left in Grindleford. I examine it for clues.

SEE YOU IN SHEFFEILD
XX

Even with the evidence in front of me, I can't see what I've done wrong. As is often the case when faced with an angry member of the opposite sex, silently chewing one corner of my bottom lip seems the most appropriate response.

'That was it, was it?' Lou spits. 'That was all you had to say?' She kicks my chair round so that I receive the full force of her whispered wrath.

'Um …'

'We spend the night together, share our thoughts, our feelings, and that's all you can be bothered to write to me? Four fucking words?'

'Your mum was running me to the station, I didn't have time to write much else. She was rushing me, I think she wanted me out of the house.'

Nor can I remember sharing many of *my* thoughts or feelings; that was all one way.

'You promised we would spend the day together. But no, you write me four words, on a piece of scrap paper, and flee.'

'I did put kisses on it. Two.'

'Oh, how very sweet. Exactly like my grandparents put on my birthday card each year.'

'Should I have added a smiley face?'

'It's not funny, Chris.'

'OK, I'm sorry. But are you really this upset about a note?' I regret it as soon as the words leave my mouth. The anger that was swirling within is released in a crazed, hushed torrent.

'You turn up at my home. I cheat on my boyfriend with you, and get myself into such a confused mess that I can't sleep all night. Then, after I finally do fall asleep, I wake up to find the person responsible for my confusion has written, on the back of a shopping list, four measly words about how he feels in return. And you dare to ask me why I'm cross?'

But you invited me to your house. And you came into my room. And you woke me up. And *you* climbed onto *me*. And you're the one who's in a relationship. And I was the one who offered to give you some space. Which I've stuck to. And your mum gave me that scrap of paper, which was helpful because I don't carry headed notepaper around with me in case of emergencies.

These are all perfectly reasonable responses, and I keep them all in my head.

'I'm sorry. I should have been more considerate.'

'And you spelt Sheffield wrong.'

I look at the note again. She's got me there. 'Like I said, your mum was rushing me.'

'If it's any consolation, she thought you were nice.'

'At least one of you thinks so.'

Lou kicks me under the table, unnecessarily hard but I think it's meant affectionately. Gingerly, I nudge her foot with mine, before moving both legs well out of her range.

'And did you make a decision about Jonathan?' By which I mean about me, but going round the houses seems like the safest route.

'We broke up. No, let me correct that: he broke up with me. As soon as I got back.'

'I'm sorry. Did he say why?'

Lou shakes her head.

'Oh. Well, I'm sorry.'

'You've said. Don't start apologising all the time, I couldn't bear it. Anyway, it's not your fault, not entirely. I'm not sure he suspects anything, but I didn't tell him. I'm assuming you didn't either?'

'Why would I?'

'That's the main reason why I'm angry. And upset. And confused.'

I no longer need to ask about her and me. It's obvious that romance of any kind is the last thing on her mind. Disappointing, but I'll survive. As I consider what to say next, another thought leaps up from nowhere.

'Where are you living?'

'I'm still in the flat. Jonathan's moved in with a friend for now, he says I can stay there for as long as I need. He's being very reasonable about everything.'

'Is there anything I can do?'

'Not really, unless you know someone with a spare room.'

'Mike's got a spare room. One of his housemates has just gone to Vietnam.'

'Who's Mike?'

'PhD student. Doesn't wear shoes. I can ask him if it's still free?'

'That would be great.' Finally, Lou smiles. She even looks grateful. 'And Chris? You've been really good about everything, too. Thank you'

'Don't start thanking me all the time, I couldn't bear it.'

'I guess I deserved that.'

She kicks my foot, but more gently this time.

'I'll go and ask Mike about that room.'

I pause before leaving. She's revealing the merest flicker of vulnerability, the first I've seen since getting to know her. If I stay, I might be able to position myself as the front runner when she needs a shoulder to cry on, or a bed to–

No. I need to do the right thing.

I leave. That's doing the right thing twice in two weeks. I'll treat myself to a beer once I've found him, to reward my newfound nobility.

* * *

Mike's day is not going well. Balls of screwed-up paper cover the floor around the bin, and he is sitting with his bare feet on his desk, furiously biting at what's left of his nails while staring at his computer.

It isn't switched on.

'Alright, Mike? You look a bit stressed.'

'I am, Christopher, I am,' he sighs, swinging round towards me. 'I had a review meeting with Dr Holland this morning. Brutal woman, brutal. She spent nearly an hour ripping apart my thesis. I won't bore you with the gory details, or upset myself further, but the takeaway message is that, in short, so to speak, I need to start again with a new proposal. Three years down the drain, not to mention eight thousand pounds.'

'Sorry to hear that. Got any coffee going? It's nearly three o'clock.'

'Coffee? Yes, apologies old boy, very rude of me, I'll put some on.'

While fiddling around with his brewing implements, Mike fills me in on the details, despite promising that he wouldn't. Given that I've called round to ask a favour, albeit one for someone else, I feel I have to listen. The problem seems to be that all the existing theories for paleo ice mass instabilities have been largely agreed upon, but Mike's initial findings indicate that the most recent ice age started fifty thousand years earlier than everyone else thinks it did. Either Mike is wrong – and he's convinced he isn't – or every other glaciologist in the world is. Including Dr Holland. I don't want to tell him – he's one of my best friends, after all – but I have a suspicion that he might lose this fight.

'Maybe your glacier formed a bit earlier than all the others?' I offer helpfully.

'It's possible, old boy, distinctly possible. Anyway, enough from the world of academic turmoil. What can I do for you? Didn't I just write your six-thousand-word opus on agricultural subsidies?'

'You did, thanks, but it's not a work question. Is that room in your house still available?'

'Indeed it is, twenty-seven pounds a week plus one sixth of the bills. Have you and Rob had a tiff?'

'It's not for me. You remember that girl, Lou Banks? She's split up with her boyfriend and needs somewhere else to live, ASAP.'

'They've broken up already? Impressive work.'

'Nothing to do with me, it happened before I even had a chance to ask her out. But they lived together, and it's his flat, so she's looking for a new place. She's very bright, so where better than a house overflowing with the finest academic minds in the city? And you, of course.'

'Very droll, very droll. I'll have to check with the others, but I'm sure that'll be fine.'

'She's in the library now, shall I introduce you?'

'Coffee first, Christopher, coffee first. Shame to let it spoil.' He hands me the "Geographers do it in the field" mug. Childish, but it always makes me laugh. 'Anyway, I know who she is. I can go and find her later.'

I give the coffee a good sniff, just as he's taught me. 'Can you not do something else for your PhD? Something a bit easier, I dunno, rain forests?'

'Not quite that simple, old boy. My funders are expecting something at least vaguely glacier-related. Anyway, enough of all that. Tell me everything that happened with you and young Louise.'

He presses me for every last detail: why she turned me down, all I know about her and Jonathan, even about her mum and their house in Grindleford. It seems like an unnecessarily thorough vetting for a new housemate, but it's their house, not mine. And I get another free coffee out of it, along with my reward beer to enjoy later. Not a bad day, all things considered.

Single Girl

One bonus of Lou moving out of Jonathan's flat – alongside the fact that I no longer have to think about them having sex – is that I now know where she lives. I leave it a week before heading along the ginnel and knocking at the back door (for as long as I've known Mike, the front door has been blocked by a stack of boxes containing the assorted possessions of PhD students lost in various corners of the globe). Footsteps thud down the staircase and the door is opened by a woman with purple-framed glasses sitting on a nest of greying dreadlocks. She's clasping a weird, misshapen mug that looks handmade, and not in a good way.

'You're Chris, aren't you? Mike's not in at the moment. You can come in anyway.'

I can't remember meeting her, but the residents of Mike's house are constantly changing. I smile broadly to disguise the fact that I have no idea who she is.

'I came to see Lou, actually. Is she in?'

'Not sure, but come in, sit down. Lou!'

She disappears back up the stairs, hollering for her newest housemate, and I look around for a place to sit in the living room. Three huge cheese plants have the armchairs in their clutches, and the rest of the furniture is under siege from a jungle of spider plants and cacti, which protrude from every bit of shelf not submerged beneath books. Overflowing ashtrays, many of which began life as jam-jar lids, nestle in the crannies in between, and the scent of stale tobacco clings to the furniture. I can't see Lou, with her spotless appearance and barely hidden sense of superiority, lasting long here.

'Hi Chris.'

She hovers in the entrance to the room, unwilling even to enter it.

'Hello. I popped round to see how you're getting on in your new surroundings.'

'Shall we go through to the kitchen? It's a fucking pigsty in here, I can't stand it. We can open the back door in there, let this stinking air out.'

She's settling in better than I expected.

'Would you like a drink?' she asks, removing two mugs from the rack, inspecting their insides then scrubbing them vigorously with a liberal dose of washing-up liquid.

'Yes please.'

'What do you want?'

'Whatever you're making.'

'I'm making whatever it is that you want.'

'Anything's fine.'

'Can you stop being so bloody passive for one minute and choose something to drink?'

I'm getting used to being spoken to like this. I know now that she isn't even that annoyed with me; she just says things that other people manage without shouting or swearing.

'OK, coffee.'

'I haven't got any coffee,' she says, looking in her allocated cupboard.

'Mike'll have some. I can steal it, he won't mind.'

'No, I've only just moved in. I can't steal from housemates already. You'll have to choose one of these instead, they're communal.'

She hands over a tin overflowing with an assortment of teabags. I search in vain for one containing actual tea.

'I don't like herbal teas,' I mutter.

'Why do you have to be so difficult?'

'You just told me not to be passive.'

'Oh, for goodness' sake.' She pulls two out at random and puts them into the now-gleaming mugs, then leans against the sink, no doubt deeming it the most sanitary part of the room. The onus is on me, as the unexpected visitor, to start the conversation. Given the lingering tension between us, I stick to the safest ground that I, or anyone, knows: geography.

'You missed a good tutorial yesterday. We made maps showing the changing forest cover of the British Isles over the past hundred years. It was fun.'

'I've already got the notes, I'll go through it this week.'

'Where were you? Not that it's any of my business, of course.'

'I was having lunch with Daddy. He takes me out somewhere every December.'

'How was it?'

I meant what did they eat, white wine or red, that sort of thing. But once again, I've tapped the keg, and she's off, telling me about these annual guilt-ridden outings with her philandering father.

'... it was always me and Bex separately, so we each got some quality time with him and got to feel special, and at first, it was a weekend away, he picked me up early from school on a Friday, much to the headmaster's annoyance and my friends' envy, and we drove to the Cairngorms, to Snowdonia, to the Lake District' – never Dartmoor, I note; the man's clearly got some sense – 'and he splashed out on expensive hotels, theatre tickets, musicals, boat trips, but I knew, even then, that it was to compensate for not being with us at Christmas, but I didn't care and in some ways it was even better, as it was time with him instead of tearful fights in front of the Christmas tree, but since he moved down south, the trips have been much shorter, he collects me on Saturday mornings, not Friday afternoons, and leaves earlier on the Sundays to get back down south, and he never asks me how I am, just talks about his new wife and her hideous children and their hamsters that keep dying, and this year we didn't even leave Sheffield, he took me to an Italian in Nether Edge, and left at four to avoid the traffic, and I wanted to tell him about everything that's been happening but he kept glancing at his fucking watch, so I ordered the most expensive items on the menu, which was childish, I know, but I'm glad I did it.'

Once again, I'm lost for words. But this time it's not diffidence; I just can't remember what I asked her. I *think* I'm supposed to ask an insightful, empathetic question, to let her know I care and she can always share her troubles with me. But she's already been banging on for over twenty minutes and the mugs of tea have long since stopped steaming.

'I'm sorry about your dad,' I offer, but she isn't listening.

'Do you know what upset me most this time? I'm like him now. I cheated on Jonathan. All those years, I promised myself that whatever I did, I wouldn't do that.'

'A bit like Meat Loaf.'

'Is that another hilarious music joke?'

'Don't worry about it. But we didn't sleep together, did we? We were just messing about.'

'It doesn't matter. And it was my fault. I acted like a stupid, selfish bitch. I'm so like him, I can't stand it.'

This must be the other side of infidelity: guilt, disappointment, shame, regret. I've got off lightly with a bit of paranoia followed by disappointment and bewilderment. Lou pushes herself away from the sink and hands me one of the mugs. I taste it and wish I hadn't.

'How's the tea?' Lou asks.

111

'It's, um, different.'

'Different? I'm not surprised, some of those things are disgusting.'

I take another sip. 'It tastes like sawdust mixed with toothpaste, with a hint of cough medicine.'

'That bad? I'll buy some teabags before you come round again, I promise.'

'Please do.'

'Chris?' she says, back at her perch by the sink. 'I wanted to thank you for helping me find somewhere to live. I appreciate it.'

'You're welcome.'

'And also for not trying anything after I broke up with Jonathan. A lot of men would have done. I'm glad that you're different.'

'I did think about it,' I admit.

'But you didn't act on it. And ... I shouldn't have taken it out on you in the library. That was unfair.'

The merest tinge of crimson brushes her cheeks. 'Is that an apology?'

'It's as close as you're going to get to one. But don't ever write me a note like that again.'

'I won't. Promise.'

'I'm glad we're friends, Chris.'

'I'm glad too,' I say, even though it's not exactly what I was hoping for.

She walks over to the back door and opens it. Again, not exactly what I was hoping for.

'I'll give you a call soon, OK?'

'Sure. Bye.'

So that's it. Friends, nothing more. In some ways, it's an overachievement. At the start of the year, my aim was to speak to her and now we're at the herbal-teas-round-the-kitchen-table stage. But I can't help thinking I've got this all wrong somehow. I've gone from naked in her bed to being kicked out without so much as a goodbye kiss, all in the space of three weeks. It's hard to see the positives.

Snow has started to fall. Not Christmas card snow, just fat, cold raindrops. I should be wearing gloves, but I don't want to be the first person in the city to crack. So I'm cold, hungry and single.

And Blur might be splitting up.

I'm not going to think about it anymore. Any of it. Instead, I let my internal jukebox kick in, to comfort, reassure, maybe provide insight into this latest setback. Music: my most trusted and loyal companion. Mum's hippy hangover meant that my earliest days were soundtracked by flower-power anthems rather than nursery rhymes; 'Where Have All The Flowers Gone' and 'If You're Going To San Francisco', plus her beloved Simon and Garfunkel tunes. I knew their entire back catalogue, word for word, by the age of six. We sang them together until Dad came home, but he needed something heavier after a busy day of council business: Guns N' Roses, Def Leppard, Poison, Whitesnake, AC/DC, Rainbow – any band that fully embraced long hair and power chords. They blasted not only from his record player, but also from the garage every Thursday evening when he pulled off his shirt and tie and put on his T-shirt with a wolf's face on it to rehearse with the rest of Bob Jovi, his rock covers band. These tunes also embedded themselves deep inside; I was thrown out of a school assembly for humming 'Dirty Deeds Done Dirt Cheap' during the Lord's prayer. I only got away with further punishment because Mr Greenwood was a big fan; he's been Bob Jovi's rhythm guitarist ever since. They still go down a storm at the village fête each summer.

Adolescence turned up uninvited and, as well as pimples and pubic hair, Cecilia and I got our own cassette player one Christmas. It was the greatest gift that either of us could have wished for. No longer were we confined by our parents' tastes. Being three years older, she got more pocket money and could afford more tapes, so her early selections were also forced upon me: Madonna, Bros, Rick Astley, Bananarama. Then she started getting boyfriends, and they brought round tapes of better bands: the Cure, the Smiths, Pet Shop Boys. I was delighted when she left home and I no longer had to compete for access to the cassette player. And she left in '93, just as Britpop arrived.

People talk of punk hitting the country with a bang, or discuss glam rock and New Romantic as if they are defined historical periods. But Britpop crept up on us. One day they were the bands on *Top Of The Pops*, the next it was A Thing, and it rapidly took over the country. The stereo in the school common room played the latest albums on repeat, often for days at a time. *What's The Story* wasn't removed for over two weeks: whoever was nearest simply pressed play whenever the final drops of 'Champagne Supernova' faded out. Newspapers stolen from the village shop were crammed with music-related gossip: Jarvis mocking Jacko on stage at the Brits; the Gallaghers arguing with each other, with Blur, with Robbie Williams, with anyone they could find. They were no longer just bands, they were celebrities. The torch I hold for rock music has never been extinguished, but that belongs to Dad and his generation. Britpop is all ours – and upon leaving school, I was desperate for more.

The obsession merely intensified at university. From surviving on a diet of copied tapes, there were now endless gigs and indie nights to slake my cravings, and a student loan to fund them. I met new people who knew of different bands;

114

everyone had a recommendation of what to listen to next. Like Cast? Try the La's, John Power's first band. A fan of Oasis? Listen to Inspiral Carpets, the band who inspired Noel. And it wasn't all about Britpop. I found out how Radiohead got their name, which led to a week spent tracking down Talking Heads albums. Music is an ever-expanding web with fat melodious flies to be found on all its quavering threads.

And music – from flower power to soft rock to Eighties electro-pop to Britpop – has never let me down. It's never led me on, never flirted with me then changed its mind an hour later. It's reliable, a safe bet, and right now my generation is creating the greatest music this country has produced for decades, written by songsmiths awash with wisdom and guidance for surviving the trials of life.

Anyone can play guitar: you're right, Thom, they can.

The drugs don't work: couldn't agree more, Richard.

Don't look back in anger; sound advice, Noel, sound advice.

I won't look back on this wasted term for a minute more. I've got half a year left as a student, and from now on, it's music all the way; girls, women, whatever, can take a back seat.

Suede belt out in my head as I walk through the snow. 'Metal Mickey', Brett Anderson explaining to his father that the girl of his dreams works in a butcher's shop.

OK, maybe music doesn't provide *all* the answers; I'm confident that Lou has never, and will never, sell heart or meat. But even this nonsense is reassuringly familiar. Are Suede due another turn as my favourite band? There is only one place to make such a momentous decision. Ignoring the snow, I continue past my house and head for the Washington, where there will be familiar faces to discuss the merits of

Suede or, failing that, a crowd of music-loving strangers to get drunk with as the tunes blare out.

13

One To Another

The last week of my second-to-last term as a student. There's toast on the plate, tea in the mug, Mark and Lard on Radio One. And I have a gig coming up tonight. Life is good and I won't let thoughts of Lou ruin it.

I hear keys. Rob. I can tell my housemates apart by the noise they make as they open the door, which is either highly impressive or deeply worrying.

'Rob, do you fancy seeing the Manics tonight?'

'Do I fuck.'

'I've got a spare ticket. Andy can't make it, he's got to work late. Come on, it'll be great.'

'No it won't.'

'Catatonia are one of the support acts ...'

'The Stone Roses could be reforming to support them, and I still wouldn't spend my evening watching those miserable Welsh bastards. Slash and burn my fucking arse.'

I take this as a no. I don't know why I ever thought he'd go: Rob's hatred of the Manic Street Preachers is as vitriolic as it is unrelenting. It's all part of being a self-appointed music aficionado. As well as liking obscure bands no one has heard of, you have to despise at least one mainstream act – and Rob's target is the Manics. I have my own dislikes – I'm not that keen on Elastica, but as they are three-quarters female I can't broadcast this out loud, in case people think I'm sexist. Being sexist is a massive no-no when you're a student. Instead, I pretend to like everyone, and over-enthuse about Sleeper, Lush and Echobelly to make sure that no one suspects.

I lift myself from the sofa to plead my case further. I hate going to gigs alone.

'This is Emma,' says Rob as he slings his coat on the stairs, nodding towards an elfin creature hanging her jacket on a hook behind him. I study her quickly while her back is turned. She's wearing a flowing, flowery dress beneath a baggy jumper that hangs off one shoulder, as well as a patterned red and green scarf. Earrings run all the way up the lobes of both ears, and a floppy hat covers her short-cut, light-brown hair. She turns round and smiles, looking at me with strikingly bright green eyes. I can't stop staring; I've never seen eyes so vivid.

'They're not real,' says a soft Scottish voice from somewhere below the eyes. 'I wear tinted contacts.'

'Uh-huh.'

'No one's eyes are this green naturally.'

'Sure, I know that. I'm Chris, by the way.'

'Hi, Chris. Rob's told me lots about you.'

This is a surprise; I've never heard Rob talk about anything except rock climbing and music. Occasionally he will explain what gay men actually do in bed, but only when my drunken curiosity gets the better of me and I beg him to tell me.

'Well, maybe not lots,' she continues. 'He did tell me that you took a girl on a date and made peanut butter sandwiches.'

'Thanks, mate.'

'Sorry,' comes the voice from the kitchen. 'Couldn't help myself. It still amuses me, even now.'

'I thought it was very sweet,' Emma continues as she pushes past me to follow Rob to the kitchen. I follow her and, when we reach the kitchen, shove a stack of old newspapers and takeaway menus from one chair before ushering her to sit down. I then shove Rob's precious climbing kit from the chair opposite, forcefully, to inflict as much damage as I can.

'How do you two know each other?' I ask, sitting down.

'We're on the same course. Actually, I do English literature and philosophy joint honours. We do some philosophy modules together.'

'Wow, that sounds fascinating,' I nod enthusiastically, trying not to stare at her eyes too much. Even though they aren't real, they're still intoxicating. Images of Kaa the snake pop into my head, but I quickly delete them, not trusting myself to keep them there.

'He's bullshitting, Emma,' says Rob, carrying over three cups of tea. 'Chris thinks philosophy is a waste of time. What was it you said, you get a 2:1 for writing your name on the exam paper, and a first for spelling it correctly? And this coming from a geographer.'

'That was a joke,' I say hurriedly, hoping Emma doesn't use the upstairs toilet, where I wrote 'Pull here for a philosophy degree' above the toilet roll holder. It was funny at the time. 'Anyway, I meant the English part sounds fascinating.'

'I like them both,' Emma replies. 'But I'm struggling a bit with philosophy, so Rob offered to help me out.' She switches her look from me to him.

'You know he's gay?' I blurt.

'Aye, he told me.'

'I'm not, in case you were wondering.'

'This is what I love about living with you, Chris,' laughs Rob, leaning back and resting his boots on my knee. 'No matter who comes round, you instantly put them in the picture about who in the house is a homosexual and who isn't. You forgot Andy, though. He's not gay either, Emma.'

Rob mashes his teabag, then expertly flicks it across the room and into the sink. It's blatant showing off and wasted on Emma, but she has, I note giddily, returned her smile to me once more. The look lasts for around six seconds, which counts as holding my gaze. She's fiddling with her hair as well.

Flirting tactics two and nine from the list (which is now safely hidden at the back of my underwear drawer, where no one, male or female, will ever willingly venture).

Normally, this is the point where I go red, make an excuse and flee to my room. But things have changed this term. I almost had sex with Lou Banks. That has to count for something. Pretty girls should no longer intimidate me.

'Emma, do you fancy going to this gig tonight? The ticket's free, Andy doesn't want any money for it.'

'Who did you say it was?'

'Catatonia, then the Manics.'

'What sort of music is it?'

'They're both Britpop bands, kind of, and both awesome.'

'It's not really my thing … I'll go if you buy me drinks all night.'

'So you get a free ticket *and* free drinks? What's in it for me?' I chuck in a laugh at the end, one that I desperately hope is cheeky rather than sleazy.

'I'd take it, Chris,' says Rob, draining his mug. 'It's the best offer you're going to get for the Manics. Come on Emma, we've got work to do. And don't come crying to me if your ears are bleeding tomorrow.'

Rob gives me a sly wink as he leaves. Emma follows but, in the doorway, pauses to give me a heart-snapping smile. Bless you Rob, for your hatred of the Manics. And bless you Andy, for your unreliability and ridiculously time-consuming course.

* * *

We stand left of stage, near enough to get a good view but safe from the chaos at the front. If this isn't Emma's usual kind of evening out – her scarf and knitted hat stand out among the sweaty T-shirts and grubby jeans – then being bashed about for two hours by pissed-up lads might put her off for good. Even I'm not brave enough for a mosh pit at a

Manics gig. But even from here, it's impossible not to get swept along. From the moment they skulk on, the Manics are sensational. As he prowls across the stage, spitting out maudlin lyrics with a venomous fury, I give serious consideration to moving James Dean Bradfield to the top of my list of greatest Nineties vocalists. Rob's musical snobbery is way out on this one.

'And, what did you think?' I ask Emma once we're safely on the tram back to the city and can hear each once more.

'They seemed very angry,' Emma muses, after a moment's thought.

'They're Welsh, all that mining and English oppression are bound to get you down a bit. Anyway, they're a rock band, they're supposed to be angry.'

'I thought they were Britpop?'

'The categories overlap. It's like one of those diagrams with two circles in it.'

'A Venn diagram.'

'That's the one. The Manics straddle the bit where rock and Britpop overlap. But did you like it?'

'I liked the first band a wee bit more.'

I laugh, and fail to disguise it as a cough.

'What's so funny?' Emma asks.

'Do Scottish people really say wee instead of little?'

'Some do. Have you not met a Scottish person before?'

'I'm from Devon, it's a long way away.'

'Aye, I suppose it is.'

'You just said "aye" as well.'

Emma reaches over and takes my hand. 'Are you always like this around girls you don't know very well?'

'Like what?' I'm not sure I want to hear the answer.

'A wee bit clumsy.'

'Yeah, pretty much. I never know what to say.'

'Why not tell me about the other bands you've seen recently.'

'I saw the Bluetones in London with Cecilia. She's my sister. They're a bit easier on the ear, cheeky rather than angry. You might like them more.'

'Cecilia … that's a very unusual name.'

'Mum chose it, she was a big Simon and Garfunkel fan. Although it's a bit weird to call your daughter that, when you think about the lyrics.'

'You got off lightly with Chris, then. You could have been called Garfunkel.'

Focus.

Act casual.

Don't give anything away. I glance out of the tram window with as much nonchalance as I can muster.

'You're not, are you?'

'Hmm? Not what?'

'Your hand tensed when I said Garfunkel.'

Hmm. Not so nonchalant after all. Still, it's a useful warning to never take up poker. Or at least not to hold hands with the other players.

'What's your real name?'

'Simon Garfunkel Christopher Henderson. Christopher after my grandad. Please don't tell anyone, I've managed to keep it a secret up here, even from Rob.'

I expect her to laugh, like everyone does. But she doesn't. In fact, she's looking at me in a way that no one ever has before, like she's examining every part of my face, reading it, searching it for clues.

'That must be where it comes from,' she says eventually. 'Your love of music. It's in your soul, it's a gift from your parents. They must have realised, even when you were a wee baby, that you have a creative spirit. Like Simon and

122

Garfunkel, they have it too. You have this amazing, vibrant aura. I saw it as soon as we met.'

I'm not totally convinced by this; music was force-fed, rather than gifted. I didn't have much choice. But Emma is now stroking my knee and I don't want to break the spell. Maybe my aura is vibrant? I'll check, once I've discovered what it is.

'Are you really not going to take the piss? I don't mind, I spent fourteen years at school being called Garfuckwit. And that was just the teachers.'

'No! It's a wonderful name. It's so unique. And I love Simon and Garfunkel, too. "April Come She Will", that's a beautiful song.'

'Wow, that's my favourite too.' This isn't true – it's a tie between 'Keep The Customer Satisfied' and 'Red Rubber Ball' – but having just confessed my darkest secret to someone I hardly know, I'm allowed a few little lies. 'Who else do you like?' I ask, keen to keep this comforting line of conversation going.

'I listen to folk music mostly.'

'Did you know Paul Simon sang in folk clubs before he was famous? He wrote "Homeward Bound" on Widnes railway station.'

'Aye, I did know. But I like that you know too.'

'He was married to Princess Leia as well, from Star Wars. Well, to the actress, not the actual Princess.'

'You're a fountain of trivia, aren't you? I always wanted to be Princess Leia when I was little. Her or Boba Fett.'

This date is getting better all the time. For the first time in my life, I've met a girl who is impressed by musical trivia and knows about *Star Wars*. If she declares her love for Plymouth Argyle, I'll have no choice but to propose.

'Who else do you like?'

'Bob Dylan's my favourite, but I also Nick Drake, Fairport Convention, a wee bit of John Martyn. I'm in a folk group back home, I play the fiddle. Oh, I like Bert Jansch of course, a fellow Scottish folkie.'

'I don't know any of that stuff,' I admit. Paul Simon apart, folk is a bit of a black spot in my knowledge.

'You should come round, I'll play you some. It's better than the Manic Street Preachers.'

'I very much doubt that.'

'Listen first. Then decide.' She squeezes my hand, and I consider trying for a kiss, but we've reached our stop. Standing on the platform, Emma turns to face me and takes both of my hands.

'I live off Barber Road. You can walk me home if you like.'

We talk more about Simon and Garfunkel as we walk. Thankfully she lives at the near end of the road, as I've run out of trivia about their songs by the time we reach her door.

'Thank you for taking me out,' Emma says. 'And for buying me drinks all night.'

'You said I had to.'

'So I did. But thank you anyway. I had fun. And I mean it, about coming round to hear some folk music. You'll love it, I know you will.'

'How about now?'

'Not tonight. Boys don't respect girls who invite them in on a first date.' Her eyes twinkle behind their emerald lenses. 'But a group of us are going to Roxy's on Wednesday. Fancy joining us?'

'I didn't know they played folk music at Roxy's.'

'They don't. They play cheesy chart music. I like that too, when I'm out with my friends. There's more to me than tin whistles and accordions.'

'Maybe I'll see you there, then.'

'Maybe you will.'

We're still holding hands. She keeps almost letting go, then catching one finger and pulling my hand back towards hers.

'Hands are important, aren't they?' she says. 'They're so intimate and sensual.'

'Hmm,' I reply, as convincingly as I can. There are at least three other body parts much more intimate and sensual in my opinion, especially if a hand or two is involved. But I don't share this.

'Goodnight, Simon Garfunkel Christopher Henderson.'

'Goodnight Emma– wait, what's your surname?'

'McMurray.'

'Goodnight, Emma McMurray. And please don't tell Rob about my name, I'll never live it down.'

'I promise.'

We kiss, briefly. She finally lets go of my hands and goes inside, waving once more before shutting the door. I think about knocking, but it's been a good date – far and away my least disastrous ever – and I don't want to ruin it. I turn and head for home, confident that my erection will last until I get there.

14

Disco Down

The lesser-spotted Andy Salisbury is waiting for me in the Washington. I need moral support for the trip to Roxy's and left a guilt-tripping note in his room, pointing out that he stood me up for the Manics gig (he doesn't need to know how grateful I am that he did). It's risky, though; while I can't face going on my own, I don't want Andy to meet Emma either. He doesn't just have a way with women; he has several ways and knows exactly when to apply each one. He can play the party animal, the opinionated intellectual, the smooth-talking ladykiller or the mysterious stranger. His most successful routine is the tortured romantic. Sipping a glass of red wine, he allows the latest target of his scattergun affections to tease out his troubles – always fabricated on the spot – before eventually "confessing" that he's been working through them by writing poetry. When the girl begs him to recite some – which they always do – he refuses three times before delivering the most beautiful couplets she's heard. All stolen from the shelves of his parents, both professors of English literature at Cambridge who between them own hundreds of books of ancient poems that no one has ever read. It's definitely a risk bringing him, but with Rob swearing he will never set foot in Roxy's again after they played a Boyzone medley on his sole visit, I don't have an alternative.

'Evening, Chris, how's it going?' Andy asks as I walk over.

'Not bad. You missed a great gig last week.'

'Ah, sorry about that, and not the first time, I know. I hate medicine. Did you know there are twenty-seven bones in your hand alone? And I'm expected to know about each and every one of them. Sometimes I think we should get rid of the NHS altogether, let natural selection take its course among the population.'

He lights cigarettes for both of us and we chat for the first time in weeks. Once our respective courses have been dealt with, the conversation moves on to our usual staples: football and music. Andy's a Man United fan, but his taste in music is far better. His current obsession is Garbage, especially their alluring lead singer, Shirley Manson – possibly the only woman he considers to be out of his reach.

'… and even though *Version 2.0* was slated by the critics, it's so much better than the first album,' he says, repeating an argument I've heard many times before.

'Evening gents,' interrupts Rob, appearing through the purple haze of the pub's smoke-filled innards. 'Still banging on about Garbage, Andy?'

'Here he is, the queerest of the queer. Smoke?' Andy holds his packet towards Rob.

'No thanks, mate.'

'Still friends with your lungs, very good to see. As a doctor, I can only approve. Unlike young Chris here, who quickly gave in to his basest instincts.'

'You're only a trainee doctor. You've still got three and a half years to go,' I point out, snaffling the cigarette that he has expertly flicked up from the packet. 'And I thought you said you'd never set foot in Roxy's, under any circumstances?' I say to Rob.

'I decided to make an exception. I didn't want to miss the chance to watch the master of seduction at work,' he replies, his grin as broad as ever. 'You heading to the bar? Excellent, I'll have a Guinness.'

Of all Rob's many affectations, this insistence on drinking Guinness is the most annoying. Not only does its inflated price leave me thirty pence down on a round, but he only started doing it so he could remark on how it never tastes the same as in Dublin. He even kept this up after I found out that he's never been to Ireland. Yet tonight this is the least of my worries. I never bargained on both of them being with me. They gang up on me, even though I'm the oldest.

'I knew there must be a reason for us heading to the world's shittest nightclub,' says Andy as I return with the drinks. 'Is this little excursion all so you can stalk that foxy geography girl?'

'No, he managed to get dumped by her before he'd even slept with her,' Rob interjects, looking disapprovingly at his foam shamrock. 'Which is impressively quick, even for him. This week it's Emma, on my course.'

'What's this one like?'

'Very hard to pigeonhole,' says Rob, stroking his beard. 'In the drama society. Works part-time in a corner shop. Reads a lot, erudite in tutorials. Short. Green eyes. Fantastic tits.'

'How would you even know that?' I shout.

'I'm gay, Chris, not blind. I can tell nice tits from average ones.'

This line of conversation needs nipping in the bud, tonight more than ever; the two of them can be ruthless when they get going and I don't want them in full flow when we meet Emma. If we meet her; Roxy's is huge and Emma is tiny. The odds of bumping into her aren't promising.

'Thank you, Rob, for bringing us up to speed. To recap, Andy, I am hoping to meet up with Emma, who is lovely, and went to the Manics with me, seeing as Rob refused and you let me down. And she asked me to come, so I'm not stalking her. Which means you can both piss off.'

'Well, it sounds like you've picked yourself a winner,' says Andy, generously 'After that leggy nymphomaniac last summer, and that posh one from your course, you're doing well for yourself lately.'

'Thanks mate, I appreciate it.'

'And it sounds like this one's keen.'

'Of course she is,' laughs Rob. 'Why else would she arrange for your second date to be in a place where there are a thousand other people about? Possibly in case she needs rescuing when you get overexcited and try to hump her leg on the dancefloor, I guess. Right, one more here before we go. Whose round? Must be yours, Chris, chop chop.'

* * *

After a wet walk through the city and a cold half hour in the queue, we are finally admitted to Roxy's, a sticky-floored, vomit-flecked, overcrowded, aggressively staffed meat market that is adored by almost every student in Sheffield. The central dancefloor is vast but still leaves little room for weaker members of the herd, who are spat out from every side if they fail to keep pace. I can't even see a way in, so tightly packed are the bodies who got here before us. Andy decides that we shouldn't even attempt it without more alcohol inside us and nobly goes to find the nearest bar.

Even after an invigorating beer and Jägermeister chaser, it's hard work getting through the crowd. The bodies writhe as if one organism, a giant beast charmed into life by the flashing lights and hypnotic beats. At the centre they are so tightly packed that it is impossible to find human-sized gaps; only via the lubricant of student sweat and spilt alcohol do I manage to squeeze through, and not without several stray elbows, both received and delivered, greeted by drunken gurns and surly glares in equal measure. It takes me three disco classics –

'Boogie Wonderland', 'It's Raining Men' and 'Hot Stuff' – to reach the other side, but there's no sign of Emma.

A new approach is needed: as Kool & The Gang start up, I set off for the balcony overlooking the dancefloor, stopping to buy another beer on the way. But the dancefloor looks little better from above. Tongues lock onto each other, hands explore any body near enough to reach, beer is sprayed in arcs, both accidentally and intentionally. Blur's vision of love in the Nineties doesn't look paranoid so much as grimy and uninhibited. I can't decide if I want to dive back in or run for my life. Right in the middle of it all, I spot Andy. He's evidently opted for party animal tonight and has a girl on each arm. How does he manage it so easily?

'You made it, then? Rob said I might find you up here.'

The shout, right into my ear, makes me spin around. It takes a minute to recognise her. Gone are the flowery dress and baggy jumper, replaced with white jeans and a very tiny, very sparkly top, which shows off her– no, don't stare, remember what your sister told you.

'You look different.' I lean beyond her ear to shout my reply, partly so she can hear me over the music but also to protect her from the full force of my beer-and-fags breath.

'What?'

'I said, you look different. Not very folkie.'

'They don't let you in wearing long skirts, so jeans are a compromise. The tight top is to show off my cleavage.' She grins at me, then falls backwards a little, spilling most of the drink she's holding. We head to one of the worn-out leather sofas that line the darker corners. It's as sticky as the floor, and I hope it's nothing more ominous than spilt Bacardi Breezer.

'Are you having fun?' Emma asks, flopping back against it.

'Yeah, you?'

'I'm a wee bit drunk.'

'Me too. What is that, anyway?'

'Cider and blackcurrant.'

'As a son of Devon, I can only disapprove.'

'It tastes nice and gets you pissed, that's good enough for me.'

'If I'm ever in Scotland, I'm going to put orange squash in my whisky as revenge.'

'Don't care, I hate whisky.'

She shuffles over to drape a sticky arm over my shoulder. This is surely my chance to kiss her, yet the cigarette breath is still strong. Would a swig of beer help? Which flavour do girls like more, beer or cigarettes? It might ruin the moment if I ask.

'Fancy a dance, sweetie?' Emma says, releasing me from the dilemma. 'Only you'll have to dance properly, none of that bobbing your head and staring at your feet. I know how you indie kids move.'

'We only do that to decent music. We get a free pass with shite like this,' I retort. Right Said Fred kick in at this very moment, instantly proving my point.

'Or, we could go back to mine? I promised I'd play you my folk CDs, didn't I?'

'Er, yeah, if you like.' It seems an odd time to start listening to folk music, but I don't know much about the genre.

'We don't have to listen to music of course, we could do something else …'

Something else sounds far better than folk music. But after recent misunderstandings, I'm keen avoid yet another disappointment.

'Emma, do you mean, um … only I've been wrong about this sort of thing before. Quite often, in fact.'

'Maybe I do, maybe I don't. I'm trying to be demure.'

'Blunt and obvious tends to work better with me.'

'Aye, I'm beginning to see that. Come on, let's go.'

Noddy Holder is bellowing out his festive greetings as we make our way towards the exit, accompanied by the most tuneless set of backing singers ever assembled in one place. People wrap tinsel around each other and toss furry antlers into the air. It's the beginning of the descent into carnage, and reason enough on its own to leave – but Emma is a much better one. As we wait in the cloakroom queue, I count the pound coins in my pockets to check that I have enough before suggesting a taxi. It's freezing outside, and the sooner we get to her house, the better.

Hopefully.

Even I can't mess it up from here, surely? I've made considerable progress this term. My ambition was to talk to Louise – Lou – Banks, and while that didn't work out all that well, being naked in her bed has to be classed as an overachievement. And things are looking extremely promising with Emma, who's still holding my hand.

If I can get hold of Blur tickets before they split up, this will go down as my most successful year to date.

15

Grateful When You're Dead

For once, it's good to be back in Devon. I'm in the unprecedented position of having two actual girls to tell my friends about. OK, the first one ditched me after one night together, and I've only met the second one on three separate occasions, but that third occasion ended extremely well. I can't remember a great deal about it – we finished off a bottle of wine beforehand, which I don't think either of us needed – but I can make up the details if they don't come back to me. I've got a few shifts at Safeway, allowing my bank balance to make a rare swing back towards zero, and Matt comes home early enough for us to catch Plymouth Argyle's last pre-Christmas home game. When I arrive back after a long session to celebrate our victory, I find Cecilia on the sofa.

'Dad tells me you've been playing with his band?' she says as I sit next to her.

'Yeah, Mr Greenwood's got a touch of angina. It's been fun, I get to jump around in leather trousers, I even do the vocals on 'Bad Medicine'. How are things with Tom the Wonder Stuff fan?'

'Awful. He broke down in tears the other day, saying how he was ruining his kids' Christmas by cheating on their mother. While we were … well, I'll spare you the details. What are you supposed to say to that?'

'You're asking the wrong person. I can check with Rob if you like?'

'Thanks, but I'll work it out. Have you seen any good bands since the Bluetones?'

'Saw the Manics last week. Catatonia in support.'

'I'm not sure I like Catatonia. Tell me about the Manics.'

I talk her through the gig. She wants to know everything: which songs they played (in order), whether Nicky Wire was wearing daft clothes (he was), what the between-song banter was like (non-existent), and what the crowd were like (drunk, aggressive). Women like this are hard to find. Wonder Stuff Tom doesn't know how lucky he is.

'Did I tell you I'm seeing a girl called Emma?' I ask, desperate to share the good news. It's the season for glad tidings, after all.

'You didn't, but it'll have to wait until tomorrow, I'm exhausted. And don't tell Mum and Dad about Tom. Oh, and this is from him. I told him you didn't approve of the Wonder Stuff and he said you should try these instead.' She hands me two CDs, *Reunion Wilderness* by The Railway Children and *Plastic Jewels* by Flamingoes. I've never heard of either of them; hopefully nor has Rob, so I can gain a few musical credibility points.

'Cool, I'll give them a listen. Say thanks, the next time you're having tearful sex together.'

'Will do. What did you get for Mum and Dad?'

'Shit, I forgot. Can you run me into Plymouth tomorrow?'

'Every year, little brother. Every year.'

* * *

The following morning, Mum joins me in the kitchen for our 'serious' chat. While her bees keep her busy, they don't offer much in the way of conversation, and the need to interfere in someone else's life spills out during trips home. Previous subjects have been money (specifically my lack of), prospects (see money) and university grades (alright, but she'd like them to be better). This year, though, it's relationships.

'Cecilia says you've been seeing someone in Sheffield,' Mum says, cupping her mug of tea in both hands and blowing on it.

'Cecilia's wrong,' I reply, not looking up from the copy of *Devon Life* I'm half-heartedly browsing through. 'I've been seeing two people.'

'That's lovely. You didn't have any girlfriends at school, did you?'

I continue pretending to read, hoping she'll go away.

'And? What are they like?' she continues, undeterred.

'Just to be clear, I'm not seeing them at the same time. It didn't work out with the first one.'

'That's a shame, dear. What did you do wrong?'

'Nothing. She was difficult, that's all. She dumped her previous boyfriend as well.' Not strictly true, but better to shift the blame onto Lou.

'Has the second one finished with you as well?'

'No, she hasn't.'

'Tell me about her.'

'She's called Emma and she's lovely. She's got green eyes, but they're not real, she wears contacts. And she likes folk music. Rob introduced us.'

'That's nice of him. You're lucky to have such a good friend looking after you.' Mum has a thing for Rob that she makes no attempt to hide. She was ecstatic when he came to visit last summer. A real homosexual, from Manchester, in her house; it was the most exciting thing to happen since Mrs Jennings was caught using chemical-based fertilisers and lost her organic honey certificate.

'Rob doesn't look after me. We're friends. And he didn't introduce us either, she just came around to ours with him two weeks ago. I did all the rest myself.'

'So she's not a proper girlfriend.'

'What? Yes, she is. Why would you say that?'

'Well, if you've only known her for two weeks, it doesn't really count. You've been at home for one of those.'

'We slept together four times on the last night of term. Does that count?' This is an exaggeration, by a factor of two, but the last thing I need is Mum picking holes in my sexual stamina.

'Don't be vulgar, dear. Not at the dinner table.'

I retreat into silence once more, hoping she'll take the hint.

'And? Was it any good?'

'Was what good?'

'The sex, dear.'

'No, no way, not happening. I know you're desperate to be one of those right-on hippy parents who talks about this stuff, but I do *not* want to be one of those children.'

'I'm only trying to help, dear, it's important to talk about your problems.'

'We're not having any problems, we've only known each other for two weeks,' I say, slamming down the magazine. 'Can't you just tell me about your bees?'

'You're not interested in my bees.'

'That's never stopped you before.'

Mum tuts and refills the kettle. Her capacity to consume tea is unsurpassed.

'Have you had any thoughts about what you'll do next year? Cecilia said you didn't have any ideas, jobs-wise.'

'Cecilia's going to get a kick up the backside when she wakes up.'

'Don't be silly dear, she went to Oxford. So you don't have any firm plans yet? You need to start thinking about it, you'll be twenty-one soon.'

'I'll think about it then.'

'What about becoming a geography teacher?'

'I don't like children. I don't even like geography that much.'

'Or something in the National Park? They're always looking for wardens.'

'I hate Dartmoor. You know I hate Dartmoor.'

'You have to do *something*, dear.'

'Maybe I'll do a master's, like Cecilia.'

'You'll need better grades to do that. Cecilia said you were still only averaging a two-two.'

'Did she really? Well, when she wakes up, ask her if she knows any Wonder Stuff fans called Tom.'

There, that's the family argument for Boxing Day sorted.

'Who are the Wonder Stuff?'

'They're like Simon and Garfunkel. Maybe I'll look for a job in Sheffield. I could work for the council like Dad.'

'I'm not sure you're the right sort of person for that.'

'Are you trying to help me find a career, or simply pointing out all the ones I'm not clever enough for?'

'We're worried about you, that's all.'

'I promise I'll think about it. Soon. Now, seriously, tell me about your bloody bees.'

She tuts once more, but knows I'll not ask about her stripy friends again so, over another two teapots' worth, she tells me about her bloody bees. I make a mental note to add beekeeping to my list of potential careers, just to keep her off my back.

* * *

When she's run out of hive-related antics, I retreat upstairs to listen to the Flamingoes CD. It's fantastic. Tom may be a love rat and a bad father, but he has impeccable taste in music. I'm warming to him already. Halfway through the second listen, Dad knocks on the door.

'Err, hello Chrissy. I just popped up to see if you've had any thoughts about a career.'

'Not yet. I'll have a think next term.'

'That's good, that's good.'

'When's the next band practice?'

'Tomorrow night. Are you coming?'

'Yeah, I'll be there.'

'Good, good. OK, well enjoy whatever it is you're listening to.' He pauses before leaving the room. 'And if your mum asks, we've had a chat about your plans for next year. OK?'

'OK, Dad. See you at dinner.'

* * *

The first week home is uneventful – they are rarely anything else in rural Devon – but Christmas Day was always going to be a bigger hurdle. We are all apprehensive about how Grandpa, prickly at the best of times, will cope. Despite their constant bickering, he was besotted with Grandma and her death last spring has done nothing to change that. Yet from the moment he arrives, late on Christmas Eve, it's the same as every year: he sits at the kitchen table and moans. About the Christmas crowds in Plymouth, about Mum's driving on the way over, about the weather, about his neighbours. He then asks how Mum's bees are doing, so he can point out everything she's doing wrong, before switching to my dad, who stopped taking any notice of him years ago. I open a bottle of cider for him – another Christmas Eve tradition – and he moves on to more recent subjects: his new carer whose accent he can't understand, the weather over the last week (as opposed to the weather in general), the couple who've moved in along the street and make too much noise.

The only two people exempt from his wrath are Cecilia and, to a lesser extent, me. He relies on me to keep him up to date with how Argyle are doing, so once the first bottle is finished, I help him to his favourite armchair in the sitting room and I bring him another. Despite never having seen most of the current team play – he's boycotted matches since his favourite player, Tommy Tynan, was sold to Torquay in 1990 – he still knows every player's deficiencies in minute detail and scoffs when I claim we're doing alright for once. He falls asleep while I'm talking him through the current selection of pies on sale at Home Park. I cover him with a blanket, then finish off his cider while watching all three *Star Wars* films back to back, my own Christmas Eve tradition.

* * *

Christmas Day passes much the same as it always has, albeit with one person missing. Cecilia and I no longer wake at six to open our presents, but we do traipse into Mum and Dad's room at nine to drink a glass of sparkling wine together. Once breakfast is over, we all make our sole visit of the year to the village church, after which Mum retreats to the kitchen to get the lunch ready, refusing any offers of help so that she can later complain about none of us lifting a finger. The tension is more palpable when it comes to carving the turkey – this was always Grandma's job, right up until last year when she could barely hold the knife steady – but Grandpa says nothing as Cecilia does the honours. I'm impressed by his resolve, but also a little sad; part of me wants him to get upset, so we can all talk about Grandma and get it out in the open.

He insists, as always, on silence during the Queen's speech, not so we can hear her pearls of privileged wisdom but to ensure we all give his heartfelt and well-worn anti-monarchy rant our full attention. Once both Grandpa and Her Majesty are through, Dad retires to his study, Mum and Cecilia go for a walk through muddy fields, and I do the washing up – another tradition I've established to give me unmonitored access to the spirits cupboard. Once finished and nicely pissed, I return to the sitting room with a generous whisky for me and another cider for Grandpa.

'Grandpa, can I ask you something?'

'I'm watching this,' comes the reply, eyes not budging from the screen.

'It's *The Little Mermaid*.'

'Nothing wrong with Disney, Chris lad.'

'I'm not saying there is, but even if I ask you a question while the film's on, I'm confident you'll be able to pick up the plot afterwards. She's a mermaid who wants to be a human. That's about it.'

'Wait until this bit's over,' he grumbles. Sebastian the crab is doing his big number. I like this scene myself, so wait for it to finish before trying again.

'How did you and Grandma meet?' I ask. I want to get him talking about her, but also wonder if there was anything about dating in the 1940s that might still be useful as I try to move things forward with Emma.

'Boy's Brigade.'

'Grandma was in the Boy's Brigade?'

'Don't be daft, lad. Her mother, your great-grandmother, ran our company. She was there and I took a shine to her.'

'How did you go from taking a shine to her to going out?'

'At the village dance. I gave her one of my cigarettes and it went from there.'

'I didn't know Grandma smoked.'

'Everyone did back then. Now can I watch the rest of my film in peace?'

I give up for now and settle in to watch the rest of the film. Personally, I've always thought Ariel should stay a mermaid. It looks like an easy life and the prince is a bit of a bellend. He also leaves his shirt unbuttoned at the top, like Jonathan. It must be some sort of badge of honour among bellends. But I feel short-changed by Grandpa. He was married for over fifty years; there has to be something he can teach me about keeping women happy.

'I've met someone at university. She's called Emma.'

'Your mum told me. Where did you meet her?'

'She's a friend of Rob's.'

'Is he the poof?'

'Yeah, but you're not supposed to say that anymore.'

'I'll say what I like, I'm seventy-nine. Tell me about her, if you must.'

I tell him what I know, but soon run out of details; having not known Emma for long, there isn't all that much to share.

'So, what do you think, Grandpa? Is she the one?'

'It'll never last.'

'Why do you say that?'

'Look at your sister, she was with that lovely lad at university and what happened? They broke up as soon as they hit a bump in the road.'

'He moved to Australia. I think that might have made things tricky.'

'She could have gone with him, if she'd wanted to. Or he could have stayed. Now she's with this married one. Your mother told me about that as well. Your generation always put themselves first, that's the trouble. This Scottish lass will too, and if she doesn't, you will. No commitment, none of you.'

'Let me guess, back in your day everyone was perfectly happy, always thought of others, and the sun was always shining.'

'No, but we did have a war going on, so maybe we were a bit more grateful for the simple things in life.'

They can always play the war card, old people; it's really not fair. He gets up stiffly to put *Aladdin* on. Time to give it one last shot before I've lost him completely to his cartoon world.

'Do you miss her?'

'What do you think, Chris lad? Of course I miss her. Every bloody day. She was my wife. But I'll be with her soon enough. If not by natural causes, then I'll do it myself. Had enough of this life, me.'

'Brilliant. And a merry Christmas to you too.'

'It'll be my last one, mark my words.'

'Well, if it is going to be your last Christmas – and it will be if you don't stop moaning, trust me – then you can do something for me.'

'What's that?'

'Come to the Plymouth game this weekend. We're at home to Exeter.'

'Alright. But on two conditions.'

'Go on.'

'We don't talk about your grandmother any more. It upsets me and I want to let her rest. You can talk about your Scottish lass if you like, but don't expect me to listen.'

'Done. What's the second one?'

'You get me another bottle of cider and let me watch my films without any more daft questions. Your mother will be back soon, and I won't get a moment's peace after that. She'll be fussing over me and talking about her bloody bees the whole time. Hasn't got a clue about keeping a hive, that girl.'

16

Songs Of Love

I return to Sheffield in a very good mood. Plymouth beat Exeter 1-0 and even Grandpa enjoyed himself. I have a ticket for Gene at the Leadmill safely stashed in my wallet and Rob rang to tell me he's got tickets for the sold-out Supergrass gig in Leeds later this term. Best of all, Emma rang during the week after Christmas. The phone line was a bit crackly, with a ten-second delay on it – I expected Scotland to be more developed – but the call went extremely well. A bit of flirting on both sides, a lot of long words on her side, and both of us saying that we couldn't wait to see each other.

I've finally managed it. I have a girlfriend, and a music-lover too, even if it is only folk. It sets plenty more questions – I'm as clueless about how to have a girlfriend as I was about how to get one – but I'm confident finding out the answers will be fun. Another ambition ticked off; only Blur to go.

My outlook becomes even sunnier when I get back to our student house to find a letter confirming a place on the environment and conservation course – and, more importantly, its six-day field trip to Kenya. Only twenty places are up for grabs and they are highly sought after. Over the years, Sheffield's geographers have established a proud reputation for drinking the hotel bar dry and I'm keen to play my part in upholding this tradition. It might also be a chance to talk to Lou again. I'm certain she'll be there: Professor Pryce is rumoured to allocate places largely based on femaleness and attractiveness. I've been lucky, securing one of the places set aside for males that ensure the university's

Complaints and Appeals department don't poke their noses in.

A trip to Africa will also mean an overdue trip away from European shores. A well-stamped passport earns considerable respect in student circles, yet all I've managed in twenty years is one week in Brittany and three disastrous weeks in India ...

* * *

A fourteen-week summer holiday takes some filling. After England crashed out of the '98 World Cup, and with weeks still to go until the Reading Festival, Matt suggested we blow our supermarket wages on a trip to Goa to check first-hand if its reputation for utter debauchery was accurate. We booked flights, stocked up on Imodium and set off in search of sun-kissed beaches, full-moon parties and foxy backpacker chicks.

That was the plan.

The one flaw with said plan was neither of us realised August is monsoon season on India's west coast. We arrived to find Colva Beach rain-lashed and deserted; everything was boarded up except one tiny bar. Its stuffy little rooms were our sole accommodation option, and its tiny restaurant the only place to buy food. The only other people around, apart from the Indians, were three wrinkled hippies who wore nothing but G-strings and flip-flops. They weren't even good hippies. I've read *The Beach*; hippies are supposed to give you maps to secret traveller hideaways where people catch sharks and get shot by drug dealers. All our hippies did was drink chai, do yoga in the rain and doze in hammocks. One of them kept sneaking off to the village telephone to check how his shares were doing. Turn on, tune in, ring your broker; it wasn't the hedonistic paradise we'd been expecting.

'This is all your fault,' snapped Matt one week in, as we sat and watched new puddles form on the floor of our room.

'You study geography. You should know about India's climate.'

'We don't just sit around and learn about the weather.'

'Didn't you do meteorology in your first year?'

'Fuck off.'

And he did. That afternoon, he took a rickshaw to the bus station, in search of LSD and a better class of hippy. I was too angry to go with him, but was now left alone, facing two weeks of rain and near-naked yoga. I couldn't even go anywhere myself, as Matt had taken our copy of the *Lonely Planet*. I was trapped, and when the hippies moved on the next day, I found myself completely abandoned. My only solace came from my collection of C90 mix tapes. They took up half the space in my rucksack, meaning I only had one spare T-shirt, but I was eternally grateful for them during those long, friendless hours.

Two days after Matt deserted me, the Walkman left me too. It chewed up my treasured bootleg copy of Oasis live at Knebworth. The tape's brown intestines had worked their way so far into the machine that it was beyond salvage. My one source of comfort, cruelly snatched away. I was left with little choice but to pace up and down the deserted beach, willing someone to turn up. In the afternoons, I sat in the bar, repeatedly explaining to the few Indian families walking past that no, I didn't like cricket and no, I wasn't still distraught about the tragic death of Princess Diana, given that I hadn't known her personally and it was over a year ago. My loneliness became so extreme by the third music-free afternoon that I even started watching the videos playing on the small TV. Ever wondered how many Bollywood films you can sit through when you have absolutely nothing else to do? The answer is three and a half, at which point sitting in a tropical storm and staring blankly at the sea becomes the better option.

At least India's food lived up to its reputation. I worked my way through every single item on the beach bar's menu, and the owner gave me double portions – he was as bored as I was, with no one else to cook for. In return I taught him how to play chess. It didn't work too well with only half a set, but he didn't seem too concerned with how each piece moved anyway.

But not even this could sustain me for ever. When I had eaten everything on his menu at least three times, and moved 143-0 ahead in our ongoing chess marathon, it was time to leave Goa.

I spent the fifteen-hour trip to Bombay hoping desperately that it would be better.

It was far, far worse.

The volumes of sewage, rubbish and traffic I'd been warned about; it was the volumes of people I couldn't cope with. On my first morning, I couldn't even step out of the hotel; there was never a big enough gap in the sea of humans to step into. After several failed attempts, I decided to confine myself to the hotel until my flight home. With no other guests about (none that wanted to spend time with me, anyway), I set about working my way through the hotel's small library. Each morning, I took up residence on the tiny terrace until it got too hot or my stomach couldn't face any more samosas. I even managed to finish their battered copy of *A Suitable Boy* – all 1,474 pages of it – while ticking off every item on a second menu of the trip.

On my last night, it felt like time to give the city one last go. A rickshaw took me to Leopold's, a café which the hotel's edition of the *Lonely Planet* insisted was the best place to meet other backpackers. This was true: I counted twelve other

Westerners sat on their own and all looking as miserable as I felt. Several had a copy of the *Lonely Planet* perched carefully on their table, like some kind of travellers' beacon. It wasn't working, though, as no one was talking to anyone else. Many of them looked skeletal; at least I'd avoided that fate. But I had no energy left to start up a conversation with a stranger. I'd come to prove I could handle India, and India had won, hands down.

After four mango lassis, I gave up. It was only while paying the bill that I realised one of the skeletons was Matt.

'Shit, you look awful. What happened?'

'Amoebic dysentery. I bought a cup of tea from one of those little kids at the bus station. I was shitting rusty water within two hours and I've spent the last week in bed. I feel terrible.'

Discovering that Matt's experience had been even worse than mine was the high point of my trip. But it did leave us with one mutual problem.

'What are we going to tell everyone when we get back?' Matt asked, as we walked – very slowly and carefully in his case – back towards my hotel (he couldn't bear the thought of being on his own again, and insisted on sleeping on my floor). 'We were supposed to have wild adventures, and between us we've done sod all.'

'Don't worry,' I replied. 'I've got a plan.'

We spent our last night picking out some key passages in *A Suitable Boy*, to be passed off as descriptions of the real India that we had both failed to find. And so I returned from my Big Trip with a heavy cold, four words of Hindi, the rudiments of yoga and an in-depth knowledge of Indian cuisine.

* * *

Whatever happens in Kenya, it has to be better. But Kenya is six weeks away and with little else to distract it, my mind meanders back to the pre-Christmas conversation with Mum. Early as it may seem, I will soon be forced to decide what I want to do with the next forty-four years of my life. And, as with so much in my life, I need someone to point me in the right direction. Rob is as good a bet as anyone and distracting him with some soul-searching questions might also help in our afternoon pool battle. I'm already four-one down.

'Rob, can I ask you something?'

'Fucking hell, not this again,' he says, sizing up a long red. 'Right, it smarts a bit the first few times, but you soon get used to it and there are all sorts of lubricants—'

'No, not that one. About me. What do you think I'll be when I'm older?'

'Less of a twat, hopefully.'

'I mean as a job.'

'Do Plymouth Argyle need any ball boys?'

'There's an age limit, unfortunately. Seriously, what can I do?'

'I'm your housemate, not a careers advisor. What's brought this on?'

'Mum, over Christmas. She says I lack ambition.'

'You don't lack ambition, Chris,' Rob replies, lining up the black. 'You actively chase it away. Your dedication to an easy life is one of the few things I admire about you.'

'My mother doesn't share that view.'

'What do you want to do?' he asks, missing his pot.

'I'm not that bothered,' I shrug, swearing as the easiest of my six yellows rattles in the jaws of the pocket.

'If you're not bothered, it doesn't matter, does it? Do anything. Now stop trying to distract the master at work.'

He sinks the black with a double, blows nonchalantly on the tip of his cue and winks. Everything's easy for Rob. Even career planning; he decided long ago that he's going to find a way to get paid to spend every day rock climbing. Failing that, he'll be a music journalist, either for *NME* or *Rolling Stone*. He hasn't bothered with a third option, so confident is he in one of the first two coming off.

'How are things with Emma?' he asks while studying the pub's menu to find the least expensive, most filling option.

'Great, mostly. I'm spending most of my time round there now. She reads books and I watch her films. And we drink lots of tea.'

'Hmmm,' says Rob, slotting twenty pence into the table to release the balls. 'And that's it? You sit around, watching telly and drinking tea?'

'I like it. It's nice. Cosy.'

'It sounds like you're living in an old people's home. As students in the first throes of a new relationship, you should be humping away on an hourly basis.'

'It's not like that. We usually just cuddle.'

'Cuddling's a waste of time,' Rob says, shaking his head. 'Tell me honestly, how often do you two have sex?'

'It's just been that one time. After Roxy's. We listened to Nick Drake afterwards.'

'Once? Before Christmas? I'm not sure it even counts if you did it to folk music.'

'She hasn't seemed to want to do it again,' I admit. 'Any idea why?'

'Not really. Maybe it's stress, but then you think she'd want a break from all the studying. You'll have to ask her about it, next time you're round there.'

'Can you talk to her? You've known her for longer.'

'I'm not sorting out your love life for you, not until you come and join me on the other side.'

'I dunno what to say, though. I never do.'

'Be casual. Don't make a big deal about it, drop it into a conversation about something else.'

'OK, I'll try.'

'Let me know how it goes. A quick summary will do, not every last detail. OK, my break, your round. And put some music on the jukebox. What were you humming on the way up here?'

'Ocean Colour Scene.'

'Hmm, choose carefully if that's what's buzzing round your head. Three good songs amid a tidal wave of shite. In fact, you get the beers, I'll choose the music, less risky that way.'

* * *

Rob's advice rattles around my head as I wait for Emma the next day. It makes sense: wait until the time is right, then raise the subject tactfully so we can discuss it like adults. Subtlety is undoubtedly the best approach, but it isn't my strongest suite.

Emma kisses me upon arrival, then goes straight to my room while I make our latest round of tea. I prefer going to hers, which is a lot cleaner and has far more food, but she says she likes our house (without ever giving any concrete reasons as to why).

She's cleared the unread geography books away from my desk and is already jotting away when I carry in the tea.

'What are you revising?'

'It's not work, it's a wee play I'm writing with some friends from the drama soc. We're going to perform it at the Edinburgh Festival. Hopefully.'

'Cool, can I read it?' My girlfriend, the playwright. I like the sound of that.

'No, sweetie. But you can come and watch us when we start rehearsing.'

'At least tell me what it's about.'

'It's about an angel who arrives in heaven only to find it's much the same as earth: work, bills, traffic, stress,' she replies, frowning. 'It's supposed to be a satire on modern life, but it's hard work writing it.'

'Please let me read it.'

'No, read your magazine. I'll come over when I've finished this scene.'

She starts scribbling again and I retreat to my bed to let her write in peace. I finish my tea.

Now seems as good a time as any.

'Emma, why don't we have sex?'

'Where's this come from, sweetie?' she says, not turning round.

'Nowhere, really. But we only did it that one time, before Christmas, and we're students, so we should be doing it all the time. Shouldn't we?'

'Because that's what everyone else does?'

'Well … yeah. That's what you do when you're going out, isn't it?'

She sips the tea, then comes over and sits on my bed, folding her skirt beneath her. 'Aye, that's what some people do. But relationships are about more than that. I want to know you as a person, I want to find out what makes you tick: what music you like, what films you enjoy, which books made you stop and go "wow". I want to know what you think about the world, what your dreams are. That's what relationships are about. Sex is just a small part of it.'

This is not good news, on any level. While I would never claim to be much good at sex, I'm far worse at deep, meaningful conversations. And far less interested in them.

'Come on, sweetie, talk to me. Tell me what you're reading.'

I glance at my bedside table, where the latest issue of *Q* sits atop a pile of football magazines.

'I read *A Suitable Boy* last summer,' I say. 'Right to the end.'

'God, I *adore* that book. What did you think?'

'It was ... long.'

'Isn't it incredible, how Seth keeps us enraptured by all those intertwining lives through so many pages? Which characters did you like best?'

Shit. I can't remember any of their names, or even what any of them did, except play cricket and go to weddings.

'Well, the boy, obviously.'

'Kabir? Isn't he wonderful? Like Heathcliff of the sub-continent, so dark and brooding. I was totally distraught at the end, I mean, how could Lata end up with Haresh, not Kabir or even Amit?'

'Exactly. Me too. Very much like Heathcliff.' I have absolutely no idea who Heathcliff is. 'Very dark and very brooding. Almost too brooding, you could say.'

'OK, sweetie, you choose the next subject,' Emma says, taking hold of my hands.

'Do you like football?'

'Not really.'

'Right, music then.' This should be easy, it's what I know best, but I can't think of a good starter. 'Well, you know what music I like. What else do you want to know about it?'

'I want to know *why* you like it,' Emma says. 'What was the song that was playing when I got here? Tell me about that.'

'"Razzamatazz", by Pulp. It's a classic.'

'And why do you like Pulp?'

'Because they're great.'

'*Why* are they great?'

This is tricky. I've never had to think about it before, it's just an accepted fact. Discussions about music rarely extend beyond the 'which' – which band, which song, which album – or how much, on a scale from 'alright' to 'good' to 'awesome'. There's rarely any more in-depth analysis; that's what the music magazines are for.

I concentrate on Pulp. What's so great about them?

'OK, so that song, 'Razzamatzz', for a start the lyrics are filthy. It's about incest. I think it is, anyway. So that sets it apart from most songs straight away. But Pulp's songs are about real life, not made-up crap. Like "Disco 2000". He, Jarvis, doesn't get the girl, she goes off with all his mates at school. Most pop songs are about relationships going badly or people breaking up, but you've got to *have* a girlfriend before you can get dumped. And that's what Pulp sing about, being awkward, being an outsider, not getting the girl. I can relate to that.'

I breathe, relieved to have got through it and surprising even myself with such a long answer.

'Not that I didn't have a girlfriend, at school,' I add quickly. 'I had loads.'

Got away with that one. Just about.

'Very good,' Emma confirms, her green eyes fixed on me. God, she's pretty. 'OK, which band do you like most?'

'Is this a test?'

'Aye, kind of. And same rules, you need to tell me why you like them.'

This one will be even harder. I've never settled on one band before, four or five usually compete for the title at any one time. 'I guess Oasis are the biggest band around, along with Blur. But that doesn't mean they're the best. Although Oasis definitely have the finest collection of B-sides, they're often better than the singles. Radiohead are definitely number one musically, artistically I mean, they're so creative. But lyrics-wise, I'd say Pulp or Blur, although Blur can be a bit sneering at times. Of course, the first Nineties band I really loved was Cast. When their first album came out, I was obsessed with it for weeks. So, there's an argument to be made for them, too ...'

And that's before I factor in live performances. The best Britpop band I've seen live is Suede. Or maybe Super Furry Animals. No, definitely Suede. I still have great affection for Longpigs, whose rise to semi-fame coincided with my moving to Sheffield. *The Sun Is Often Out* is still in my top three albums, but they haven't released a second one. Can I count them as my favourite band on such a limited output? I've been listening to a lot of Charlatans lately, although that's at Rob's insistence, so I can't claim them for myself. And Supergrass are getting better all the time, the early singles from their soon-to-be-released album are better than anything they've done before. And then there's the newcomers, Embrace, Travis, Mansun, who have all burst onto the scene in recent times. But the Longpigs rule applies there, there's too little to judge them on.

Emma is looking at me, expectant. Hang on, what did she ask me? I lost track of our conversation somewhere between the Charlatans and Supergrass ... Oh yes, favourite band.

'Sorry, I can't do it. I can't pick one. And that's what I like: there's so much music about. There's always a new album to look forward to, or a new band, or a new single from an old favourite. Is that enough of an answer?'

'Aye, I suppose so, but also a wee bit indecisive. OK, next one. If you had to pick one song to play to me, which would it be? It doesn't have to be your favourite, but the one you'd choose for me. And no saying you can't decide this time, you have to pick one.'

This will be even harder; it's challenging enough to pick the tracks for a mix tape, and you can usually get nine or ten tracks on each side of the tape. And I have to choose just one? Jeez. My most-listened-to song is probably "The Man Don't Give A Fuck", but Rob has vetoed it from any list of great Britpop tracks because it rips off a Steely Dan song. (And it's not even the Super Furries' best song; "Demons" is.) My favourite *bit* of a song is the guitar solo after the third chorus in "Champagne Supernova", when Noel starts wigging out and doing his own thing and everyone else be damned; it's quite possibly the greatest bit of music ever. Although the bassline to "Girls and Boys" runs it close, Alex James' finest work without any question. Still, I have a feeling Emma might be expecting a whole song, not just a riff.

"Four Walls" was an early favourite, capturing everything I felt as a teenager about being desperate to escape (although I suspect it's about being stuck in prison rather than Devon). I could try and look clever by choosing something obscure like "Mum's Gone To Iceland" by Bennet, or an overlooked album track; "Let It Flow" by Ash is an underappreciated classic. But she'll see through me if I try too hard. And this feels like a Significant Moment. "Saturday Night" by Suede? I love it, but Rob says that the moment rock bands start doing ballads it's the beginning of the end. Wonder Stuff Tom recently sent me a Teenage Fanclub compilation, but do they count as Britpop? Did Emma even specify that it has to be Britpop? I can't remember, but it needs to be my choice.

"'On & On' by Longpigs. That's the song I'd choose for you,' I declare after several minutes of silent consideration.

'Play it.'

I dig out the mottled blue CD, skip to track four, then jump back onto the bed. Emma is lying down, her eyes closed. I lie next to her as the guitar intro builds up and take her hand as the drums kick in. Crispin Hunt begins his most heartfelt, tender vocal performance.

The lyrics aren't ideal, I realise now – about a break up, I didn't think about that – but Emma's hand is tightening around mine.

'It's beautiful,' she says as the final chord fades. 'Play it again.'

I stretch my left leg and prod the backwards button on the CD player with my toe, not wanting to leave her side. By the time it's finished for a second time, she's nestled in the crook of my arm, head on my chest.

'You see?' she says. 'We're really communicating now, getting to know each other. For me, that's the best part of being with you. There's so much more to enjoy than the physical side, don't you think?'

An image flashes into my head. My mother, sitting at our kitchen table, both hands around a mug of tea, the week before I left for university. She was imparting parental advice to her eighteen-year-old son before he prepared to leave home. 'Always be honest with girls, Chris. That's what relationships are built on: trust and honesty.'

I smile at the memory; she always wants the best for me.

Although it's a mystery how she's managed to stay married for twenty-five years believing bullshit like that.

'Of course I agree, Emma, one hundred percent. That's what I like most, the talking.'

'I'm glad you think so, Chris.' Her hand moves lightly across my stomach.

'Do you want to talk some more now?' I know I'm supposed to say it, even though it's very hard.

'What do you want to do?'

'Maybe we could have sex, then do some more talking afterwards. Or listen to more Longpigs. It's an incredible album, there's this song halfway through, "All Hype", which is just as good, and–'

'Let's listen to it later,' Emma says, climbing onto me.

17

Saturday Night

It's official: Emma and I are now a couple. Our abstinence problem in now firmly behind us. She is my girlfriend.

My first proper girlfriend.

It's a significant milestone, and one achieved just before another comes around: my twenty-first birthday. Rob and Andy kick the day off in style with my favourite breakfast: two tins of beans with grated cheese, four slices of toast and tea from Rob's treasured pint-sized mug from a climbing café in Wales. I'm rarely allowed to touch it, but get special dispensation to use it on days like this.

Once Andy has dashed off to the hospital, Rob sits down with me.

'And here's your present,' he says, passing over a small parcel wrapped in newspaper. I rip it open to reveal *Leisure,* Blur's first album and the only one I don't have on CD, and a bootleg recording of one of their concerts in Japan. It's nearly impossible to get hold of a copy, and must have cost him a lot.

'Brilliant, thanks, mate.'

Yet the CDs have jogged a memory supressed these last few weeks. I haven't asked Rob about the rumours of Blur splitting up, simply because I don't want to have them confirmed. Even now, I try to convince myself it doesn't matter. But it does. Blur are hugely significant; in many ways, they *are* Britpop. I need them to complete the set. Dad saw all the big bands in his day – Led Zeppelin, Deep Purple, Black Sabbath, even the Stones – and I won't be able to look any kids Emma and I might have in the eye if I miss the defining band of my decade. Even if they can forgive me, I'll never forgive myself. I need to know what Rob knows.

'Did you hear that rumour about Blur?' I ask, as nonchalantly as I can muster.

Rob shakes his head; he's already taken the CDs back from me and is scrutinising the track listing from the Japan concert.

'Something about Graham leaving,' I continue. 'Cecilia mentioned it when I was in London.'

'I've not heard anything. Let's hope not, I'd hate for your pin board shrine to be left with a huge hole in the middle,' he says. He doesn't sound overly concerned, but then he's seen them twice; they were better the first time, naturally, on the Rollercoaster tour in 1992. Still, if Rob doesn't know anything about it, perhaps it is just a rumour. 'And while I've got your attention for once, there's something I've been meaning to tell you,' he continues.

'You're gay, I know. It's no big deal, get over yourself.'

'No, but it is gay-related. I'm seeing someone.'

'Really? Who?' This is a surprise; Rob is usually too busy climbing to bother with relationships.

'He's called Seth. First year. I met him at an LGB night about a month ago.'

'You've been seeing someone for a month and not told me?'

'You never asked.'

'What's he like?'

'Short, thin. Into music. You'll like him.'

'Are you going to bring him to my birthday meal?' I haven't made any special plans, sticking to the established cheap-meal-out-and-drinks formula, an unspoken agreement among third years to keep twenty-first celebrations affordable.

'Not tonight, you'll be hammered before we get there. I'll arrange something in the next week or so.'

Rob's right; I'm plastered long before we reach the restaurant. Yet I can just about focus for long enough to look around the table as we eat a mix of dishes of imprecise Mediterranean origin. Everyone important to me is here: Rob, Andy, Mike, Joe; my football team, some mates from halls; Emma (and her irritating housemates, who I felt obliged to invite). It's reassuring; I may be average at geography, shit at football and clueless with women, but at least I've got friends. And most of them have bought me a drink, judging by the long line of spirits surrounding my hot'n'spicy pizza. I've given up hope of making it through the evening without vomiting; if I can manage to keep it down until we're out of the restaurant, it will be an achievement.

And I very nearly do.

* * *

Rob's in the living room when I wake the next day, wading through some climbing-related paperwork.

'How're you feeling?' he enquires.

'Awful. I've got a thumping headache. You were supposed to look after me.'

'You're twenty-one now, you can look after yourself,' he grunts, turning the sheets of paper ridiculously loudly. 'By the way, why didn't you invite Lou to your birthday meal?'

'I thought it might be a bit weird, with Emma being there. My girlfriend and my ex. Well, my girlfriend and the woman who turned me down. I decided not to mention it to her in the end.'

'That makes sense,' Rob says, stapling a wad of receipts together with a deafening thud. 'She knows anyway. And about Emma.'

'Shit. How?'

'I told her. She was here yesterday, looking for you. I assumed you'd asked her. The Emma bit just slipped out, sorry.'

'How did she take it?'

'Hard to say. She was only here about two minutes. Are you two friends or not?'

'I don't know. I've not spoken to her for a while, she said she needed some space.'

'When was that?'

'December.'

'Possibly she's had enough space by now. Anyway, she wants to talk to you about something. She seemed a bit worked up. Oh, and she brought you this.'

He chucks a small parcel over, neatly wrapped in shiny paper, unlike his slapdash recycled effort. I remove the paper to reveal a copy of *Ocean Drive* by the Lighthouse Family.

'Fucking hell. I'm sorry, mate,' Rob says, shaking his head sadly.

'You know what the worst thing is? I've got two copies now. Grandma gave me one for my twentieth. The last present she ever gave me. Why do people think I like the Lighthouse Family?'

'Search me. Is there a receipt with it?'

'Nope.'

'Ouch. Well, keep it away from your other CDs, you don't want to risk any cross-contamination.'

Rob returns to his accounts and I sip my tea gingerly, an extra-strong two-bag effort in the hope it eases the hangover. But it doesn't: my problems are stacking up. Not only do I now technically have a collection of the worst album of the 1990s, I'm also thinking about Lou again. Talking to her again was always going to be difficult, but Rob's big mouth has made it even trickier. Will she be annoyed that I've met someone else? Will she even care? And now I have to talk to her, if only to say thank you for the shit birthday present. And it will have to be in the next few days, I can't put it off any longer. Or next week, maybe. But I definitely have to talk to her, and sooner rather than later. Maybe. Definitely maybe.

18

Rocks

Spring finally emerges from beneath the mouldering duvet of winter. To welcome in the new season, I'm lying in bed with The Verve on – I've forced myself to take a break from *13*, the new album from Blur (which thankfully contains no detectable evidence of internal band strife) – when my inertia is interrupted by the doorbell. I'm tempted to ignore it – I know it isn't Emma, she has classes on a Monday morning, and I'm not interested in seeing anyone else. But when they ring again, I force on an Oasis T-shirt and go to answer it.

On the step, staring at our dandelions, is a pale-skinned, malnourished-looking youth. A greasy black fringe sprouts from beneath the hood of a baggy black sweatshirt that is several sizes too large. He looks like the bastard son of Brett Anderson and Brian Molko, if such a thing were possible.

'Can I help you?'

'Rob in?'

'Dunno. Who should I–'

'Seth,' he mumbles, before I can finish my question.

'Come in, I'll see if he's around somewhere.'

As I call upstairs, Seth loiters in the hallway, staring at our mat. He's not what I expected. I haven't met many of Rob's boyfriends – he rarely stays with them long enough for me to be introduced – but I expected someone a bit, well, healthier. But I need to make an effort, get to know him. The jangling, post-addiction angst of *Urban Hymns* floats out of my room. Rob said he liked music, didn't he?

'Are you a fan of The Verve? Rob and I saw them at the Leadmill.'

He shakes his head, still staring at the mat.

'I love this album,' I say, trying to breathe life into this flagging conversation. 'Rob says it's not as good as their early stuff. No surprise there, I suppose.'

No response; not even a flicker.

I plough on bravely. 'Do you like the same bands as me and Rob, then? Indie, Britpop, whatever we're supposed to call it.'

'Nah. Britpop's over.'

It's early days, but I'm pretty sure Seth and I aren't going to get on.

'Morning Chris, morning Seth. Do you two fancy some climbing at Stanage?' Rob hurtles down the stairs just in time to save me. Seth shrugs, which apparently means yes. I would happily leave them to it and return to The Verve, but Rob's look – raised eyebrows, eyes staring – indicates that he wants me to come too. This is evidently his way of introducing me to Seth. And he gets to spend the day climbing. He's a sneaky bastard at times.

'Sure, why not?' I say, with as much enthusiasm as I can muster.

Rob heads back to his room to sort out the kit and I nod towards the kitchen to inform Seth, in his own language of silent head movements, that I'm putting the kettle on and he's welcome to have a cup despite the fact that he's a miserable prick. No one speaks as the kettle boils, nor while the tea brews. Silently, we sip our drink to test how hot it is, even though it's clearly just been made with boiling water. After a few blows to speed up the cooling process, I give Seth another chance; he is, after all, my best friend's new boyfriend.

'Who do you like, then, if not The Verve?'

'All sorts,' Seth grunts.

'Heard the new Blur album?'

"S'alright. Not great.'

'Wrong. It's fantastic.'

Seth ignores this and stares at his tea.

'What about Oasis, then?' I continue. 'I suppose they're rubbish as well?'

'They were ripping off the New Seekers on their debut album. Says it all.'

It sounds like a well-rehearsed line (it's also a good point) but he's so, so irritating. Especially the oily smirk on his face as he eyes my T-shirt. He's in my kitchen, drinking my tea – and he's openly mocking me.

'Bull. Shit. They're the most iconic band of our time. One of the greatest of all time. You have to accept that.'

'You two ready?' asks Rob, before Seth has time to shrug a reply. 'We can walk to the station, save money for tea and cakes in Hathersage. And it will give you two more time to continue this highly entertaining musical squabble.'

The animosity intensifies as we head through the city. Seth dismisses Suede, Pulp, Cast, Ash and Radiohead, each passionate tirade met with a sneering reply, alongside chortled amusement from Rob. Even when I name-drop the bands that Wonder Stuff Tom has introduced me to, Seth has a snide response ready. I'm losing the argument. Badly. The little civility I displayed earlier has long since been discarded in favour of swearwords and derisive snorts. I give up on bands and move on to albums, hoping I might catch him out.

'What about *All Change*? Twelve perfectly formed pop songs. Or *1977*? Ash were doing their A-levels when they wrote that. You're honestly saying that no one will remember those in the future?'

'All years ago. Like I said, Britpop's over.'

'That's bollocks.'

After remaining neutral this far, Rob finally enters the fray. I'm willing him to take my side. 'OK, Chris, what was the last really great album you heard? Not one you hoped would be great because you like the band, but one that blew your mind on the first listen.'

I can't say *13*, Seth has already disregarded that, even though it's only a week old. I almost blurt out *Be Here Now* but manage to stop myself in time; I love it but everyone else has now decided it's atrocious, overblown nonsense. *OK Computer*? Too obvious; he'll shoot that down instantly. Most other big bands have also been dismissed. I rack my brains for something more obscure.

'*Radiator*, Super Furry Animals' I state, finally. It's a safe bet. Rob is a massive fan of that album, he has to back me up now. But it's Seth who replies, with the longest answer he's managed all day.

'Eighteen months old. And what's been good since then? Most bands are already putting out their greatest hits collections. The biggest band today is Travis, which says it all.'

'What's wrong with Travis?' I'm not too fussed either way by the latest media darlings, but at this point I would even defend Elastica to the death, just to win the argument.

'Nothing, if you like pub-rock Byrds tribute acts.'

This is descending into a war; it's time for Rob to pick sides.

'What do you think, Rob? You failed to defend *Radiator*, even though I know it's in your all-time top five. Want to offer an opinion on Travis, given that you love their first album?'

'I think young Seth's assessment of them as "pub rock" is a touch harsh,' he replies, massaging his beard thoughtfully. 'Personally, I consider Mr Healy to be one of the finer vocalists of our era. But overall, the argument stands. If Travis are all we have these days, then Britpop, or at least the best of it, is behind us. And who knows for how long, or indeed if, we shall mourn its passing? I've been listening to more expressive and meaningful material of late. Elliot Smith, Jeff Buckley, it's superior in almost every way.'

'You're both wrong,' I snap back, before adopting a sulky silence as we approach the station. I need time to gather my thoughts. Clearly Rob isn't going to defend me, or the bands we've worshipped for years. I'll have to try a different angle. As we jump onto the train, I give it one last shot.

'OK, if the very best *is* behind us, then what's coming next, Seth? What should I be listening to?'

'Up to you,' he shrugs.

'No, come on, if you're such an expert, name some names.'

'Try listening to something other than Britpop. You'll soon find out.'

'Oh, he does,' interjects Rob, a wicked glint in his eyes. 'I've heard all sorts of horrors pumping forth from his stereo, usually when he thinks I'm out. Guns N' Roses, Dire Straits, even Meat Loaf on one occasion. And while he tells everyone that his first gig was Longpigs in Sheffield, it was actually Bon Jovi at Wembley. The full stadium rock experience: lighters in the air, glossy programmes and warm, pissy five-quid beers.'

Seth cackles loudly, an unpleasant, nasal splutter that sounds like he's choking. I stare at Rob in disbelief; I can hardly believe this betrayal. Grandpa was right all along; homosexuals aren't to be trusted. Admittedly he makes the same accusation of Greeks, maths teachers and Postman Pat, but in this instance, he's correct.

'How do you even know that?'

'Your sister told me in Devon last summer,' Rob grins. 'You'd passed out from too much cider and we spent the night talking about you. Well, about ten minutes, then we talked about more interesting stuff.'

'And? So what? As your boyfriend just told me, everyone should listen to more than one type of music. What's wrong with rock music?'

'Shall I begin, Seth? OK, let's start with Mark Knopfler, who is, to all intents and purposes, Dire Straits. A great guitarist, no question, but he dresses like a colour-blind bag lady. Guns N' Roses have a couple of vaguely passable songs, granted, but they would sound so much better if Axl Rose remembered to have a shit before he went on stage. The poor man sounds in agony. Meat Loaf is, well, Meat Loaf. And it's difficult to know where to start with Bon Jovi. There's the lyrics, which read like the angst-ridden poetry of a dysfunctional teenager. And of course there's his weird misconception that he's a cowboy. But hey, if you like them …'

'I do. So you can both fuck off.'

I give Rob one last, cold stare to let him know this loathsome act of treachery will not be forgotten. I then pointedly turn to look out of the window. Unfortunately, the train enters the Totley Tunnel and I have to spend the next five minutes staring at blackness. Still, it gives me time to consider whether Andy or Mike should be promoted to the recently vacated slot of best friend. And to revise my opinion of Seth from bellend to wanker.

* * *

My sulk continues as we walk from Hathersage station to Stanage Edge. I hang back, hands shoved as deep into pockets as they will go. I'm seriously considering withholding Rob's ticket for Gene at the Leadmill tomorrow night as punishment for his behaviour. But it's Seth who has really got under my skin. I detest him, not just for his musical opinions, but for ruining my good mood. Things have been going so well recently – meeting Emma, turning twenty-one, Blur not splitting up – and then this greasy, anaemic social inadequate wanders in to piss all over my campfire. I can't understand why Rob likes him; he's scrawny, sullen and over-opinionated. Why pick him out of all the gays in Sheffield?

By the time I reach the rockface, Rob is already fitting Seth's harness. Danny, one of his faithful entourage from the climbing club, is sorting out ropes. We nod at each other; I recognise him from various climbing events I've tagged along to. He looks like Davy Jones, the Monkee who could only play the maracas, and I suspect he has a crush on Rob, given how devotedly he follows him around. But seeing as Danny never speaks, it's difficult to know for sure.

'You finally made it,' Rob says as he adjusts the harness straps. 'I thought you'd got lost. Danny's already got a route set up, so Seth's going up first, OK?'

'Whatever,' I mutter, wandering off to find a comfortable-ish rock to lean against and simmer. While I can ignore Seth's many failings as a human being, I can't shift one tiny, nagging and terrifying doubt. What if he's right?

What if it's all over?

I can't think of a recent album that is anywhere near as good as early Britpop. Even *13* doesn't quite hit the mark of Blur's earlier work. The thought of Seth being right is nauseating enough, but the thought of the greatest musical era ever being finished is far harder to swallow. And there are no guarantees as to what might come next. Dad told me once how devastating it was when Led Zeppelin split in 1980, but did he and their millions of fans expect the void to be filled by Shakin' Stevens and Bucks Fizz? Almost certainly not. The current number one in the charts is a Boyzone cover of a Billy Ocean song. The signs are not promising.

At least I have a view to enjoy as I wallow. The deep blue of Ladybower Reservoir stands below, the distinctive table top of Kinder Scout beyond. Mam Tor is out there somewhere, the location of an utterly tedious first-year field trip about rotational slip. Grindleford, too, but I've got enough to occupy my mind without venturing there. Instead I lose myself in happier thoughts – music, Emma, beer, what I might have for tea – until they are interrupted by an anxious-looking Rob hurrying towards me.

'What's up,' I ask.

'Nothing serious,' Rob says quickly, as Seth waddles within earshot. 'Just a tricky bit at the end there.'

I look at Seth. His eyes are glazed over and he's rocking back and forwards. Pale to begin with, he's now whiter than Michael Jackson. He looks really shaken; this day isn't a complete write-off just yet.

'He's not a natural climber, then?'

'Nope,' Rob whispers. 'I think he shat himself.'

'Really?' This is fantastic news. I give up trying not to look pleased.

'Can you take him down to the café in Hathersage?'

'No, I can't stand him. You take him.'

'I can't, he was almost crying back there, saying he's ruined my day out. So I told him that he hadn't and that I'll do a couple more climbs with Danny.'

I wrinkle my nose; Rob's betrayal is still fresh in my mind.

'Please, Chris, help me out.'

'You've been taking the piss out of me all day. Why should I help you now?'

'Emma. You'd never have met her if it wasn't for me.'

He has a point. Still, it doesn't fully excuse him. 'Tell me you still love *Radiator* and I'll consider it.'

'Come on, you know I do. It was a bit of fun, that's all.'

I can see Rob is desperate. Over his shoulder, Seth finally has some colour in his cheeks, but it's a yellow-ish green. It'll be even harder for us to bond if he starts throwing up everywhere. Rob rubs his temples, exhausted with the situation.

'Right, here's money for the café. I'll be no more than an hour, I promise. I know he likes Supergrass, he's got a poster of them in his room. Stick to them and you'll be fine.'

'OK. But this cancels out the Emma favour – you can't use that one again. Deal?'

'Deal.'

Half an hour later, we're in the café. Seth heads straight for the toilet and stays there for another fifteen minutes, but looks a bit better when he finally emerges.

'Tea?'

He shrugs. It's hard to tell if that means yes or no.

'I'll get us some cake as well, Rob gave me a tenner. What sort do you like?'

He shrugs again. I order a pot of tea for two and a slice each of the ginger cake and the lemon drizzle, hoping he won't like either.

'We're going to see Supergrass in a few weeks,' I say, placing the tray on the table. 'Rob says you like them.'

'Nah,' he says, taking the lemon drizzle.

'Not even the early stuff?'

'They're only famous because of the fuzzy-felt sideburns.'

Even the cheeriest, most amiable band of our times fail to escape his scorn. I give up and retrieve the latest edition of *FHM* from my bag to indicate that our chat is over. From the corner of my eye, I see Seth pull a notebook out of his pocket and start scribbling away. I'm desperate to know what he's writing, but too proud to ask.

The minutes tick by. As I consider buying myself more cake to help speed them up, Rob and Danny walk in.

'Any more tea in that pot?' Rob asks, squeezing in next to me. 'Come on, budge up.'

'There's plenty of room. It's not my fault you've got a fat arse.'

'You need a big hammer when you've got a big nail. Isn't that right, Seth?' Rob winks across the table, shaking the teapot to check if any was left. 'Not even a drop? Greedy bastards. I'll order some more. What about you, Danny?'

Danny nods in reply. He's about as chatty as Seth; where does Rob find these people?

'Don't we need to get going?' I say. 'There's a train leaving in a few minutes.'

'No rush,' says Rob. 'Danny's offered us a lift back to Sheffield. And personally, I think it's best if we wait for an hour or so. If we're going back in his shitty little Ford Fiesta, I'd prefer it to be under cover of darkness.'

'I'll get something else as well, then, if we're all staying' I say, pushing past Rob. The bacon rolls at Hathersage café are legendary, and one of Rob's weaknesses. I'm certain he'll have impressed his vegetarian principles on Seth and the thought of him having to watch me eat one – two, in fact, there's still enough change left from his tenner – will allow me to end a miserable day with a victory. A small one, admittedly, but they all count.

19

Strumpet

I head straight to Emma's house, not wanting to spend a minute longer in Seth's wretched company. She asked me to give her some peace to focus on her play, but that was two days ago; she's probably finished it by now. Plus I urgently need to bitch about Seth to someone who will listen.

I want to see her anyway. Things are going extremely well. It feels like an adult relationship, which makes me feel like an adult. And I like that feeling. Like everyone else, I experienced teenage angst; not quite at Placebo levels of intensity, but still plenty of moody silences and slammed doors. But this last year, I've done a significant amount of maturing. I did the right thing, however reluctantly, with Lou; I got to know Emma by talking to her; I even went to London on my own.

The day's frustrations drift away as I walk up the hill. I love her house; not only is it mould-free and full of food, but her room overflows with CDs that I don't know. At first, I was sceptical; most of the covers feature old men with beards sitting on stools and holding guitars. But collectively, they have quashed my prejudice against folk music. Tim Buckley, Christy Moore, Luka Bloom; all new to me, and all wonderful. Dougie MacLean has quickly become a favourite. He looks like the bloke who fixes motorbikes in Tavistock, but sings about Scotland with such tender passion that I have an overpowering urgency to wander among those lochs and glens, even though I've never seen them. I dismissed folk music without giving it a fair crack, but Emma's collection has offered me the chance for redemption.

Her video collection is equally intriguing. I've heard of many of the old classics on her bookshelf – *Casablanca*, *Brief Encounter*, *Wuthering Heights*, *To Kill A Mockingbird* – but never watched them, so, in between the folk, I've been setting that right. I'm thinking about which one I'll pick tonight as I ring the doorbell.

'Hi sweetie,' Emma says, opening the door. 'I thought I said I'd call you when I'm free?'

'I wanted to see how the play's going. Have you got any food?'

'There's salad in the fridge. Help yourself.' She heads back upstairs and, after filling a bowl and nabbing an apple for dessert, plus a packet of ginger nuts for later, I follow. She's already back at her desk when I get there.

'How's it going?' I ask.

'Badly. Really badly. I'm crossing out all the bits that don't work, and there's hardly anything left. It's a wee bit dispiriting. Writing a play is very, very hard.'

'Can't you perform one that's already been written? One by Shakespeare, or …' – come on, think of another famous person who's written a play – '… or Blyton?' She wrote loads of books; some of them must have been plays.

'Do you mean Byron?'

'Yes, Byron, sorry.'

'He was more of a poet, sweetie. God, I love Byron, he's so emotive, so vivid, don't you think?'

I nod with a mouth full of salad, which is about as much as I can contribute to a discussion about poetry.

'You know, there are some days when I simply *have* to read Byron,' she continues. 'Which are your favourites?'

'Well, I'd be doing the man an injustice by just choosing one,' I splutter. 'I, err, generally like his earlier stuff.'

I only just manage to avoid saying 'albums'.

174

'God, me too. *She Walks In Beauty* is my favourite, isn't it wonderful? So evocative, yet so restrained. But I want to perform *my* play. I want to see posters plastered around the city, with "A Play by Emma McMurray" on them.'

'Is that the title?'

Even I could come up with something better than that.

'No, of course it isn't, sweetie. I haven't managed to come up with one yet. What I meant was, don't you ever want to put your thoughts down in writing, to share them with the world?'

'Not really.'

'You don't even want to write songs on your guitar?'

'They'd be rubbish. There's enough shit music out there already, no need for me to add to it.'

'You should try some time, sweetie. I'm sure you'd be good at it,' she smiles. 'Now can I please work for a bit?'

'Shall I think of a name for your play?' I ask through a mouthful of apple. 'You'll have to let me read it, of course.'

'I appreciate the offer, sweetie, but I'd just like to concentrate for a bit. In peace. Why don't you watch a film, then, if I manage to write something half-decent, I'll read it to you and you can tell me what you think.'

'I've watched all of your films.'

'Why not check again.'

It's an instruction, not a question. Right at the end of her shelf of videos is *Out Of Africa* which, according to the blurb, is set in Kenya. Perfect. I might pick up some useful tips ahead of the field trip. I slot the video into the machine, turn on the TV, then open the biscuits.

It doesn't look much like Kenya.

Everyone is white and they're all wearing fur coats, standing about in the snow. Kilimanjaro, maybe? I turn to ask Emma if she's mixed up the boxes, but she said she needs some peace and quiet. Ah, there's Meryl Streep, and she's on the video case. It must be the right one.

I shovel in two more ginger nuts.

'Can you eat those biscuits a wee bit more quietly, sweetie?'

'I'm just eating them.'

'I know. But if there's a way to do it without making so much noise, please do.'

'Biscuits are naturally crunchy. That's what the name means, apparently. It's French for 'twice as crunchy' or something.'

'Twice cooked. And it's Latin. Please try. For me.'

The film is quite slow-moving, even for one from Emma's library. All they're doing is growing coffee and sitting about on a veranda. I hope Kenya's a bit more exciting in real life.

'Did I tell you I'm going to Kenya next week?'

'Aye, you have mentioned it. *Please*, Chris. I need half an hour without interruptions.'

The film picks up a little. Robert Redford arrives and they start shooting lions, then go and visit some mountains.

'Kenya looks amazing. We could go there together, if you like. Or somewhere else in Africa. Maybe in the summer.'

'Mmm,' comes the non-committal reply from the desk.

'Have you been to Africa?'

'I went to The Gambia at Christmas.'

'Really? This Christmas just gone?'

'Uh-huh.'

This is odd; did she mention that?

No, she didn't. I'm sure of it.

A small, uncomfortable niggle begins to gnaw at the back of my neck.

'Who did you go with?'

'I went with Angus.'

The niggle gets a little stronger, edging its way down my spine.

'Who's Angus?'

'My boyfriend from Stirling.'

Emma and I got together just before Christmas; why was she going on holiday with an old boyfriend?

'You never mentioned him. When did you break up?'

Emma puts her pen down, very carefully, and turns towards me. For once, her eyes aren't sparkling, and a frown is forming on both mouth and brow. The gnawing sensation leaves my spine and claws its way round to my stomach.

This is bad, very bad.

'We haven't broken up. He's studying history at St Andrews. We've been together for four years.'

She walks over and sits on the floor next to her bed.

'So you've already got a boyfriend?' This isn't making any sense. 'If you've got a boyfriend at home, then what are we … what am I?'

'We're friends.'

'Friends? But we sleep together.'

'Sometimes friendships get wee bit complicated.'

'When were you going to tell me?'

'When the time was right.'

'So I'm your term-time boyfriend?'

'We never said we were a couple, sweetie. Things aren't always that clear-cut.'

Did we not say that? I'm sure we did, but now I think about it …

Damn.

I can't remember if we did.

'Does he know about me?' I ask.

'Angus and I have an open relationship. We agreed before university that it was unrealistic to be faithful for three years and that we should be honest about it.'

'That doesn't answer the question.'

She pauses, then shakes her head. 'No, not yet. I haven't discussed it with him yet.'

'You didn't discuss it with me either.'

'I've not known you for all that long, sweetie,' Emma replies, rubbing my leg gently. 'I'm sorry if it's a wee bit out of the blue. These past few weeks have been very confusing for me.'

'Poor you,' I snap. But another unpleasant revelation now thumps me. 'Was he there, when you rang me over Christmas? Is that where you rang me from?'

She nods. The delay on the line makes more sense now, as does her insistence on speaking quietly. 'I don't want to argue with you, Chris. Listen, why don't you go home, think about what you want, and then we can talk it through.'

She sits next to me on the bed and strokes my neck gently. I wanted an adult relationship, but I'm regretting the decision now. I'm desperate to flounce out with a tortured expression wrought across my face. But if I leave now, will I dare to come back? Will she want me to? I'm not convinced, seeing as she's the one saying I should leave.

'I want to watch the end of the film,' I say, trying to buy a little more time to decide if and when to flounce. Emma nods and, after one final neck rub, goes back to her desk.

I try to concentrate on the film. Meryl Streep is now being treated for syphilis. She must have caught it from Robert Redford, the filthy bugger. Or the other one, who is possibly her husband; I haven't been following that closely.

'What about Aids?'

Emma sighs and looks up. 'What about Aids, Chris?'

She's no longer calling me sweetie, I notice. 'If you're sleeping with this Angus, and you're sleeping with me, how do I know I haven't caught anything? One of them died from Aids in *Trainspotting*. The tall one, who wasn't on the posters.'

'That was a film about heroin addicts, not a documentary about Scotland. And *Trainspotting* was set in Edinburgh and filmed in Glasgow, while Angus and I both live in Stirling. Besides, I'm careful with both of you.'

'Does he take heroin?'

'No. His interests are listening to radio plays and writing poetry. He plays the accordion in our folk group, too. Does that make you feel better?'

It does. It makes me feel much better. I've been picturing some giant, flame-haired Begbie-esque nightmare, but Angus sounds like a right wanker. I fancy my chances if it comes to a fight; it certainly sounds like a much closer contest than it was with Jonathan. I'm not prepared to let her off quite yet, though, not until I'm sure how open relationships work.

'What if I wanted to start seeing someone else?'

'You're free to do what you like, Chris.'

'And you won't be upset?'

'I might not like it, but I will respect your right to be with who you want to be with. I don't see relationships as exclusive, I explained that when we met. I think it's possible to have feelings for more than one person at a time.'

'What about in Kenya? Lou's going to be there. What if something happens between me and her?'

'Is she the one who turned you down last year?'

'Well, yes, but … she might have changed her mind.'

'It's a risk I'll take.' She's staring at me again, but it's no longer a warm, concerned stare. She looks as close to annoyed as I've seen her. I stare back, having run out of counter arguments. I can either accept it or walk away, and I'm not ready to do either.

Not yet.

'I'm not happy about it.'

Emma walks across her room once more. Sitting next to me on the bed, she cradles my pouting face, holding it firmly so I can't look away.

'You don't have to be happy about it, sweetie. It would be a wee bit strange if you were. But you do have to accept it. For now. Think about how you feel, what you want. Why don't we have a break from each other until you're back from Kenya? We'll meet up then and see how things are. I promise. I don't want this to be the last time we talk, OK?'

I don't want to leave, especially now she's stroking my cheek and I'm "sweetie" again. 'Can I watch the rest of the film?'

She reaches over, presses eject, then hands me the tape.

'Take it home and watch it. You'll enjoy it, it's one of my favourites. And I can work on my play. I've been too focused on it, I know, and it's not fair on you. When it's finished, things might be clearer.'

'So your play's more important than me?'

'I didn't say that.'

She doesn't deny it either. But she does kiss me on the cheek. 'Come and see me when you get back. Promise?'

'Promise.'

'Have fun in Kenya.'

'Yeah, I suppose.'

I buy four cans of bitter on the way home. I open the first one on a garden wall near the shop. Focus on the positives: she didn't actually break up with me; my latest love rival sounds like a dick; Seth shat himself. The day hasn't been a complete disaster.

I skull the second can, then start on the third. Emma told me to think about how I feel and what I want. So how do I feel? I'm not as angry as I thought I'd be. In some ways, it fits with her arty, free-spirit personality.

And yet I know that I'll never get used to it. If this is what adult relationships are like, I'm not ready for them.

The house is empty and I head to the living room, cracking open the final can and wishing I'd bought eight instead of four. Yet by the closing credits of the film, I've cheered up immensely. In little over a week I'll be in Kenya, which looks beautiful. And if the film is anything to go by, those hot, dusty landscapes speckled with lions get women in the mood. Could something happen between me and Lou? There'll never be a more romantic place for it, and I'm due a bit of luck. Emma will just have to accept it. Yes, this could be my chance to play Robert Redford to Lou's Meryl Streep.

Without the lion hunt, of course, I'm not too keen on that. And preferably without the syphilis.

Or dying in a plane crash.

I lie back and close my eyes, ready to dream of my African paradise.

20

Sun Hits The Sky

The cobalt ocean glistens in the sun, each wave crashing gently on a crescent of coral reef, its mesmeric rhythm broken only by the syncopatic plop of coconuts from the date palms that border an unending stretch of white almost too dazzling to look at. Tiny translucent crabs leave neat patterns in the sugar-like sand as they search for scraps before scurrying nervously below. Far on the horizon small fishing boats move about lazily in search of the day's catch, drifting gently in the tropical breeze …

'Absolute fuckin' waste of time, man.'

Chemical Joe slumps down next to me, forcing me to share what little shade is offered by the trees. Even at nine-thirty in the morning, the sand is already too hot to sit on. He picks up a shell and throws it at one of the crabs. The crab dodges it easily, disappearing into the nearest hole in the sand before quickly reappearing and scuttling down the beach.

'She won't talk to us either?' I ask, aiming my own shell at one of the crabs. I miss and it runs past my bare feet, flicking V-signs as it goes.

'Nah. No one will unless we buy a sarong or one of those stupid wooden animals. Hand-carved by Maasai warriors my arse. Mass-produced in a Bangladeshi sweatshop, more likely.'

I look over at the latest person to decline the opportunity to complete one of our neatly typed questionnaires about the environmental impacts of Kenya's tourism industry. The woman is sitting on a plastic red chair beneath a sunshade made from discarded carrier bags. She waves, then beckons me to come and look at the collection of souvenirs spread out on her multi-coloured blanket. I hold up my hand, a gesture I've learnt quickly which means 'thanks, let's pretend that I might come and look later, even though we both know I won't'.

'At least people are friendly,' I shrug.

'Fuck friendly, man. We're supposed to have a hundred of these things done in the next three days, and so far we've got one, from the security guard in our hotel. And he only answered two questions, his name and his age, before giving up.'

Joe's good spirits, usually unshakeable, are plummeting by the minute. I've never seen him this agitated. I suspect it has little to do with our slow progress and more to do with his failure to locate any drugs in the two days we've been here. I've never seen anyone go cold turkey before; it's fascinating to watch.

'Why don't we just make them up?' I suggest.

'I think Pryce might notice if we hand in 100 questionnaires all in the same fuckin' handwriting.'

'True,' I reply, looking along the beach for anyone else to pounce on. A man is walking slowly along the sand, carrying a string bag full of mangoes.

'What about him?'

'Already asked him. He told me he doesn't speak English. In English, obviously.'

Joe fishes a crumpled packet of cigarettes out of his pocket. I shake my head when he holds them towards me. I had one yesterday and can still feel it. The local brand may be dirt cheap, but the back of your throat pays the balance. Joe closes his eyes and pulls his beanie hat – which hasn't once left his head, despite the heat – over his eyes.

It's an odd friendship. We've known each other since being put in the same tutor group in our first term. He even played for my football team for a bit, although I had to drop him eventually (a goalkeeper who spends the game sitting against the post and smoking a joint doesn't create the right impression, even when you're bottom of the league.) But our friendship has never developed beyond lecture halls and football pitches. His interests are drugs, dance music and more drugs. But I'm with Liam and Noel on this one: cigarettes and alcohol are more than enough for me. Joe does at least share my liking for beer, so I stand up and kick his foot.

'Come on, let's get a drink.'

The nearest beach bar is a low-slung effort with three whitewashed walls that support a roof made of wooden beams and dried palm fronds. The fourth side opens onto the sand and the owner is already putting out a selection of sun-bleached cushions on the wooden loungers, each of which lies next to a small but beautifully carved wooden table. He waves in recognition – we asked him yesterday to fill out a questionnaire (he declined, naturally) – and, as we descend on the loungers, potters off to fetch two half-litre bottles of Tusker beer. We don't even have to ask; it's all anyone drinks here. Nor does drinking before ten o'clock raise an eyebrow. Heat notwithstanding, Kenya is my kind of country.

Joe drains half his bottle then shuts his eyes once more. I stare at the beach, using the downtime to consider the best way to approach Lou. It's already day three of six, and I've not yet spoken to her, merely shared a couple of awkward smiles in the hotel restaurant. She's as cool as always, but to everyone, not just me. I've kept a close eye on Jonathan and she's definitely not on good terms with him. The path is clear, but making a move is even harder this time; I've used up all my best lines and moves. I need some advice, but Rob, Mike and Cecilia are the other side of the world and Joe is usually asleep. I *have* to make something to happen, though, not least to get back at Emma. While I'm warming to the idea of an open relationship – it makes you sound very cool – it'll only work if it's open on both sides, not just hers.

As I debate a second beer or a nap, a youngish man walks over. He's wearing an Arsenal shirt (a few seasons old, I note) and beaming as if I'm his long-lost brother rather than a complete stranger. Kenyans are the friendliest people in the world, right up until you ask them to fill out a questionnaire.

'Hey brother, how's it going? Enjoying Kenya?' he asks, dragging a lounger over to sit with us.

'It's good, thanks. Bit hot. How are you?'

'Good, brother, good. Why you two white boys out this early?'

'We're from Sheffield University. Doing research on the tourism industry. Trying to, anyway. I'm Chris.'

'Leonard.' He offers his hand, but when I go to shake it, he tries to snap off one of my fingers. It all gets a bit confused, so he opts for a fist bump instead.

'Sheffield, huh?' he continues. 'Sheffield Wednesday! Good team, brother, good team. Chris Waddle. Him I like.'

'He's left now. But they're better than United.'

'Yes! The Blades. See, I know English football. Who is your team?

'I'm a Plymouth Argyle fan. Heard of them?'

'No. Me, I'm Arsenal. So, I work in tourism, what you wanna know?'

'How tourism affects the environment,' I explain. 'But no one wants to talk to us.'

'Sure, sure. People here, they talk about other stuff. Maybe you ask them about football?'

'What do you do, exactly?' I ask, wondering if he might agree to an interview if I buy him a beer. We're supposed to be doing interviews as well, I now remember.

'I arrange things, man. For tourists. Diving tours, safaris, taxis, hotels, anything you need, brother, you ask for Leonard.'

Joe erupts sharply from his coma. 'Have you got any drugs?'

'Sure, brother, sure. I have a friend, he can help you.'

Joe immediately sets about establishing exactly what is on offer, and I leave them to sort out the details, moving away slightly so that I can deny knowing either of them should the police turn up. The bar owner heads over with another round of chilled Tuskers. We drink a third while Leonard tells us about his corner of Kenya, and a fourth as I tell him about Tavistock. He's the first person I've met who seems even vaguely interested.

By midday, a sea of empty bottles around us, Leonard moves to get up, then thinks better of it and sits back down with a thump.

'My friends, we play football every evening on the beach. Wanna join us? Kenya against Plymouth. The Pilgrims!'

We arrange to meet outside the hotel. With half the day gone, Joe argues that there isn't much point in attempting any more work, so after Leonard has left, we order two more Tuskers and spend the next few hours trying to hit crabs with bottle tops.

* * *

I always get twitchy before a game of football, but this is even more nerve-wracking. England v Kenya, an international fixture – and I'm captain (Joe acquiesced, given he's too drunk to remember anyone's name). We had little trouble persuading the others to join in; in fact, every male on the trip is playing –

including Jonathan, unfortunately – and most of the females have come to cheer us on.

Including Lou. She's sitting under a palm tree with her friend Maria. As the two teams introduce themselves, I head over. It feels like the right moment to talk to her: before leading my country to a glorious victory (which is inevitable, Kenya have never even qualified for a World Cup). I swagger over, all cool and casual – think Richard Ashcroft in the video for 'Bittersweet Symphony'. Perhaps the day's alcohol has given me a little extra strut, but I'm also aware there's been a shift in the dynamic between us. She's the single one now, while I'm in a relationship. OK, not an exclusive one, but she doesn't need to know that.

'Hi, Lou. Hi Maria.'

'Hello,' Lou replies flatly. Maria just looks amused.

'I've not seen you for a while,' I continue, ignoring Maria and focusing on Lou.

No answer.

It wasn't technically a question, but I can feel my late-found self-belief slipping away as quickly as it arrived.

'I, er, never said thank you for the birthday present.'

'No, you didn't.'

'Well, thank you.'

She lifts her sunglasses and fixes me with a look similar to the one she gave me at the start of the year: like she's trying to decide if I'm worth bothering with. Eventually, the balance tips in my favour, but I sense it was close.

'Did you like it?' Lou asks.

'I did, yeah,' I lie. 'Something a bit different. It's good to broaden your horizons.'

'Mike said you'd like it.'

Mike, you evil bastard. I've always suspected there's a cruel streak under that jovial, friend-of-the-people veneer. But I can deal with Mike later; right now, I need to relocate that swagger.

'So, I was wondering if ...'

I glance quickly at my fellow footballers, willing one of them to beckon me over, to save me from this. No such luck; they're all too busy learning the Kenyan handshake.

'... if you maybe, if you've got time, we could have a drink later. Just as friends, of course, I've got a girlfriend now. But only if you want to.'

There's another agonising delay as she continues to survey me with a cool detachment. 'Alright. I need to talk to you about something anyway.'

'Great!' Relief and joy race over me, with relief the clear winner. 'I'll find you after the match.' I start jogging back to the pitch, before remembering my manners. 'Bye, Maria.'

'Bye Chris. See you later for our drink,' Maria says.

'Sorry, I just meant me and Lou. Not you.'

'Ooh, mean. I thought you wanted to just be friends with me, too.' They both start laughing. This must be what passes for female humour. I laugh weakly, wondering why all women – even ones I barely know – feel obliged to make my life difficult.

Leonard is laying the finishing touches to the makeshift pitch, meticulously marked out with coconut shells and driftwood for goals. He shakes my hand, captain greeting captain. The other players shuffle round.

'So, Leonard, do you want to choose ends, or–'

'Hang on, we haven't picked teams yet,' a deep voice interjects.

Jonathan.

'I thought ...'

'Surely we're not going to play locals v foreigners? Come on, it's not Happy Valley.'

A couple of Jonathon's friends laugh at this. I have no idea where Happy Valley is but know better than to ask. 'But how will we tell who's …?'

I catch myself before finishing the sentence; I know how it will be interpreted, even if it's a perfectly reasonable point. Any hint of racism, even unintentional, is totally unacceptable at university. I look up at Leonard, desperate for a lifeline. He's grinning; is there anyone who doesn't enjoy seeing me squirm?

'I think Chris means we don't know each other,' he says, winking at me. 'Not names. Come, we play shirts and skins. Chris, you can be shirts, you pick first.'

Praise the Lord, and more importantly, praise Leonard that I don't have to take off my top and reveal my scrawny torso. I pick Joe first, out of loyalty more than expectation. Leonard picks Jonathan, and after we've gone through the rest of the players, the match gets underway.

Within minutes, I tuck away a scrappy toe-poke to put my side one-nil up: the perfect start. I look across to Lou, but she's not watching. Which is possibly for the best, as I then proceed to miss several easy chances and we are swiftly three-four down. Then, a flurry of tackles on the seaward side of the pitch, a cross from a Kenyan and I power home a header from eight inches out. Four-four.

'Nice header,' Jonathan says as we trot back towards the coconut-shell centre spot.

Maybe he's not so bad, after all? On reflection, he's only ever treated me decently. I can hardly say the same. 'Thanks,' I reply, but he's already halfway up the pitch.

The score moves on to seven-all, the sun drops quickly behind the beachfront hotels, and Leonard suggests that the next goal is the winner: playground rules extending across the globe. I'm more than happy to agree; I have my date with Lou to prepare for and my legs are aching from running on sand for over an hour. As I take a breather on the halfway line, one of my team valiantly heads clear two corners in a row. Then, on the third, he hoofs the ball in my direction. It bounces on the sand in front of me.

I look around quickly: there's no one near. I'm through on goal.

This is it, my chance to score the winner, complete a hat-trick and lead my team to victory. Even Lou will have to be impressed.

I take one touch to control it – a good start, I usually need three – and check where the keeper is. Perfect: too far to his left. All I have to do is tuck it to his right, then celebrate briefly with the team before marching over to Lou for a triumphant kiss beneath the setting sun. I couldn't have planned this better.

I steady myself, draw back my right leg, then listen to the loud crack my left leg makes as it disappears from underneath me.

21

Sulk

'I can't believe you got knocked out by some sand, man. That is fuckin' tragic.'

Joe and Lou sit beside my hospital bed. Joe's grinning, but Lou looks worried, her head cocked to the side, her hand resting on mine. My hospital-issue pale blue pyjama suit is far too small and its scratchy, overly starched material chafes at my armpits and groin. It only reaches halfway down my arms and legs, and I check quickly that it isn't revealing anything else.

'How are you feeling?' Lou asks, sounding genuinely concerned.

'Bit groggy,' I say. The plaster cast sticking out of my left pyjama leg is raised up on a winch and looks suitably injured. I can't feel a thing, thanks to the painkillers being piped into me, but I'm keen to milk as much sympathy from Lou as I can, especially while there's hand-stroking involved. 'And my ankle's killing me, obviously.'

'Do you need me to get a nurse?'

'I'll be OK,' I reply stoically. 'Who won the match?'

'We decided to call it a draw,' Joe says. 'Leonard fuckin' furious with Jonathan, it looked like they were going to have a scrap. We had to pull them apart, but everyone's friends now.'

'Jonathan fouled me?' I assumed I must have tripped on one of the coconuts. But no, it was Lou's ex …

'Yeah, man,' Joe confirms. 'He won the ball, just happened to smack your ankle as he did. How bad it is? It looked properly fucked, it was hangin' at this weird angle, man.'

The doctor told me it was just a chipped bone, not a break, and should heal in two to three weeks. Nothing serious, they were only keeping me in until the swelling went down, and the cast was just to keep it secure. But I don't share this information. I'm stuck in a hospital in Mombasa and now I discover it's all Jonathan's fault. Was it revenge? Lou swore he didn't know about the two of us.

'They're still testing to see how bad the break is,' I say. Lou grips my hand even more tightly, only releasing it when the door swings open and Professor Pryce puts his balding head around it.

'OK you two, we need to leave promptly or we'll be stuck in the Mombasa rush hour. Not recommended, trust me. Henderson, how are you feeling? The doctor says you'll live. Maybe even walk again, God willing. I'll pop up tomorrow and sort out the paperwork. Come on, let's go.'

Joe stands up, but Lou stays seated.

'I'll come and see you tomorrow, OK? Sleep well.' She places a soft kiss on my sweaty forehead. I don't want her to go.

But she does. I lie back against the brick-like pillow, wishing the air conditioning in my room worked.

The door opens again. Joe's beanie-hatted head pokes around it.

'I left you a little present, under your bed. Don't let the nurses find it.'

I lean over and lift up a plastic carrier bag. Inside are four bottles of Tusker; he's even remembered to put in an opener. Good old Joe. I pop one open and things don't seem so bad. Lou has, finally, revealed that she does care about me on some level. Plus a spell in a foreign hospital will provide a few good traveller stories. The sun casts a gentle orange glow onto the whitewashed walls of my tiny room, and the call to prayer starts up from the nearby mosque, managing to outdo the traffic; an enchantingly exotic atmosphere. I take another sip and think about that kiss from Lou and what it might mean.

* * *

Mombasa doesn't get any cooler once the sun's gone. Nor any quieter. And four bottles of beer don't mix well with anti-malarials and painkillers. I wake up several times in a hallucinatory panic, room spinning, sweat cascading. At one point I scream out so loudly that three nurses rush in to see what's happened. One spots the empty beer bottles – I couldn't hide them properly with my leg strung up – and admonishes me severely.

At three am, a mosquito starts to plague me. At first it buzzes around my ear, then settles down on my stomach for a feed. I nearly tumble off the bed during one particularly ambitious attempt to squish it. It's hours before I manage, its body bursting my blood onto the bedsheets. As soon as I manage to fall into an exhausted sleep, the five o'clock call to prayer wakes me. My head is a fuzzy mess for two more hours, when another knock clatters the door.

'Ah Henderson, how's the ankle doing? Good, good,' Professor Pryce blusters, sitting in one of the chairs. 'Now, I need you to sign these forms to confirm it was all an accident, and I'll fax them over to the department in Sheffield. They'll sort out the hospital bills with the insurance company, nothing for you to worry about. You have to sign here and here.'

He puts a pile of photocopied forms on my stomach and places a biro on top. I stare at them. I ache from my head to my chipped-not-broken ankle. I have a multitude of throbbing mosquito bites that I can't reach. I have an exceptionally unpleasant psychedelic hangover.

'What if I don't?'

'Don't what?'

'Sign them. What if I don't think it was an accident?'

'Like that, is it? OK, let me think.'

He stares out of the tiny barred window for a minute. 'Right, how about this. If you sign these forms, I won't have Everitt kicked out of university for selling drugs on this trip. You, in return, keep your mouth shut about any possible intention on the part of Gilbert. At least until you both leave Sheffield, after that I couldn't give a monkey's what any of you do. How does that sound?'

'Why do you care if he gets into trouble or not?'

'I don't, but it's a lot more paperwork for me if there's a full investigation.'

It's the best offer I'm likely to get, and I know I'll never make a formal complaint about Jonathan. I can't prove anything and I'm not sure I'd come out of it well. He had a motivation, after all, even if he doesn't know about it.

Which I'm starting to suspect he does.

'OK, deal.' I sign the forms without bothering to read them.

'Very good, very good. Can't say I blame either of you, of course. She's a fine-looking girl, that one. Well worth fighting over. May the best man win and all that. Right, I'll check in again tomorrow. Oh, and there's someone else here to see you.'

He leaves and I straighten myself out in the bed in readiness for Lou's arrival. As much as I like Joe, I hope she's alone this time. But it's not Lou.

It's Jonathan.

He sits down silently in the recently vacated chair and studies my plastered leg, as if examining it for clues. Eventually, he speaks.

'I'm sorry about your leg. I didn't mean to actually break it.'

It's the 'actually' that gives him away. Is he always this honest? He'll never make it as a politician if he doesn't learn to lie a bit more naturally.

'Have they told you how long it'll take to heal?'

'Anything up to three months,' I lie. 'It's a bad break, the doctor says. One of the worst he's seen.'

'That's not good.' He's still staring at it. Then, after less than half a minute in the room, he gets up. 'I won't stick around, I'm sure you need to rest. I brought some stuff to get you through the day. Joe's coming to see you later. And Lou.'

Not a flicker of emotion crosses his face as he mentions her; the political career might yet be on track. He hands me a plastic bag containing a bunch of tiny bananas, a book, a football magazine, a portable CD player (plus a set of spare batteries) and some Leonard Cohen CDs. They're useful, thoughtful presents. He's a hard one to read.

'Thanks.'

'You can keep the magazine, I've finished with it. The book belongs to Maria, so she might want it back.'

He gives my leg a quick final stare, then leaves. I don't bother saying goodbye.

* * *

A day passes slowly when you're confined to a rock-hard bed, unable to turn over and with a number of itches you can't scratch. The hands on the clock barely move; by mid-morning, I don't dare look at them, in case they are going backwards.

I put on one of the CDs Jonathan left me, but while I can appreciate Leonard Cohen's music, it doesn't exactly make the hours fly by.

I try the book, but it's rubbish, full of pointlessly long words.

I flick through the magazine but feel too tired to read.

I trace the cracks in the walls, trying and failing to make it all the way around the room without a break.

I count the flattened mosquito corpses in the room, conceding defeat at two hundred when I'm no longer sure which ones I've already included.

I try to sleep, but whenever I drift off a nurse comes in to take my blood pressure, or check my temperature, or adjust my drip. It's annoying when they arrive and heart-breaking when they leave as it means I'm on my own again. I'm stuck in a constricting room in a far-off land where time stands still, and I have nothing to except eat undersized bananas. Even worse, I'm trapped with nothing but my thoughts, and the unwelcome realisation that there aren't enough of them rattling around in my head to get me through a whole day.

Evening eventually turns up, dragging its heels like a petulant toddler. I could cry when Joe marches in, followed by Lou. When she kisses my forehead I do actually cry a little bit, but manage to wipe the tears away and pretend they're sweat.

'How's it goin', man?' Joe asks, putting his feet up on my bed and knocking my good leg against the minorly injured one. I remember to let out a yelp of pain.

'Awful. Nothing happens in hospitals, I've been so bored.'

'I can get you some more beers if you like? Or some weed? Leonard's mate has got some awesome stuff.'

Lou fixes him with a glare and he shuts up, but winks to confirm that the offer still stands.

'Did the doctors say anything more about your ankle?' Lou has reassumed her look of concern, but I'm too tired to stretch this lie out any longer.

'I'll be fine. I can travel back with the rest of you, they're just keeping me in until then.'

She bites her lip but doesn't take my hand like last time. Disappointed, I turn back to Joe. 'How's the work going? Did you get any of the questionnaires filled out?'

'All in hand, man, all in hand.'

'Really? How?'

'Leonard's sister. She's a teacher in the village school and her students are gonna complete them as their English homework. By this time tomorrow, we'll have 200 completed questionnaires, all in different handwriting. I think Leonard might be the greatest person I've ever met.'

'That's genius,' I say, grateful for this sliver of good news. 'How about yours, Lou?'

'Maria and I spent the day interviewing tourists about their views on the environmental impacts of hotels along Diani beach. They all think it's a bit of a shame that the coastal forest has been decimated, but they also like an uninterrupted sea view. So the endangered wildlife can go fuck itself, apparently.'

'I saw one of them black-and-white monkeys doing that earlier,' interrupts Joe. 'He was having a quick fiddle, at least.'

'That's more than I've seen today. Nothing apart from these four walls. Watching a monkey have a wank would have been a welcome change.'

'I'll try and get you a photo tomorrow.'

Lou gives us both a look that is at least ninety-nine percent contempt, but most is directed towards Joe this time. 'OK, boys, I didn't sit in Mombasa's traffic for over an hour to discuss simian masturbation. Joe, go and read that magazine outside so I can talk to Chris. Alone.'

He picks up Jonathan's football magazine and heads off. Is this the moment when Lou finally declares her true feelings?

Not quite. Instead, she updates me about how all the other students are getting on with their research, on the markets in Mombasa, on what might be going on between the barman at the hotel and Maria, and where Professor Pryce is rumoured to spend his days (the most popular theory is that he has a woman somewhere in Mombasa and that she's the only reason he organises field trips here each year). So not exactly a declaration that her love will no longer be kept under wraps, but it's good to listen to her voice again, especially as for once it's not cross with me. I curse silently when Professor Pryce arrives and tells her they're leaving.

'Will you come and visit me tomorrow?' I ask, hoping I don't sound too needy.

'I can't, sorry. Leonard's arranged for everyone to visit an elephant sanctuary. We're all heading there straight after we've finished work.'

I make no effort to hide my annoyance.

'I won't go, if you want me to come and see you,' she says after a pause.

I do, desperately, but know I can't say it. 'No, you go, it sounds great. Wish I could be there.'

She kisses me again, on the forehead again, nowhere even close to the lips. I'm alone once more, with no prospect of a visit tomorrow.

I stare at the clock: six thirty-five.

Sleep is still several hours away, if it comes at all. The traffic blares, the mosque wailes and tonight's malaria-ridden tormentor is already sizing up my dewy flesh. Thoughts turn briefly to Emma, now back in Scotland and no doubt sleeping with the poetry-loving, accordion-playing, non-heroin-addicted Angus. They return to Lou, soon to be out beneath the star-swept African sky, fire crackling, lions growling. No doubt snuggled up under a blanket with Jonathan as they act out my *Out Of Africa* fantasy. Or Joe. Or Leonard. Or Professor Pryce.

And Britpop is over, according to Seth.

And Blur are splitting up, according to Cecilia.

And I have no idea what to do for a career.

And whatever I choose, I'm not good enough for it, according to Mum.

Six-thirty-eight.

It's going to be an insufferable night. The porter will be along soon with the tea trolley; I search in my wallet, desperately hoping I have enough Kenyan shillings to bribe him to bring me some beer to wash down my various medication. If I'm going to be abandoned by everyone, I might as well kill the time with another DIY acid trip.

22

Headshrinker

I thought nothing could be worse than those two days in Mombasa hospital.

I was wrong.

Even after the eleven-hour flight is over, my fellow geographers are still preoccupied with recounting everything that happened on what was, evidently, the Greatest Night Ever – elephants, beer, drugs, snakes, more beer, more elephants, monkeys, more drugs, a bonfire, and several fumbles in the jungle. None involving Lou, it seems, but they're still nauseating to hear about.

But worse is to follow at Manchester airport. My parents are waiting. Mum hurriedly tells me that the university rang and explained what happened, but before she's finished, she rushes away to berate Jonathan, who apologises politely and walks off. Undeterred, she moves on to Professor Pryce, accusing him of failing to protect his students and all manner of other personal failings. He simply walks off. Everyone else disappears without so much as a goodbye. Lou does pause to give me a brief wave, but she's the only one who can be bothered to bid farewell to their fallen comrade. Only Joe escapes my wrath; he was called to one side by a customs official and hasn't been seen since.

My mood fails to brighten during a long week in Devon, and by Friday, everyone is avoiding the sitting room, where I've taken up a self-pitying residence on the sofa. It comes as little surprise and widespread relief to everyone when Dad offers to drive me back to Sheffield a few days early.

And it's here that I finally begin to calm down. With the start of term still a week away, and Rob and Andy nowhere to be seen, my days are free to enjoy my favourite non-footballing sporting event of the year: the World Snooker Championships.

I have Grandpa to thank for my love of this noblest of games. Taking a rare break from his Disney films, he spent hour after hour in front of the screen each spring, only lifting his gaze to grunt in acknowledgement when Grandma brought in tea and cake. In my tenth Easter, with the rain preventing me from going outside to decimate the flowerbeds, I decided to sit with him and see what all the fuss was about. Instantly, I was mesmerised: the barely audible clacking of cue against ball; the slow, unhurried movement of the balls as they trundle around the table; the satisfying plop as they drop into a pocket; the soporific, whispered commentary. Once Grandma started bringing me cake and squash along with Grandpa's tea, I saw little reason to move for the fortnight. Especially when I discovered that some matches went on beyond midnight – and that my parents would let me stay up if they thought I was hooked. Soon enough I was, and I've marked out two weeks in my calendar ever since.

I begin my preparations early, ready for a full Sunday of uninterrupted coverage on BBC2: a full pot of tea (the first of many), a packet of Abbey Crunch stolen from Rob's cupboard, and plumped-up sofa cushions, ready for twelve hours live from the Crucible Theatre. It's Ken Doherty and Nigel Bond up first. But as Doherty walks up to break in the opening frame, the doorbell rings. I ignore it, but when my unknown caller rings again, I lift myself off the sofa with a reluctant sigh.

'Oh. Hi Lou.'

'I thought I'd come and see how you are.'

I'm not in the mood for company and want to tell her I'm busy. But it's a Sunday morning, I'm wearing tea-stained jogging bottoms and the sound of the snooker is clearly audible. There's a slim chance she won't believe me.

'I bought you some biscuits,' she says, holding out a packet. Milk chocolate HobNobs, a far superior biscuit to the humble Abbey Crunch.

'Come in.'

Lou insists on making herself a fresh cup of tea, despite my protestations that the pot has only just brewed. After ten minutes fussing about in the kitchen – she's been scrubbing our mugs, I'm certain of it – she returns and takes the armchair by the window.

'What are you watching?'

'Snooker. Ken Doherty and Nigel Bond.'

'Which one's which?'

'Do you care?'

'No, but tell me anyway.'

'That's Bond at the table now.'

She nods and concentrates on the screen. The players trade blows in a tense safety exchange before Doherty sinks an ambitious long red and is rewarded with the first opening of the day. As he gets going, I steal a quick look at Lou, whose finely manicured brow is knotted.

'What's up?' I ask.

'Nothing.'

'Go on, ask me.'

'Why does the one dressed like a penguin keeping putting the balls back, once the other two have got rid of them in the corners?'

'He's the referee. And they're pockets, not corners. That's how the game works. You put the colours back each time, until they're the only ones left at the end. Then you pot them as well.'

'OK. I'll shut up now.'

She does.

Briefly.

'He's not putting the red ones back, though. The penguin fellow.'

'No, only the colours go back on their spots.'

'Red's a colour.'

'Not in snooker. In snooker, reds are reds and the rest are colours. Except the white, which is the cue ball.'

'That's far too confusing.'

'It's really not. I understood this game at the age of ten.'

She continues watching but the look of confusion remains in place. I nudge her with an outstretched toe, checking that it isn't the leg that's supposed to be injured (I've kept the bandage on, just in case I need more sympathy).

'Come on, what else don't you understand?'

'It's not important.'

'Ask me anyway.'

'Why is only one of them playing?'

'Eh?'

'That one, who looks like he's never seen daylight, he's the only one doing any shots now. The other one isn't getting a turn.'

'He's building a break, trying to get enough points to win the frame. That's the whole point.'

'That's not fair. How's the other one supposed to get any points if he never gets a turn?'

'You do realise that this is the snooker World Championships, not an after-school club? They're trying to determine who the best player in the world is, not make sure everyone has a jolly time.'

'I liked it better at the start, when they were taking turns nicely,' she says, pouting. There's little point trying to explain it; I realised many years ago that people either appreciate snooker or don't; there's no convincing anyone of its charms. Doherty misses a green, but Bond, with the merest flick of his head, concedes the frame. The knowledgeable Crucible crowd reward both players' effort with a gentle ripple of applause. As the table is being reset, Lou stands up.

'Right, they've finished. I'll take you out somewhere, it's a beautiful day.'

'They haven't finished.'

'Why is everyone clapping?'

'That was the end of the first frame.'

'How many of these frames, whatever they are, do they have to play?'

'Twenty-five.'

'Fuck. That. We're going out.' She switches the TV off and picks up the empty mugs. I sigh loudly, but I'm secretly delighted. The snooker is on for another two weeks, but it's not every day I get Lou to myself.

* * *

She suggests that we go to the Peak District, but we stop at Tesco first after I fail to convince her that two packets of biscuits are sufficient sustenance for the day. The fridge of pre-packed sandwiches is near the main entrance and I pick out a chicken and sweetcorn, then add apples, crisps and a bottle of Coke to the basket. Yet as I head to the check-out, Lou is still with the sandwiches. I walk back over, remembering to hobble for effect.

'What's wrong?' I ask.

'I can't find what I want.'

'Choose anything, they've got loads. It's just a sandwich.'

'That's true, Christopher, but I've always thought that the best thing for a picnic in the Peak District is a peanut butter sandwich. Preferably a soggy one.'

She barely gets to the end of the sentence before breaking down in a fit of laughter. There are tears coming down her cheeks.

'Ha ha. How do you even know about that?'

'Joe told me in Kenya.'

'How does *he* know?'

'Everyone knows. I heard about it in the first year, I just didn't know it was you.'

'Brilliant. So everyone knows about that, yet no one knows about the gorgeous older woman I was sleeping with last summer.'

'Suzanne Harrison? Every man in the geography department slept with her. Half the women too, apparently. She almost got kicked out for giving people hand jobs in the library.'

'What? She wouldn't do that.'

Not to me she wouldn't, anyway.

'Aww, did you think you were the only one?' Lou teases. 'Don't worry, I'm sure you were her favourite. Now come on, let's get going. I'm starving.'

'I'm waiting for you, remember? You've already wasted ten minutes coming up with the weakest joke in the history of humanity. One that I've heard a hundred times before, by the way. Just grab anything.'

Still laughing, she opts for ham and pickle. I hope she's willing to go halves; ham and pickle is a much better choice than chicken and sweetcorn.

We drive to Ladybower Reservoir. Lou has a tartan rug stowed away in her car, which seems a little middle-aged but then I'm in no position to criticise other people's picnicking etiquette. After lunch (no sandwich sharing, sadly) she tells me about her Easter, her sister, her time at school. No big revelations, no mention of Jonathan. It's comfortable, relaxed; it's almost like we're friends. When it's my turn, I tell her about the bands I've seen and promise to make her a CD so she doesn't have to listen to any more Robbie Williams. Things are going well, but as I begin to tell her about Plymouth's faltering promotion push, she closes her eyes and lies down.

Once I'm certain they're properly shut, I take the chance to admire her up close once again: her legs, her breasts, those perfectly formed ears, her unblemished skin. Slowly, very slowly, I reposition my non-bandaged foot so that it's touching hers.

She doesn't move hers away.

'Why didn't you talk to me the first time we met?' Lou asks, not opening her eyes.

'I did, didn't I? I apologised about eighty times for kicking a stone at you.'

'I don't mean then. I mean in the first year, at that cheese and wine party.'

'You remember that?'

'Of course I do. And answer my question.'

Standing next to her for thirty seconds was memorable for me, sparking off an infatuation that persists even now, but I never imagined she remembered. Especially as she met the love of her life at the same event. This has to be a promising sign, surely? But her question has caught me off-guard; with no time to work out a clever, charming reply, I'm left with no option but to tell the truth.

'I was nervous, I suppose. It's nerve-wracking talking to beautiful girls when you're unremarkable yourself. It's hard enough talking to ordinary ones, if I'm honest. I'm better at it

206

now, but not by much. It's not just shyness, it's that … I dunno, I've got nothing interesting to say. I'm from a small village in Devon. I got three Bs at A-level. My dad works for the local council, my mum's a retired veterinary nurse who spends all day with bees. It's not exactly gripping stuff, is it?'

Lou doesn't reply. Instead, she starts twiddling a daisy in her right hand.

'This is the point where you're supposed to say "No, Chris, you've always got loads of interesting things to say".'

'Let's not be silly, Christopher, we both know that's not the case.' She flicks the daisy at me. 'But I do wish we'd got to know each other back then. Next time a girl approaches you, try to say something.'

'Even if I had, Jonathan would have come over and said something better.'

'Perhaps. Perhaps not. If I'd been talking to you, he might not have done.'

And who knows what might have happened? She doesn't need to say it; we're both asking ourselves the same question. I am, anyway. And for the first time, the answer isn't "almost certainly nothing".

'You didn't talk to me either,' I retort. 'It's 1999, it's all supposed to be about equality these days.'

'It was 1996 back then. And sometimes a girl likes to be charmed. We're talking now, that's something, I suppose.' She sits up and looks at me, and seems – what was that word Emma used, whimsical? No, the other one; contemplative, that was it. Abruptly, she moves onto her knees, indicating that this intriguing line of conversation is closed. Not permanently, I hope.

'It's getting late. We should head back,' she says. 'Have you got any food at your house?'

'Nothing except two packets of biscuits. One and a half packets, to be precise. How about I buy you dinner?'

'OK. Nothing with peanut butter, though.'

I suggest we head for the King of Tandoori, a Sheffield institution that has carved out a profitable niche in serving huge platefuls of curry to students too pissed to notice that everything on the menu tastes the same, i.e. of chillies and garlic and not much else. My motivation is not the quality of the dining, though, but rather to engineer an opportunity to demonstrate my sophisticated man-of-the-world credentials by showing off my encyclopaedic knowledge of all things curry-related. I make a start as we walk to her car.

'You know, most of what we think of as Indian food comes from Bangladesh. It's richer, more tomatoey, than Indian food. And of course the dishes they cook in the southern states of India are completely different.'

'Hmm,' Lou murmurs.

'Most of the recipes have been adapted for our Western palates. More cream, less spice. The dishes out there are much drier. Did I tell you I went travelling in India?'

'You did mention it. Goa, wasn't it? One of the tourist beaches?'

'There are touristy ones there, but we tried to get off the beaten track, see the real India, y'know.'

'And did you?'

'Did I what?'

'See the real India.'

'I saw the Goan bit. Sometimes you've got to follow your dreams.'

The raised eyebrow is all contempt this time; I should have known I could never pull this one off.

'OK, you've got me. I hated it. I had more fun in Newquay the year before. The food was the only bit I enjoyed.'

Lou laughs. I don't often make her laugh; usually I only manage to amuse her, which isn't the same thing.

'OK, one more fact, then I'll stop talking about curry, I promise. Did you know they make Cobra beer less fizzy than other lagers? That way it's easier to drink with spicy food, meaning people drink more. A lot of the profit in these places comes from the drinks.'

'I didn't know that. I've learnt a lot from you today, Christopher. Mostly about snooker, curry and lager, but all girls are secretly fascinated by those subjects. Don't let anyone tell you otherwise.'

We both laugh this time. This feels good; this is the most comfortable we've ever been with each other.

This could be the moment.

I need to make it the moment.

'I've had a great day, Lou. Thanks for taking me out.'

'So have I. And you're welcome.'

I steel myself for the next bit. 'We could meet up again, if you like. I'm free tomorrow, if you are?'

There's no reply. I try again. 'Lou, I'd like to take you out somewhere. I'd like us to try again. You and me.'

'Chris …'

'Sorry, it's OK. If it's still too soon after Jonathan, I can wait. You said you needed time. There's no rush, I just got a bit carried away. Too much fresh air.'

This is deeply confusing. The signs were all there; what have I done wrong?

'I'm seeing Mike,' she says quietly as we reach her car.

'Mike? Who's Mike?' The realisation is delayed, but gets there before long. 'What, my Mike?'

She nods.

'I can't believe this. My Mike … and you?' I squeak.

'He's not actually *your* Mike.'

'He's my friend, I introduced you to him. How could … how did this even happen? He's my friend!'

Was my friend, the bastard.

'I was having a bad time, and he was very supportive. We've been spending a lot of time together lately, and–'

'You've been in Kenya!'

'It started before that.'

This can't be happening. And if they'd been going out for this long, then it's inevitable that …

'Are you sleeping together?'

'That's not really any of your business, is it?'

'Yes. Yes it is my business, because he's one of my best friends, and … why did you act as if you still liked me all day? What was all that shit with the daisies and remembering the first time we met?'

'I've been trying to tell you all day. For a while.'

'You could have told me during the snooker. Then I'd have spent the day watching that instead of wasting it with you. Is that the only reason you came round?'

'No. I also wanted to see how you are.'

'After this? Not so good. And I'm going to have a busy week as I've got to find two new friends.'

'We can still be friends, Chris. So can you and Mike. It's not like you and I were ever–'

I need to leave, to get away from her. There's a bus back to Sheffield that leaves from somewhere near here. I scan the car park, but there's no sign of one. I set off anyway.

'Chris,' Lou pleads. 'You can't walk home with your ankle.'

There's nothing left for me to lose. Dignity left the building a while ago, around the time I emitted the second 'My Mike?' in a high-pitched, bats-only squeal.

'It's not even broken, just a chipped bone. I've been milking it, hoping it might bring us a bit closer. Which was a waste of time, clearly.'

I storm off, desperately hoping that a bus will turn up and I don't have to hitch a lift. It would be typical of my luck to get into a car with a crazed serial killer on the same day I learn that one of the two girls of my dreams is almost certainly sleeping with my joint-third best friend.

23

Monday Morning 5.19

Sleep eludes me. Partly because a chicken jalfrezi and eight pints of lager don't sit well together (I went to the curry house on my own, no reason why I should miss out). But mostly because I'm unable to stop thinking about Lou and Mike.

Together.

At it.

They're probably in bed together right now, their shared mockery of me spurring them on to filthy new heights of ecstasy.

Yet as the night ticks into the early hours, something unexpected happens: I think solely about Mike. I assumed it would be Lou, my obsession of close to three years, who would dominate, but it's him. I can't decide if he's done anything wrong – Lou and I were never a proper couple – but I still feel desperately let down. And I need to pinpoint why, so I know exactly what to accuse him of. If they've been together for a while, then I've seen him since it happened and he's not said anything. That's wrong, surely? He's not even acted any differently, not that I've noticed, despite having a dark, wicked secret. Does he not care, or is he just better at acting than he is at glaciology?

Light creeps through the gaps beneath the thick red curtains. I open them to reveal our back yard, which is filled with a large stack of bricks and several thousand dandelions. It's been a useful spot for a good, long brood in the past, but today I need more. Despite the earliness of the hour, I decide to go for a walk, to clear my head and hopefully decide what to do – about Mike, about Lou and about Emma. Perhaps even the decline of Britpop, the potential end of Blur and what I'm going to do when term ends in a few weeks; it depends on how long the walk is.

I head north, away from the well-trodden route towards campus. Out here, Sheffield is completely different. I pass through streets I've never walked before, seeing the city in a new light. Quite literally: I've never been out when the dawn is breaking. The rows of pale-brick houses look cosy, nestling neatly into each other as they slope down the steep hills. There are flowers in gardens, sown in careful rows. These are people's homes: the thousands of people who aren't students passing through the city, but the ones who actually live here.

The quietness is striking. Before the traffic builds up and the residents wake up, an urban soundscape usually muffled takes centre stage. An early tram, hidden from view, rattles in the distance while the birds chirp noisily as they flit from tree to lawn to tree. A blackbird swoops to grab a particularly fat worm, carrying it high into the branches to slurp down at leisure. And the trees; there are so many trees, in gardens, streets, parks. How have I not spotted them before? What have I been doing? Where have I been looking? There's a living, breathing city here and I've barely noticed it.

After passing a padlocked builder's yard, I stop on a bridge over a wide, shallow river. Four mallards weave their way between a shopping trolley and a traffic cone. The primroses and daffodils add a dash of yellow to the river bank, but cannot compete with the kaleidoscope of crisp packets. A fox trots towards me, pausing to size me up before deciding I'm no bother and walking straight past, just a few centimetres away. A country fox would run a mile at the sight of a human; even the wildlife has that self-assurance that comes from growing up in a city.

There's a newsagent across the bridge and I need a little something after walking for over an hour. Two skinny teenagers crouch on the floor, carefully packing huge fluorescent bags with the day's deliveries. One is wearing a Wednesday top, the other United; they put aside their sworn rivalry to accomplish the noble act of sorting newspapers. Gladdened by the good that can still be found in this world, I put a Twix on the counter, slide over a fifty-pence piece; the newsagent hands me my change. We nod at each other and I depart; the two delivery boys don't even acknowledge my fleeting presence. There's a serenity to activity at this hour and I'm beginning to like it.

Yet Sheffield's hills are unforgiving and my legs ache after their longest workout in weeks. I head for the bench next to the river and unwrap the chocolate bar. I break off a small piece and crumble it onto the pavement for the pigeons. I crumble a bit more for the sparrows that have gathered expectantly. Taking a bite for myself, I look around the city. My city.

And it's there, sat on a bench, that it hits me.

I have absolutely no idea where I am.

I climb on to the bench, hoping that a bit of additional height will enable me to pick out a familiar landmark, but there's nothing. A street sign points to a greyhound stadium; another informs me that Hillsborough is a kilometre away (which increases my respect for the paper boy in the Blades shirt). But I don't know where either of those are in relation to home, the university or the city centre, or anywhere I know. I'm lost, just a couple of miles from my house. Not very impressive for a third-year geography student.

'You alright, luv?' A milkman peers over the garden wall next to my bench. He's holding the empties in huge, bear-like hands, from which run arms that are a mix of grey hair and blue skin, his many tattoos having long since faded into each other.

'I'm a bit lost,' I admit. 'I've been walking for over an hour and don't really know where I am.'

'This is Owlerton, luv. Are you at Hallam or the proper one?'

'The proper one.'

'I can drop you at the tram stop if you like, you can get back to the centre from there. I've got a few more deliveries to make first, mind. Hop on.'

Before setting off, he leans into the back and picks out a bottle of orange juice, an act of human kindness that I appreciate greatly. I remove the foil top and take a long, refreshing swig as we trundle four metres down the hill. The bottle is finished by the time he's returned from the next delivery.

'How did you know I was a student?' I ask.

'There's not many locals that don't know where Hillsborough is, luv. But you've got that look. Scruffy hair, T-shirt, jeans and trainers. You all look the same to me. Except them ones that only wear black, what d'yer call them?'

'Goths.'

'That's them. My niece is one o' them. Lovely girl.'

We chat in short bursts, interrupted by him having to get off at every other house. I could offer to help, but it doesn't really seem like a two-person job.

'What brings a student out to Owlerton at this hour, then?' he asks, sitting back down. 'Girl trouble is it?'

This guy is like Inspector Morse and Sherlock Holmes combined. He's wasted in the dairy delivery sector.

'Kind of. There's a girl I like. We weren't together, but she's started sleeping with one of my best friends. And I'm not sure what to say to either of them.'

I can still hardly believe it, even hearing it out loud. If it was Mike and Emma, it would make sense; they share several weird habits, like enjoying poetry and cooking food with lentils in. But Mike and Lou? He has less in common with her than I do.

'Which one do you care about more?' asks the milkman.

'Not sure. My friend, probably.'

'I'd sort things out with him first, luv. Worry about her later.'

The milk float speeds up slightly on a downhill stretch, and with the milkman's prudent words to chew on, I feel more upbeat than in a long time. It's partly the unhurried pace of life at this hour, but also the general ambiance of the task at hand. Park the float, carry up the full bottles, bring back the empties, stack them, then drive down the road a bit. And repeat. He's never away for long enough for clichéd sex with bored housewives, but the few people we pass all smile and say hello. Everyone likes milkmen.

Maybe I could be a milkman?

This could be fate at work, my guiding star kicking in: today's walk has nothing to do with romantic tribulations, but is to point me towards a future career as the reality of finding employment creeps ever closer. OK, it won't make much use of my geography degree, and my parents won't be overly impressed, but this simple life is very appealing. I add it to my mental list of potential careers: shelf-stacker, barman, beekeeper, milkman.

'Right, a few more to do, then that's it for the day,' my new role model says, stacking the latest collection of empty bottles.

'You finish this early in the morning? It's only just gone eight.'

'Aye, it gives me plenty of time on the allotment. I can't complain.' This job is sounding better by the minute. 'But you have to start at two-thirty. It's not for everyone, that.'

OK, perhaps not a milkman.

We soon reach the last house on the street and he carries up the order – two pints of blue top and a carton of single cream – then returns and points down the street.

'There's the tram stop, luv. There'll be one along in a minute.'

'Great. Thanks for the lift. And for the advice.' I hold out my hand, and he shakes it, chuckling.

'I've been married twice and both had their ups and downs. But I've had the same best friend since I were four years old. Worth something, that.'

I understand what he's saying. 'I'll go and see him now.'

'Want a pint of milk, get yer strength up?'

'Thanks, but let me pay for this one.'

'Nah, y'alright. I've enjoyed a bit o' company. Ta-ra luv.'

He hands me a bottle of milk and shoots off at eight miles an hour. He's right: I have to talk to Mike.

* * *

I haven't worked out what I want to say by the time I reach Mike's office. Nor have I checked the time; it's only nine o'clock, a good hour before he usually turns up. He eventually arrives at quarter-past ten to find me dozing against his door.

'Chris, old boy, you're here early. Come in, come in. Coffee?'

I follow him in and make my way to the windowsill, finding a spot between his many stacks of papers. Mike switches on his kettle, then his computer, before hanging his battered fedora on the door hook.

'How's the ankle?' he asks, cheerily.

'Alright, thanks. I went for a long walk on it earlier. Ended up at Hillsborough.'

'What took you out there?'

'Couldn't sleep. It was interesting, though, a whole side of Sheffield I've never seen. Like the *proper* city, you know? Not just the student bits.'

'Ah, what us old timers refer to as "Full Monty Land". Did you know the average student only walks along nine roads during their time here? Incredible, isn't it? One of the other postgrad bodkins is doing research into it. It seems we all stick to what we know. Fascinating stuff, it really is.'

'Have you explored much?'

'Me? Oh, I've been all over the place. A few chaps I know took me round a steelworks once. You wouldn't believe some of the machines they used to use. All closed now, of course. There's a real history here, yet most of us pass through this fine city and never see it. A great shame. So what have you been up to? Seen any interesting new bands recently?'

'I saw a band called Muse at the Foundry.'

'Never heard of them. Are they any good?'

'They were alright,' I say, thinking back to the gig. 'They're from Devon too, but I can't see them lasting. Two albums at best. I'll copy you a CD if you like.'

'Much obliged. I'm heading off for more fieldwork next week, I'll need something to listen to when I'm huddled up in the Arctic for six months. What will I do without you and your expert recommendations?'

The kettle approaches the boil and Mike leaps up to flick the switch off.

'Right, that's the pleasantries over,' he says, pouring it over the finely ground beans. 'You're here to talk about Lou, I assume?'

I nod.

'Let me start by expressing my regret. I should have told you. Bad form, very bad form. Technically I am not guilty of a crime, as the two of you were not together and you were of course preoccupied with the lovely Emma. But I acknowledge that matters of the heart are far more complicated, and a certain level of decency is expected between gentlemen such as ourselves. I failed in my duties as a friend, for which I can only apologise. I'm sorry, old boy.'

'That's alright.' I've already forgiven him. It's impossible to be cross with Mike for long. 'So what's the story with you two?'

'The story's finished, old boy. She ended it last night. Came back in tears and told me it was over, whatever it was that was going on. I was never quite sure, if the truth be known.'

'I'm sorry.'

'Don't be. It's one of those things.'

Tension diffused, hurdles overcome, just like that. There's just one more thing I need to know. I wait until he gets up to pour the coffee, so his back is turned towards me.

'Did you sleep with her?'

'Ah, now, as James Bond said to Dr Kananga, that's not the sort of question a gentleman answers.'

'I'm not Dr Kananga. Which one was that, *Octopussy*?'

'*Live And Let Die*. Would you be annoyed if we did?'

'Yes. Very.'

'What would annoy you more, knowing that we had or not knowing either way?'

'Knowing you had.'

'Sorry old boy, but I'm not going to tell you.'

'OK, not knowing either way.'

'I'm still not going to tell you. Private business and all that.' He puts down his coffee and kicks off his shoes, swinging his bare feet onto the desk. 'Listen old boy, for whatever reason, it seems that she likes you. Either you or your ankle-snapping, politically motivated predecessor. She wasn't clear which, I'm not convinced she knows herself. But not me, it seems. Go and talk to her, see how things lie.'

'You won't mind?'

'I will, but I'll survive. Best of British and all that.'

I stare at my coffee. I don't like relationships and friendships getting muddled up like this. It's confusing and stressful and disrupts my pursuit of an easy life.

'While you're here, I've got something for you as a late birthday present,' Mike says, reaching under his desk and pulling out a small cardboard box. A brand new French Press.

'Ah, thanks Mike, that's brilliant.'

'It's a big, tough world out there, old boy. You'll need some proper coffee to get you through it. Also, I need to ask you for a favour.' He searches in his desk and withdraws a stubby key. 'It's for my office. I need someone to look after my chilli plants while I'm away.'

'Me? You'd trust me to do that?'

'Wouldn't trust anyone else. The instructions are all typed out on this card,' he says, handing it over. There are specific notes for each individual plant. He's even laminated it. 'And I expect regular updates on how they're doing. You can email me, once a week will be fine.'

'I haven't quite mastered emails yet,' I confess.

'Then it's about time you did. They're the future, trust me.'

I watch Mike while we drink our coffees. His hair is as messy as mine, but in other ways he's distinctive: the wooden beads, the lizard tattoo, the baggy trousers with brightly coloured self-repaired patches, the earring in the right ear. And of course the hat. I can see why Lou was attracted to him. I, on the other hand, am easily identifiable as a student, even to random milkmen. Unremarkable, one of a crowd, nothing to see here. That must be where I've been going wrong and is therefore where I need to make a change.

'Mike, one last question …'

'Fire away, old boy.'

'Where did you get your hat?'

24

Junk Shop Clothes

'What the *fuck* are you wearing?'

Rob hurtles down the stairs to find me trying on my new purchase in front of the cracked hallway mirror.

'Don't you like it?' I ask, adjusting the black pork pie hat I've spent hours hunting down. 'I thought I should try a new look. Something a bit less studenty.'

'You look like you're auditioning for *Stars In Their Eyes*. Tonight, Matthew, I'm going to be a shit Bono tribute act.'

'I like U2,' I grumble.

'You like everyone, you're the least discerning muso I know. You'd listen to nursery rhymes if they were sung to drums and bass guitar. But I'm sorry, the hat has to go. Take it back while you still can.'

'I'm not sure Oxfam do refunds. What's wrong with it, anyway? Mike wears a hat and he's cool.'

'No, Mike is an unkempt hippie who suffers under the misapprehension that Sheffield is located near the Equator. How else to explain his insistence on twatting about the place without shoes on?'

'He slept with Lou' I say, sulkily. 'He might have done, anyway. Neither of them will tell me.'

'Your Lou? Ouch. She really is dropping her standards. From Jonathan to you to Mike. That's quite a decline. You have to wonder how far she'll sink before the end of term.'

'You don't even know who Jonathan is. And she was never my Lou. Mike thinks she might be though. He said I should talk to her and find out.'

'And you bought that hat to help? Fuck me.'

'Thanks. Again.'

'Anyway, forget about her, I need your help to get the house ready for tonight. Your first task is to make space in the kitchen for all the booze. Leave the hat in your room, I don't want it anywhere near my stuff.'

In my Mike-and-Lou-induced turmoil, I've completely forgotten about the big party. Andy and Rob's birthdays are only a few days apart, and they've decided to celebrate their twenty-firsts together. I dislike student parties generally, but ones in your own house are especially unpleasant: there's no option to leave early and every spillage, whether beer or bodily fluids, is something you'll be cleaning up later. And I always end up with the group discussing something interminably dull, like art or science. Given that the guests at this party will mostly be medics, philosophers and rock climbers, the likelihood of tedious conversation is even higher than normal.

This one has even greater guest-related risks. While I'm not looking forward to the prospect of meeting Seth again, I'm also wondering if Rob has invited Emma. I haven't spoken to her since our kind-of break up, not being willing to do so until the relationship is open on my side as well. While moving all breakable items from the kitchen to the relative safety of the cellar, I decide that the best approach is to spend the entire evening squatting in my doorway. While uncomfortable, this will provide the perfect vantage point from which to survey the guests as they arrive, meaning I can avoid Seth, the worst of the climbers and spot Emma if she appears. It will also prevent people from entering my room unmonitored, protecting it from excess vomit and anyone wanting to steal my CDs.

It's an excellent plan, and one that would have worked perfectly if I'd remembered that we have a back door.

'Why are you sitting there?' Emma asks from halfway up the stairs. She's wearing her floppy hat and a jumper that drops teasingly off her shoulder. I wonder how long she's been there, how long she's been watching me guzzling cans of Stones and glaring at arrivals.

'I'm guarding my CDs,' I explain. 'I don't want anyone to steal them.'

'Is that a big risk?'

'Not if I sit here all night.'

'Can I join you?'

I shrug, hoping this won't look overly keen but won't put her off. It works; my understanding of the female mind is slowly gathering pace.

'How was Kenya?' she asks, offering me a swig of her Strongbow.

'Shit. I broke my ankle and spent most of the week in hospital.'

'Aye, Rob told me.'

'You didn't come and see me, though,' I say, more petulantly than intended. I remove my new hat and pick at its frayed rim.

'I wasn't sure if you'd want me to,' she says. 'You were all set for a wee fling with whatshername.'

'Yeah well, she's—' I stop myself from blurting out the latest developments with Mike. While I would happily receive a sympathetic arm around the shoulder, maybe even a cuddle, it doesn't make me look very good. And now that she's here again, I realise I still want to look good in front of Emma. 'We decided to be friends. For now.'

'Do you want to go to the living room?' she asks, offering me another sip of warm, flat cooking cider. 'Rob's dancing naked on the table.'

'Seen it all before,' I snuffle. 'It's nothing to write home about. And the music's awful.' Andy's let one of his medic friends DJ for the evening, and it is truly appalling. There have been four Spice Girls songs already. It's only a matter of time before Steps come on.

'Let's go to the kitchen, then. That's where the best parties are, isn't it? "You'll always find me in the kitchen at parties", who sang that one?'

'Can't remember. I'll have a think.'

'A think in the kitchen?' she says, hopefully.

It's tempting, very tempting. She's the same person I fell so easily for, and I want to be with her now more than ever. I remember how reassuring it was to spend time with a girl who didn't constantly see all my shortcomings, or at least didn't keep pointing them out. Emma seemed to enjoy my company, to be interested in what I thought about films, music, everything.

But nothing has changed, not really. She still has a boyfriend in Scotland. Whatever we talk about, however much we laugh, it will always be on my mind – and not at the back, but pounding away at the front. It's hard to turn her away, but it'll be even harder if we get close again.

'I might stay here,' I say. 'CDs don't look after themselves.'

'OK, sweetie. You know where to find me if you change your mind.'

It's torture, sitting in my doorway knowing she's just a few feet away. I don't dare look into the kitchen in case she's talking to another man, but not knowing if she is or not makes the torment even worse. My painful, lonely vigil is only broken when Danny from the climbing club comes over and asks, in a barely audible mumble, if he can sit in my room. I'm not keen, preferring to wallow in solitude, but he has a full bottle of Midori. I shrug – another pair of eyes watching over the CDs

225

can't hurt – and he sits down to look through my collection, picking out *Different Class* and reading the sleeve notes while it plays.

Several hours later – how many exactly, I'm not sure, Midori can have that effect on you – Emma walks past once more. I'm slumped against the bookcase, empty bottle in one hand. Danny has fallen asleep, his head resting snugly in my lap. My new hat is squashed where he sat on it. I know, without needing a mirror, that my skin has taken on that pre-chunder paleness that afflicts anyone who's drunk most of a bottle of melon-flavoured liqueur on top of several cans of warm bitter. There is absolutely no way we're a pretty sight, yet you wouldn't know it from her expression, which is as non-judgemental as ever.

'I came to say goodbye.' She looks incredible, of course. All three of her, dancing in my doorway.

'Jona Lewie,' I blurt.

'I'm sorry?'

'The song. About kitchens. Jona Lewie. He did "Stop the Cavalry".'

'I knew you'd get it. My little musical genius.'

'Yes. Genius.'

'See you, Chris. Come and say hello. Any time you like.'

I nod. Opening my mouth again at this point would be a serious risk and, having spent an entire evening protecting my bedroom from vomit, it would be a shame to spoil it this late on. I wait until she's left, then shift Danny's head and lurch for the bin.

Drug Drug Druggy

That's it. I've had enough.

I know I've said it before, but this time I'm serious. Enough of Lou, enough of Emma, enough of all of them.

I've already achieved what I set out to do this year. I've talked to Lou – I've done far more than talk to her – and Emma fulfils the girlfriend ambition. Even if she was only ever half a girlfriend, we were together for twelve weeks, which makes six in total. So more than three. Job done. And I've been checking the music press diligently; there's no news of Blur either touring or splitting up. Nothing more I can do about that one.

I only have one task left to accomplish in my final six weeks as a student: analyse two hundred questionnaires about tourism. I accept Joe's offer to do the work at his house, as it provides a tantalising peek into a previously unseen world – the world of dedicated substance abuse.

I've often wondered what druggies do all day. It turns out they take drugs, talk about taking drugs and watch films about taking drugs. And that's it. I always thought making a joint was a simple task: put cannabis and tobacco into a cigarette paper, roll it up and light it. But Joe and his friends treat it with an earnestness approaching religious observance, using an array of strange-looking devices and making whispered, awed observations throughout the process: the roller's technique, the quantities used, the relative merits of different papers, which tobacco works best and, of course, their preferred strain of drug.

The constant stream of people passing through his house also makes a welcome change to the monastic silence of my own. I can't tell who actually lives there and who simply turns up for a smoke, and nor do I learn many names; people don't waste words introducing themselves, restricting their non-drug-related conversations to commenting on the constant stream of videos playing in the corner. Which are, without fail, about drugs. In the two days I've been here, we've watched *Scarface*, *Goodfellas* and *Donnie Brasco* twice each, plus *The Usual Suspects*, *Midnight Express*, *Fear and Loathing in Las Vegas* and *Easy Rider*. Drug-taking is illegal in much of the world, and largely frowned upon by most in society, yet it forms its own vast cinematic genre. Why are there no films about more wholesome pastimes, like birdwatching or cookery?

'Don't you ever get bored of it?' I ask Joe when we've torn ourselves from the screen to make some tea, and possibly do some work. 'Getting stoned, I mean.'

'Nah man, I love it,' he replies, handing me a Leyton Orient mug. He has about twenty of them. 'I'll do it for as long as I can. My brother, he spent the year after uni getting wasted in Asia. Thailand, Laos, Cambodia, all over, man. All he did was eat noodles, sleep on the beach and get stoned. Know what he does now? He files insurance claims in a trading estate in London. Guess which one he finds boring?'

'Fair point,' I admit. 'Is that what you're planning on doing? Travelling?'

'As soon as I can, for as long as I can. I'll get a job back home, save up some cash and hit the road. You know how much it costs to live in Thailand? Five quid a day, big bruv reckons. If I can save up a grand, that's what, two hundred days? And if I can save two grand, that'll be …'

'Four hundred days.'

'Exactly, man. Exactly.'

We clink mugs.

'Why not come with me, man?' Joe continues. 'We don't have to smoke all day if you ain't into it, we can do other stuff. There's snorkelling, hiking in the jungle, all sorts of shit. My bruv never got round to any of it, but he said it's easy to organise.'

It's a tempting offer: no new career options have materialised, meaning milkman is still top of the list. A year of sitting on a beach sounds much more up my street than working. And with Joe around, I'll have my very own hippy in tow, so there'll be no repeat of the Goan debacle. But before I can answer, the door opens and one of his coterie of stoners looks in.

'Sorry to disturb, like, but Joe, man, we need you. We're planning for tomorrow night.'

I follow them into the sitting room, which has switched from a junkie's ghetto to a very small stock exchange. Money sits about in piles, while the previously horizontal residents are all sitting upright and showing far higher energy levels than they have previously. I listen to their discussions, which are of course drug-related: who wants which drugs, how many, how much, who owes money and/or drugs from last weekend, where to get them, who's offering the best rates for x, y and z right now. The pages of a notepad are filling up rapidly with names and orders; they've even turned the TV off. Joe, who is in charge of collecting the money, notices me staring and grins.

'What about you, Chris? You comin' tomorrow?'

I don't know anything about proper clubbing other than it's a very different kind of music to Britpop. Dance, trance, rave – it has various names, but the end result is the same: tuneless, repetitive shite. Still, my time as a student is nearing its end; what harm can it do to cram in a few new experiences?

Since Christmas, I've broken my ankle, been in an open relationship and ridden on a milk float. Going to a proper nightclub, with real drugs, will be another notable badge of honour. It will also give me something to crow about to Rob, whose anecdotes about the Hacienda are, I suspect, hand-me-downs from his brother; they're always lacking in detail, and thirteen is a bit young to be plausibly snorting cocaine in the toilets with the DJ. Even for someone from Manchester.

'Sure, why not?'

'Come on then, man, we need to get a few things sorted, know what I mean?'

I don't know what he means, so once we're outside and I won't look stupid in front of his friends, I ask him where we're going.

'Supplies, man. Time to get sorted for E's and whizz, as your man Jarvis would say.'

'Drugs? We're going to buy the drugs? Now?'

'Yes indeed,' Joe grins, giving me a brief flash of the wad of crumpled fivers in his pocket. I know little about drug deals beyond what I've learnt from his gangster film catalogue (and the video for 'Ebeneezer Goode', once it was finally shown on *Top of the Pops*) but even so, I'm petrified. I've stayed clear of drugs since the local policeman arrived at a party at Matt's house. I was holding the badly rolled spliff at the time and had thus borne the brunt of the angry lecture that followed. I nearly cried when he pressed me to tell him whose it was. 'Caught By The Fuzz' still brings me out in a cold sweat.

'Shouldn't there be a few more of us, in case things go wrong?' I ask.

'Don't worry man, I'm packing heat,' says Joe, suddenly looking serious and patting the chest of his hoodie.

'What? You've got a gun?'

'I'm joking, man' he cackles. 'Fuckin' hell, your face. Don't worry, I've been buying from this guy for years. He still lives with his mum. We'll be alright, trust me.'

'I'm still not sure,' I confess. I don't want to be present at any sort of drug deal, even a tame suburban one.

'OK, man, you wait here. Keep an eye out the police. And machine-gun wielding Cubans,' he laughs, walking up the path of an innocuous-looking terraced house. Five minutes later, he's back, seen off by a middle-aged woman wearing an apron. It turns out drug dealers' mums look much like everyone else's. The whole experience is a let-down, in fact. Not a single person got shot. I can't help concluding that *Scarface* is a little bit far-fetched.

* * *

The drug deal may have been underwhelming, but it's nothing compared to the next disappointment: the club. I was excited as we made our way there – a feeling heightened by the fact that I was walking through the city with a group of people all carrying illegal substances – and when we first step inside, it's undoubtedly impressive: big, noisy and much glitzier than the Leadmill. There are hundreds of people inside and they all have peculiar outfits. Some have T-shirts with curious patterns on them, others wear plastic flowers round their necks, and several have bobble hats despite it being the hottest building I've ever been in. A sizeable number are wearing very little at all: naked male torsos glisten with sweat and peculiar luminous markings, while female flesh bursts out of tiny dresses made from bin bags and tin foil.

But I can't enjoy it. I'm far too aware of how out of place I look. I thought a Charlatans T-shirt and ripped jeans were a safe bet for any sort of club, but I stick out badly. No one told me it was fancy dress. Even more incomprehensibly, everyone has a whistle hanging around their neck. And people keep hugging each other; they just walk around, hugging anyone nearby. How do they all know each other? When they're not hugging, they work their way through a series of extravagant hand movements, like a massive puppet show without the puppets. I can't work out what's going on, but it's clear that shoe-gazing and head-bobbing will cut very little rug in these surroundings.

Yet by far the worst thing is the music. My expectations were low, but even these aren't met. There's no beginning or end to any of the tracks, just a constant thudding beat with an array of weird noises played over the top. Every so often, a woman singing a completely different song will chime in, or there'll be a keyboard solo laid over the top of the drums, in most cases played by a sausage-fingered primary school child. I soon feel nauseous and, having long since lost Joe and his friends, set about finding a bar where at least I can drink a beer and the monotonous thumping might be a tiny bit quieter. OK, this is exactly the sort of comment Grandpa would make, but that doesn't mean it's not true. Besides, an eighty-year-old Disney obsessive in a knitted tank top would blend in better than I'm managing.

With the reassurance of beer in hand, I find a vacant sofa and try to make myself a bit more conspicuous; pill-popping, trip-hopping raver girls seem to be much freer with their affections than the others I've met, and I may as well get a few hugs out of the evening.

I must be doing something wrong, though. Several hours and many more bottles of Becks later, I'm still on my own. It's soul-destroying: I'm stuck in a vast warehouse crammed with people having the time of their lives – and I don't get it. Drunk, rejected and with the onset of a headache, I decide to cut my losses (which are notable – at ten quid to get in, the night has hit my wallet as hard as my self-esteem) and brave the dancefloor to say goodbye to Joe. The crowds are still dancing with an energy I've never had in my life, let alone at five in the morning, but eventually I find him. It's a welcome surprise when he says he'll leave with me. After a round of hugs – I failed to secure any from foil-wrapped females, but can't escape them from his band of slippery, stinking friends – we venture into the early morning air.

'Where are we heading?' I ask as we pass Hallam University, moving away from our side of the city.

'You'll see, man' Joe says with a wink. Minutes later, we're outside a tiny café that seems to cater solely for overweight truck drivers and bleary-eyed clubbers. 'Best part of the night,' he says, pushing the door open. 'The post-rave fry up.'

Despite our musical differences, Chemical Joe and I have much in common (well, geography and football) and my affection for him increases further when he asks the waitress to give us fried bread not toast with our breakfasts, even though it isn't a menu option. Our plates soon arrive, so full that the rashers of bacon are barely clinging to the sides. We both pile in, and only when his plate is near-empty does he speak again.

'So, man, your first big trance night; what did you think?'

'Honestly?' I say, a dribble of grease escaping down my chin. 'Not my thing. It was good to experience it, but I don't think I'll be coming back. No offence, but trance music is awful.'

'You just need the right stimulation. I saw you necking the beers at the side. Doesn't work, man. You should try something a little different.'

'I think I might stick to indie music.'

'Fair enough,' he says, then points to my plate with his fork. 'How's your breakfast?'

'Excellent.'

'Best fuckin' sausages in Sheffield, man. And I recommend a dash of tabasco in the beans.'

He adds a splash to both our plates. He's right, it's delicious. We order another pot of tea from the passing waitress and I polish off the last of my fried bread while we wait.

'Anyway, I'm guessing the music wasn't the real reason you came,' he says.

'What do you mean?'

'I reckoned you were hoping to bump into Lou. Haven't seen her there for a few months, though. Not since last November.'

'Lou? Why would she be there?'

'Are you kiddin', man? She's a proper raver. A regular in the first year, she was out every weekend. She started comin' again last autumn, until her little accident. Bad fuckin' night, that, bad fuckin' night.'

'What happened?'

'You don't know? Shit, man, she totally OD'd. It was full on. Not sure what she took, some speed, pills, maybe a bit of coke. There were police and everything, and those ambulance dudes in green, like on *Casualty*. I thought she'd gone for good for a moment. You didn't know about it?'

'When was this?'

'Just after readin' week last term, man. She had to get her stomach pumped in the hospital. So I heard, anyway.'

That night. When Rob and I went to see Pulp in Manchester. The ambulance, the police, the chaos outside the nightclub. Was that Lou on the stretcher? I wanted to go and help, and now desperately wish I had. My head is spinning, too many thoughts demanding my focus. The most prominent is surprise – I never knew Lou liked trance music – and it's followed swiftly by wondering whether she has one of those bin-bag dresses, and how good it must look on her (when she isn't spewing drugs down it, of course). But once I've dealt with those, there's the shock of discovering that Lou takes drugs – and far too many at once, it seems.

Next comes disappointment. Partly in myself – I can't shift an overwhelming desire to know all the gory details about stomach pumping; how does it actually work? Is it like a bicycle pump, or more like one for your car? Where do the tubes go, in the top or in the bottom? – but also with her. All those hours I've spent worshipping her are tarnished by the realisation that she isn't perfect. Lucid images pass through my mind: Lou collapsed on the floor of a grubby nightclub; Lou throwing up in an ambulance; Lou in a binbag dress ... no, stop, focus on what's important here.

'She was there, going proper crazy on the dancefloor, then she kind of collapsed. It was pretty fuckin' freaky, man. I was gonna go with her to the hospital, but she must've asked someone to call Jonathan, because he turned up to look after her. Even though it was three in the morning and they'd broken up. Top bloke, that Jonathan. Apart from your ankle, I mean.'

I push my plate away, unable to finish the last half egg. Here it is, the next thump in the guts: even then, right after they broke up, she turned to him in her hour of need. Not me. It's a lot to contend with at such an early hour and I'm grateful when Joe pours us each a fresh mug of tea from the pot.

'Cheer up, man,' he says kindly. 'It's no big deal. Loads of people have overdone it on a big night out. I bet you've chucked up from the booze before now.'

'Yeah, but ... this is drugs. I didn't think she'd be into all that.'

'Come on, I've taken bucketloads of drugs over the years, and you don't think any less of me, do you?'

'Yeah, but you're Chemical Joe. I expect it of you. I thought she was different.'

'Shit happens, man.'

'I suppose. I just didn't think it happened to her.'

'You really like her, don't you?' he says, spooning sugar into his tea. I count five going in before he stops.

'Yeah. We almost got together around that time, but nothing serious happened. She even started seeing one of my friends recently, although he says it's over. I don't know what she thinks of me to be honest. I can never work it out.'

'She likes you, man. Told me in Kenya, when we were waiting for you to wake up.'

'Jonathan's the problem, though. Whatever I do, it's not as good as what he does. He even saves her from overdoses. Even though they're not together, I can't compete.'

'Have you tried?'

'Tried what? To compete?'

'Yeah, man. Show off a bit. Take her somewhere fancy, show her what a classy dude you are. Got to be a better option than moanin' to me.'

Joe's right. I've never tried to compete, not properly. I've settled meekly for second place, ever since that cheese and wine party. There are only a few more weeks left; it has to be worth one last try.

She has to be worth one last try.

I pick up my knife and fork to finish off the egg, knowing I'll need every last drop of energy for the next step, one I've only attempted once before when sober: asking a girl out on a date.

26

Goldfinger

Twelve hours later, I'm on a date with Lou.

I waited until mid-morning before calling, confident that she'd be in the library or a lecture, and I could leave a message with a housemate which she'd never get, allowing me to slip back into melancholy in the knowledge that I've done all I could. Except in the fug brought about by beer, Red Bull and trance music, I forgot it's Sunday. She picked up on the third ring.

'Hello?'

'ItsChriswouldyouliketogofordinnersometime?'

To my surprise, and no little horror, she accepted and suggested we meet this evening, which leaves me with little time to prepare. The first issue is where to take her. I know she likes Italian food, because she's mentioned Jonathan taking her to Italian restaurants, but I don't want her making that comparison from the off. In a rare flash of inspiration, I head to the tourist information centre and ask for recommendations. The woman behind the counter looks highly suspicious when I say I'm a businessman in town for the week, but provides me with a list of the city's finest eateries nonetheless, and I set off in search of a happy compromise between price and poshness. After reading through several menus, and forcing myself on principle to dismiss anywhere offering two-for-one deals, I settle on Bistro Paris, a small French place near the city centre. It has candles stuck into wine bottles and the waiters wear bowties. If that doesn't impress her, nothing will.

The next problem is how to pay for it. I've calculated that I'll need between forty and fifty quid, which will take me perilously close to my overdraft limit. So, with a heavy heart, I open my desk draw and withdraw the fifty-pound note that Grandpa sent a few weeks back. I've been saving it to put towards a festival ticket for the summer, once Rob's decided which one we're going to. But that will have to be paid for another way.

The last item on my mental tick list is what to wear. After last night's clubbing experience, I'm coming to the reluctant conclusion that band T-shirts aren't suitable for all occasions. In a panic I ring Joe, who comes round with a selection of shirts. He also brings round *Goodfellas* and pauses it on each restaurant scene to talk me through what to do and how to behave. Once he's happy that I'll be OK on my own, he departs and, after a long bath – the occasion justifies it, I decide – I set off for the city centre.

Lou arrives ten minutes after seven and looks utterly devastating. She's wearing a light grey jacket over a tight white dress, and her hair is tied back instead of loose. The only shame is that there are so few people about to appreciate her (and to see me with her).

'You look incredible,' I say, hoping this is in no way sexist.

'Thank you. I've not seen you in a shirt before.'

'I wanted to make an effort.'

'I appreciate it. You look very smart.'

I take a moment before we enter the restaurant. Think *Goodfellas*. Think de Niro, Liotta, Pesci. Be calm, be courteous, be charming. And if the waiter disrespects you, shoot him in the kneecap.

No, no, don't get carried away. Just be yourself.

Your gangster self.

As instructed by Ray Liotta via the medium of Joe Everitt, I hold her chair out, just beating the leering waiter to it. He gives me a superior look and departs, then returns swiftly with two menus. First blood to me.

'Or perhaps you'd like to see the set menu, sir? It is very reasonable,' he says, sneering; round two to him.

'Order whatever you like, it's my treat,' I say to Lou.

'Shall we go for the set menu? It's a lot cheaper.'

'Doesn't matter.'

'Chris, I'm a student too. We're all on a budget, there's no need to show off. Wasting money doesn't impress me.'

'Well … if you're sure.'

'Of course I am. And it means I can order the most expensive wine', she remarks, picking up the wine list.

I hope she's joking about the wine. Some of the prices are utterly ridiculous. The waiter brings over two set menus and gives me another sneer, this one brimming with arrogance. I return it with interest: nice try, my friend, but I'm the one having dinner with her. So piss off.

I study the menu carefully. Normally when eating out, I choose a dessert first and work backwards from there, knowing how much space I need to keep free for the most important course. But I've never eaten French food before, at least not in a restaurant. How big will the portions be? What comes with them? A lot of the options are fish-based; I don't like fish, especially when it comes with the head on, which is exactly the kind of thing the French would get up to. At least with pizzas they tell you how big it is; an Italian would have been safer. I opt for boeuf bourguignon and hope for the best.

'Shall we get starters as well?' I ask. Fortunately, Lou has selected a cheapish bottle of white wine and, with two courses for ten pounds, I know I have enough money for dessert.

'We don't need to.'

'It's not about need, it's about want. I want to spoil you.' The waiter is smirking again. He can clearly spot a pretender. As Lou muses over the starters, I catch his eye. Having not yet perfected my mad-eyed Joe Pesci stare, I mouth 'fuck off' at him, slowly and clearly. Not very classy, but it does the trick.

'I don't know why you want to spoil me,' Lou says. 'I'm not always very nice to you.'

'That's not true.' It is true, but I don't want to annoy her when we've got off to a good start. 'And the last time I asked you out, we didn't even get to the restaurant. I want you to know I can make it through the first course at least. I'm trying to impress you.'

'You are. But you don't need to try so hard. Tell me what you've been up to.'

'I talked to Mike. He said you're not together anymore.'

It spills out before I've even considered whether it's the best subject for a romantic meal. Maybe that first sip of wine loosened my tongue. That or the three beers I sank on the way here to calm my nerves.

'I'm not sure Mike and I were ever *together*. It was just a … thing.'

'He said you wanted to get back with me. Maybe.'

'I don't think *we* were ever together either, Chris. We spent one night messing about and you ran away before I'd even woken up because you were scared of my mum.'

'True enough. Although it was the cat that scared me, not your mum.' I fiddle with my wine glass for a moment. 'What happens now?'

'Between you and me? Or Mike and me? Or do you mean Jonathan and me?'

The mention of his name makes me jump. I assumed he was out of the picture, except as the ever-present spectre of boyfriends past. Is she getting back together with him? I've only just seen off the latest rival for her affections, and now the old one has reappeared. It reminds me of a wildlife programme I saw about a red deer stag who had to continually fight off the other males after his herd. By the end, the poor sod was so knackered that he just wandered off into the hills, one antler hanging off. I'm beginning to understand how he felt.

'Which one of us are you going to go for?' I ask eventually.

'I haven't decided yet. Maybe I'll arrange for the three of you to have a joust on Devonshire Green. The winner takes the fair maiden home and fucks her.'

'I'm not sure Devonshire Green's big enough for a joust. The horses need quite a long run-up.'

'I'll find somewhere else, then.'

'I'm not sure fair maidens say "fuck", either.'

'This one does. Fuck fuck fuck.' She laughs as the elderly couple on the next table look over in disgust. 'I might give up on men altogether and become a lesbian.'

'It doesn't work like that, apparently. Rob says you're either one or the other. Like in Sheffield, you're either an Owl or a Blade.'

'What on earth are you on about?'

'I mean everyone in Sheffield, the locals anyway, supports either Wednesday – the Owls – or United, they're the Blades. You can't be in the middle, or flip between them. Anyway, the Owls are called that because they're from Owlerton, and United are the Blades because ... I don't know actually, something to do with steel I expect. Sorry, I'll shut up, I know football's not your thing.'

'I know one of them has red stripes and one has blue stripes,' Lou offers, taking a breadstick from the jar.

'Do you know which is which?'

'No. Nor do I care.'

'United are the red ones. Anyway, the point is you can only be one or the other, and it's the same with being gay. So Rob says.'

'What about bisexuals?'

'Dunno. Maybe they're the Barnsley fans. It's not really my area of expertise.'

'What are your areas of expertise, Christopher?'

'Music. Plymouth Argyle. Not women. Definitely not you.'

'You're not supposed to work us out, that's part of our charm. And congratulations on turning a discussion about me becoming a lesbian into one about football in under four seconds.'

The starters arrive just in time to save me. I manage to negotiate some very gooey Camembert without spilling too much down Joe's shirt. Lou, who annoyingly didn't order a starter despite it being part of the deal, takes a tiny bite of her breadstick before letting it sway in front of her. It takes every ounce of willpower not to pick one out and challenge her to a lightsabre fight.

'What are you thinking about?' she asks.

'Nothing.'

'Yes you are. You're staring at my breadstick. Explain yourself.'

'Did you know there's a new *Star Wars* film coming out?' I say, quickly. 'About Anakin Skywalker when he was young, before he became–'

'I don't want to talk about *Star Wars*, Chris.'

'No, of course not. Sorry.'

Silence resumes. Lou nibbles a little more of her breadstick and I finish my hot cheese. The old woman next to us continues to stare at Lou disapprovingly; her husband just stares. Eventually, the waiter brings over our mains. Lou's fish still has its head on, as I predicted. Why do the French think this kind of thing is acceptable?

'You can ask me if you like,' says Lou, halfway through her fish. 'About my overdose.'

'How did you know that I know?'

'Joe rang me earlier. He warned me that you knew, and would probably ask me about it. He also asked me to apologise on his behalf for going behind your back, but says it's probably better this way, and no need to thank him, unless you want to buy him a pint when you see him.'

'Ah.' There are lots of things I want to know about that night, but I don't know where to start. 'Erm, so why did you do it?'

'It wasn't planned. A miscalculation, let's say.'

'Was it because of what happened between us in Grindleford? Y'know, feeling guilty about cheating on Jonathan?'

'No. I was already a mess before that, as soon as I knew things weren't working out. I already suspected he was going to break up with me. It wasn't anything to do with you. Things just got out of hand.'

'So you OD'd because of Jonathan?' I'm unsure if I want it to be about him or me. Which is better, causing someone to overdose or not causing them to overdose? Another one for Rob to muse over with his philosophy chums.

'I think "overdosed" is a little melodramatic. I fell over – collapsed, you could say – and my friends told the bouncers, who rang an ambulance. It happens. It's happened to other people as well. I regret it, but please don't expect me to apologise or try to justify it. I had a lot of good nights clubbing, one went wrong. That's all. There's no great mystery to unravel.'

Normally this would count as a ticking off, but for once the undercurrent of annoyance is missing. I am, finally, being treated as an equal. Or as close as she gets to having equals.

'You could have called me,' I say. 'Afterwards, I mean. If you needed someone. You didn't have to call Jonathan.'

'I didn't call anyone, I was unconscious. One of my friends called him.'

'Well, if it happens again, you can call me.'

'It won't happen again. Now, can we talk about something else? Like dessert?'

Among all these adult themes, I've forgotten about dessert. My main was so large and delicious that I'm nearly full. After a silent self-admonishment to make sure it never happens again, I plump for tarte au citron. Lou chooses the same and we manage some trouble-free small talk while waiting for them to arrive. She tells me about the master's course she's applying for at Oxford, but as I start updating her on my own post-Sheffield options, she interrupts.

'The reason I didn't tell you about the overdose was because I didn't want you to know,' she says, more quickly than normal. Is she nervous? There's a first time for everything. 'I liked the way you looked at me. You put me on a pedestal and I wanted to stay there. So I didn't tell you.'

'That's OK. Like you said, you don't have to justify anything.'

'I do. A little bit.'

I reach across the table and take her hand. 'I know now. And I won't ever ask about it again. I'm sorry for being nosy. It's partly because my own life's been so uneventful I guess, I can't help but be curious. You know, I grew up in Devon and—'

'You've already done the poor little country boy routine, Chris. I grew up in the countryside too, remember, and I'm fantastic.'

'Did I tell you about the day we lost our guinea pigs?'

'You did not.'

'That's kind of the whole story, actually. They were only missing a couple of hours, then the neighbours brought them back. They hadn't gone further than the first patch of marigolds they found.'

'That's a superb anecdote. Well done.'

She's laughing at my inadequacies once again. I've missed it. She then picks up her fork and removes a pointlessly small piece of dessert.

'So, in summary, my life has been uneventful, guinea-pig traumas aside, but I guess I'm lucky overall,' I say, subtly eyeing her barely touched dessert.

'You are. Very lucky,' she replies, passing over her plate.

'You're lucky as well, you know.'

'And why's that?'

'Being out for dinner with a fine, upstanding citizen like myself. Honestly, if my parents knew I was wasting my money on a broken-home junkie like you, they'd be furious.'

She swings her foot towards my shins, but they're already out of range. There's still a lot I don't know about her, but I've learnt the basics.

'Did you really have your stomach pumped?'

'I did. And don't say it so loudly.'

'What's it like?'

'It's fun. Like being tickled inside.'

'Really?'

'No, of course it isn't. What do you think? It's unpleasant and degrading. And we're not talking about that any more, remember? Tell me how your friend Rob is, I like him.'

'He's got a new boyfriend. Called Seth.'

'What's Seth like?'

'He's a wanker. And he shat himself rock climbing.'

'Now *this*, Christopher, is a proper conversation. Tell me more.'

So I do. And for once, she listens, properly listens. There are no glances over my shoulder to see who else is about, no barely disguised sighs, no arched eyebrows. I've spent years wondering what to talk to her about, and all she wanted was gossip. After Rob and Seth, I tell her about Joe's house, how he's the king among his stoner friends and they all seek his favour. Next, I fill her in on Andy's seduction techniques (making them seem pathetic rather than successful, and keeping quiet about his Hugh Grant resemblance). She still wants more, so I tell her about the time Mike tried to seduce his supervisor at a post-grad social event and she reported him to the university (I've forgiven Mike for his fling with Lou, but not for telling her I like the Lighthouse Family). In the space of a few minutes, I betray all of my closest friends in return for the attention of a beautiful woman. If I'd known it was this easy, I'd have sold them out years ago.

The waiter comes over and asks curtly if we want anything else. I ordered two espressos without even checking if Lou wants one, just as Joe instructed. As he brings them over I demand the bill, receiving a scowl for making him go back and forth. I casually slip the fifty-pound note into the small leather-bound wallet without even checking the amount; I've kept a mental tally of the cost of each course, so know it comes to forty-nine pounds fifty. The evening is going so well that I don't even ask for the change. This is all textbook Mafioso behaviour; Joe will be impressed.

Hopefully Lou is, too. She finishes her espresso, and I leap up to hold out her coat. She thanks me politely before pointing out that it isn't hers, hers is the grey one. I escort her to the door, winking smugly at the waiter as we leave arm in arm.

'Thank you for tonight, Chris,' she says as we reach Mike's/her house. 'I had a lovely evening.'

'You're welcome.'

'Are you still seeing that Scottish girl?' she asks. She fixes me with a look I've not seen before, one I can't read.

'No, I'm not. We ... we're just friends.' Are we? I'm no longer sure. And I'm not sure it matters any more, as Lou takes my hands.

'You've changed this year,' she says, the strange look still in place.

'In a good way?'

'You're ... slightly less awkward than before.' In one movement, she kisses me on the cheek, lets go of my fingers and pulls away. 'Goodnight, Chris.'

Then she's gone, leaving me standing in the last light of day.

Slightly less awkward; I'll take that.

27

What Do I Do Now?

Except slightly less awkward clearly isn't enough.

After a day of dancing round the house, smug satisfaction plastered across my face, I spend the next two waiting increasingly impatiently for her to call. Then two wondering what the hell is going on. By Saturday, I'm very angry and extremely confused. What did I do wrong? Did I do anything wrong, or not enough things right?

I have nothing left up my sleeve, no one else to turn to now that Joe's gangster-tinged approach has failed. Nor have I heard from Emma since the party. My final days as a student look decidedly empty. I wake up. Lie in bed. Have breakfast. Extend breakfast with an additional round of toast. Watch *Neighbours*. Make a mug of tea. Put a CD on. Watch afternoon repeats and moan about the lack of decent programmes, even though there are now five channels to choose from.

At least there's music. There's always the music. And Rob and I are going out on a high, with tonight's Supergrass gig in Leeds our last as students. It's an important one, too, as I've only seen them at festivals up to now. They were superb, naturally, but it's not the same as seeing them on tour. They're Supergrass: I need to have a ticket with their name on adorning my pin board.

Rob's been occupied with climbing club duties, so I have been left to plan the evening in fine detail: train to Leeds, get a curry somewhere, then go to the gig and head back to Sheffield, hopefully in time to round things off at the Leadmill's legendary indie night. I've even bought him an *I*

Should Coco T-shirt as a belated birthday present. I'm wrapping it on the bed when he barges in.

'Are we leaving now? It's a bit early, isn't it?' I ask.

'Yeah, about that, I've got something to ...' He stops and stares at my stereo. 'Are you listening to Fleetwood Mac?'

'I am indeed,' I state proudly. '*Rumours*. It's their best album.'

'Finally taking up Seth's advice, then? An odd choice, but it's good to see you stretching beyond your usual diet of Britpop and poodle rock.'

'It's got nothing to do with him,' I snap. 'Emma gave it to me for my birthday.'

'Did she? Well, it's not their best album. Fourth best, I'd say. Anyway, I'm going to have to let you down tonight, I'm afraid.'

'You're kidding me. Why?'

'Climbing business. Danny just rang, they need someone to help out at the climbing wall tonight.'

'And?'

'And so I said I'd help.'

'Why does it have to be you? This is Sheffield, every other person's a climber. Ring him back and tell him you're busy.'

'I can't,' Rob says, scratching his beard. 'I've already promised.'

'You promised me first. You promised we were going to watch Supergrass together. We've not been to a gig together since Gene and that was months ago.'

'Chris, some things are more important than music.'

'True, but rock climbing isn't one of them. Friendship is, though, and you keep letting me down.' I flop against my pillow for dramatic effect. Rob stares at his feet, then sighs loudly.

'You're right. I'm sorry, I'm letting you down. But the climbing club is important to me, now more than ever, they're electing the next president in two weeks. I thought you understood that.' He digs into his pockets. 'Look, see if you can sell my ticket. You can keep the cash, spend it on a CD or something.'

He gives me a half-apologetic shrug and turns to go. But he's not getting away with this so easily.

'Name them,' I demand. 'All three of them.'

'What, Supergrass? Alright, if I must. Gaz Coombes, Danny Goffey, who is the driving force behind that band, incidentally, and–'

'No, not that. The three Fleetwood Mac albums better than *Rumours*. You said it's only their fourth best.'

'Do we have to do this now? I'm kind of busy.'

'You are so full of shit,' I shout, no longer able or willing to hold back my anger. 'I started listening to them because of Emma, not you, and you can't stand it. And instead of admitting it, you make up more of your stupid muso crap about how you hate their greatest album and prefer all the shitty B-sides they did before they were famous.'

It feels like an age before he speaks.

'I'd put their eponymous album of 1975 at number one. It contains several of their classic tracks, interspersed with some underappreciated gems. *Tusk* is at number two, a placing that recognises not just its undoubted excellence, but also the bravery of stepping outside of their commercial comfort zone. It's their equivalent of *OK Computer* in that respect. *Rumours* probably ties with *Tango In The Night* at number three musically, but I prefer the upbeat nature of the latter. Is that enough, or do you want me to continue through all of their albums?'

I remain slumped against my pillow, feeling foolish. 'How do you know so much about Fleetwood Mac? You've never mentioned them before.'

'My sister was a big fan,' he shrugs, turning to leave.

'Ha! Bullshit, again! You don't even have a sister!'

Once more, he stares at me, but no longer looks irritated; instead, his face displays a mixture of sadness and disappointment. He hasn't looked at me like this for a while, not since I suggested Kula Shaker might be the Beatles of our generation. Carefully, he takes a small photo out of his wallet.

'That's Caroline, Caz to most people. She was a big fan of Fleetwood Mac when we were growing up.'

I look at the crumpled passport-sized photo. Through the cracks, a girl with tangled ginger hair smiles back at me, with a much younger Rob squeezed in beside her. I wonder why he's never mentioned her …

Why he said she *was* a fan ...

The awful realisation hit me.

'She's dead, isn't she? That's why you've never mentioned her.'

'What? No, she's not fucking dead. She works for the NHS in Rochdale, I went climbing with her last week. She taught me to climb, in fact. She's basically an older, female version of me, beard notwithstanding.'

'Is she a lesbian?'

'No, Chris, it's not hereditary, we've been through this so many times now.' Rob flings himself next to me and puts his arm around my shoulders. 'Look, I'm really sorry about tonight. I've let you down, I know. I'll make it up to you somehow, I promise.'

'How come you never told me you have a sister?'

'You never asked. You've never asked me anything about my family. Except when we went to stay with my brother, and you asked what music he liked. That's it.'

I want to refute this but can't recall anything to use as a counter argument. Am I really so self-centred?

'There are some old Fleetwood Mac albums in my room somewhere,' he says, getting up to attempt once more to leave. 'I'll dig them out for you. They're only on tape, but you get the idea.'

'Thanks,' I say, doing my best to smile in an I-forgive-you kind-of way. He nods back, half-heartedly, and departs. I consider chasing him to patch things up, but I'm still unsure which of us is in the wrong. Instead, I head to the Washington.

I can't enjoy the first pint, too preoccupied with worry about how many other friends might have sisters I've never asked about, and whether I should skip the gig to ring them all and check. But by the dregs of the second pint, I conclude that the onus is surely on other people to tell you about their relatives, not the other way round. Which means Rob is in the wrong and I'm entitled to be angry with him. Relieved, I set off for the station determined to have a good time in spite of him.

The unscheduled pints mean I don't have enough money left for a train ticket, so buy two cans of cheap lager instead and lock myself in the toilet. The hour-long journey passes quickly, filled by warm alcohol and reading the graffiti scratched onto the toilet walls. Not knowing where any curry houses are in Leeds, and having no money anyway, I head straight for the venue and quickly sell Rob's ticket outside for its full value. With ten fresh pounds in my pocket, I sink a further five pints while the warm-up band does their stuff. The lights dim, the tension mounts, and with nine beers inside me, I'm ready to venture where only the bravest, hardiest and drunkest souls dare tread.

It's a curious thing, a mosh pit. If someone asked you to list the least pleasant places from which to enjoy live music, the gyrating armpit of an unwashed teenager, whose sweat stinks of stale lager and kebab meat, would probably be near the top. But once you're in, there's no other place to be. The opening bassline of 'Richard III' kicks in and we throb and move as one organism. Supergrass race through their set, classic followed by thumping classic, and we respond eagerly to each new wave of ear-shattering noise: sway forwards, sway backwards, sway left and right, overpowering anyone or anything that gets in our way. We bounce, we jostle, we sing and roar. I'm elbowed, kicked and coated in various liquids dispensed from my fellow moshers, including a sticky white streak across the back of my neck that I sincerely hope is saliva. I rub it off and wipe my hand on the person in front. It can't be anything worse than saliva, I tell myself; no one likes Supergrass *that* much.

And then, ninety minutes later, it's over. The doors open and the crisp evening air rushes in to do battle with the stench inside, and I follow the crowds towards what I hope is the station.

* * *

My head is still thumping the next day. Supergrass make a hell of noise, considering there are only three of them. But somewhere beyond the banging in my skull, I detect faint voices in the living room. One of them is Andy. He's been at home more often of late, finding time in his packed schedule to watch his beloved Manchester United assemble the luckiest haul of trophies in sporting history. It isn't football that has his attention today, though; it's yet another girl, who is being subjected to the tortured poet routine. This in unsurprising;

like most animals, he becomes more sexually active in the spring. What is a surprise, as I walk in to spoil his fun, is the latest target of his affection.

Cecilia.

'What are you doing here?' I ask my sister indignantly.

'Making an impromptu visit to spend some time with you, little brother,' she says, removing Andy's hand from her knee.

'You've come all the way up from London?'

'I was in York for a workshop,' she admits. 'I thought I'd pop in on the way back down.'

'Hmm,' I grunt, still half-asleep and fully hungover.

'Don't mind him, he's always like this when he wakes up,' Andy smarms, casually returning his hand to her knee with an over-familiar pat. I frown at the pair of them as she lets him keep it there.

'He's often like it for the whole day,' Cecilia adds. 'Especially when Plymouth have lost.'

'I'm making some tea,' I grumble, heading out of the room. If they're going to be rude about me, they can do it on their own.

'I'll help,' Andy says, leaping up and shoving me out of the living room.

'What's up with you,' I snap as we reach the kitchen. 'I can make tea on my own.'

'Chris, you've got to help me. I'm in love.'

'Who with?'

'Cecilia, of course! She's the most amazing woman I've ever met.' This is praise indeed; Andy has met a lot of women. Not all for very long, but still a lot.

'I'm not going to help you seduce my sister.'

'You don't have to help. All you have to do is disappear.'

I scowl at him. It isn't the thought of what he's planning to do, although that does make me a little squeamish. No, it's the

254

unfairness of it all. He's better-looking than me, but not by all that much. And medicine might be more impressive than geography, but he isn't any better at it than I am. Yet he has this unshakeable belief that all he needs to do to sleep with someone is meet them. I envy his confidence and curse, once again, the diffidence I was born with.

'Please Chris, I'll be forever in your debt. I'll do anything, name your price.'

'There is one thing you can do for me.'

'What?'

'Not sleep with my sister.'

'It may not come to that. I just want to spend some time with her. She's so intelligent and funny and ... and incredible.'

'Alright, whatever,' I sigh. Cecilia's big enough to make her own decisions. We head back to the living room where she's thumbing through a back issue of *Melody Maker*.

'Change of plan, sis,' I mumble. 'I'm a bit busy today, so Andy's going to look after you.'

'I thought we could start with a guided tour,' he says, quickly resuming his position as her personal limpet. 'Followed by a late lunch somewhere, there's some delightful places in the city.'

'A guided tour? Does Sheffield have a lot of must-see sights?' Cecilia asks.

'Well, there's the botanical gardens and ... what else is there, Chris?'

'There's the town hall,' I suggest. 'But I don't know if you're allowed inside. It's alright from the outside, I suppose.'

'Sheffield is more a place to be absorbed slowly,' continues Andy, the charm oozing from him like an oily discharge. 'And I'd be more than happy to be your chaperon.'

'That all sounds fascinating, but what I really want to see is this pub my little brother's always telling me about, the one owned by the drummer from Pulp.'

'Excellent idea, we could start in the Washington for a snifter,' enthuses Andy. 'And from there we could–'

'OK, stop right there, the pair of you,' Cecilia interrupts, removing his hand from her knee, more firmly this time. 'First things first: when you two are working on your next cunning plan, remember to shut the door. Sound travels and I heard every word. Secondly, you'll need to come up with a better excuse than Chris being busy. He's a third-year geography student with no hobbies; I've known him for twenty-one years and he has never once been busy.'

'But …' Andy is floundering, completely lost for words.

'Don't worry – Andy, isn't it? – you can use the afternoon to look up some more eighteenth century poems to pass off as your own. I'm sure it usually works wonders, but I did a master's in English at Oxford. I've written essays about several of the poems that you recited. And you, little brother, should be quicker to defend my honour in future,' Cecilia scolds, turning to me. 'Right, I need to freshen up before we go. Have you got a towel?'

'They're all on the radiator in my room.'

'Are any of them clean?'

'No, I don't wash them.'

'You don't wash your towels?'

'I only ever use them when I've had a shower, so they don't get dirty, do they? There's no point.'

'OK, I think I'll manage without. Go and get dressed, I'll wait outside.'

She grabs her bag and departs. Andy looks crestfallen.

'You never told me your sister did English,' he says, mournfully.

'You never asked,' I shrug. 'In fact, you've never asked me anything about my family. You're so self-obsessed, Andy.'

I go to find a cleanish T-shirt, feeling triumphant and relieved. For once, I'm not the biggest romantic failure in the house. Joint last, perhaps, but it's good to have some company there.

* * *

A miasma of smoke and stale beer greets us as we enter the pub, which is near-empty with the lunchtime rush over. Cecilia surveys the surroundings slowly; I sense disappointment. Fortunately, the CD player moves on to 'Show Girl' by the Auteurs, one of her favourites. She nods in approval, buys two pints of cider and joins me at our regular table.

'How are things with you and the Wonder Stuff fan?' I ask.

'Awful. He's the reason I'm here. We were supposed to stay on after the workshop – we booked a bed and breakfast in the Yorkshire Dales – but one of his bloody kids had a fight at school and he had to go back. I couldn't face a weekend on my own in London, so I came to see you.' She nudges me affectionately. 'Sorry, I should have called.'

'Doesn't matter. You were right, I'm not busy. Haven't been for weeks.'

'What happened to your two little girlfriends?'

'I don't want to talk about it,' I pout.

'Yes, you do.'

I do.

I tell her all about Lou and Jonathan and Grindleford, about Emma and Angus, about Lou and Mike and wasting fifty quid on a meal that didn't go anywhere. And, with a dramatic, heart-rending flourish, I finish by declaring how I feel lost, unsure of who I anymore and can she possibly help me work it all out. Please.

'You're such an idiot, Chrissy.'

'Thanks. That's exactly the kind of help I was looking for.'

'Isn't it obvious?'

'No. That's why I asked for help.'

'OK, let me spell it out. You have spent the last year chasing two girls. They both know about each other. The message they are receiving is that you'll take absolutely anyone who'll have you. Girls like to feel special, like we're the only ones you've ever cared about, not just the nearest one at hand.'

'I thought it was better to keep my options open, given how few I usually have.'

'You thought wrong,' she says, firmly. 'With this Lou, you should have ignored the mother – who's clearly got an inappropriate crush on the ex-boyfriend, by the way – and stayed to fight for her affections. With the folky one, you should have gone straight up to Scotland at Easter and ordered the accordion player to step aside. Instead, you told her you'd go to Africa and have another crack at your ex. It's not what a girl wants to hear.'

'So what do I do?'

'Be decisive. Think about what you want. *Who* you want. And make it clear to her, instead of dithering. Otherwise you'll be back in Devon this summer, working in Safeway and complaining to Matt about how there aren't any nice girls around. Be decisive'

'OK, I'll try. Thanks, sis.'

'If you want to thank me, you can buy me another pint.'

Relief washes over me. It all makes such simple sense now. I need to choose. I need to decide.

There's only one question left.

How do I do that?

28

Tied To The 90s

I've failed to come up with an answer by the time I'm back in the Washington. On my final day as a student, I wake to find Rob has shoved a note beneath my bedroom door, asking me to meet him here at lunchtime. He's at our table when I arrive, already on his third pint judging by the empties. And, I can't help noticing, wearing my pork pie hat.

'What can I say? I've grown to like it,' he beams as I point at his headwear. 'And it looks much better on me.'

'You owe me twenty quid.'

'You paid twenty quid for this?'

'No, I paid five, but it's a seller's market.'

'I'll think about it. But never mind that, I've got several bits of news to tell you. Get the beers in first, we'll need them.'

I return with our drinks and sit down. 'Come on, what's this big news?'

'You, my friend, are now drinking with the president of the University of Sheffield Climbing Club.'

'Hey, congrats! That's brilliant,' I say. 'When did you find out?'

'Last night. I won by twenty-nine votes to three. I was one of the three, it didn't seem right to vote for myself.'

'Very noble. Who were the other two?'

'Dunno, but when I find out, they're gonna be sorting through dirty kit for a year. Anyway, that's only part of the good news. The next bit is that I am staying in Sheffield to do a master's next year. And, having spoken to our landlord, he's fine for you to stay on too, as long as you don't tell anyone you're no longer a student, it causes problems with the university housing officers or something. So you don't have to go back to Devon. Andy's staying too, so it'll be the three of us. What d'you think?'

What do I think?

Our house is messy and mouldy, and freezing from October to April. Rob will be even busier with all things climbing-related now, and Andy only ever turns up for Man United matches or to try it on with my relatives. I've been bored stupid for weeks, and next year I won't even have three hours of lectures a week to break up the monotony. My only alternatives so far are backpacking with Chemical Joe, or heading back to Devon; I need money for the first and cannot contemplate the second. Yet my student loan and grant will both soon cease, and I have no job. Then there's my overdraft, which recently broke the two-grand mark ...

'Yeah, why not? Sounds great.'

I raise my pint in acknowledgement.

'Cool, that's settled then. Now for the best bit of news.' Rob reaches into his pocket and slaps down two tickets for the T in the Park festival.

'Isn't that the one where mad Scotsmen chuck piss over you for a weekend?' I ask nervously.

'It is indeed. But do you know who's headlining?'

'Nope.'

'Four Essex lads, talk like they're extras on *EastEnders* ...'

'No way. Blur?'

'Blur indeed. Your last big Britpop fish.'

'Ah, Rob, you're the best,' I can hardly believe my luck, but elation is short-lived. The fifty quid set aside for a festival has gone on a pointless and expensive French meal. 'When do you need paying back? I'm a bit short at the moment.'

'That's the best bit. Seth bought them for my birthday, but we broke up last week and he told me never to contact him again. If I can't contact him, I can't give them back, can I?'

'You two broke up?'

'Yeah. Well, I dumped him. You were right, he's a miserable little twat. And useless in bed, like a Dachshund going at a Mini Milk.'

'That's a lovely image, thanks. They must have cost him a lot, though. It doesn't seem right to just take them.'

'I thought you'd say that. Which is why I brought you this.' Rob hands over a thick, badly photocopied pamphlet. I read the headline on the front cover.

TIED TO THE 90S: THE BRITPOP FANS WHO CANT ACCEPT ITS OVER

Below is a photo of me in my Oasis T-shirt. The day we went to the Peak District. It has to be, it's the only time I met him. I didn't even notice him taking it.

I turn the page and read on.

Seth has basically typed up our whole argument from that day, but with extra waspishness and sarcasm. This is a hatchet job, which continues for page after page: ridiculing the bands I worship and listing the newcomers who will replace them, except in the minds of fools such as me who are too stupid to know better. The names are vaguely familiar: Gomez, Elbow, Doves. At least the Britpop tradition of short, one-word names lives on. I'm still reading when Rob brings over another round of drinks.

'What a cunt,' I spit.

'A cunt indeed.'

'Did you know he was writing this? It's issue three, apparently.'

'I knew he wrote a fanzine, but I didn't know he was doing a special edition on you.'

'It's even got my photo on the cover. People all over Sheffield will be reading this.'

'Not exactly. He only sold four copies, and two of those were to me.'

'It's not even well written,' I continue. 'I bet he doesn't know what half these words mean. We could write a better fanzine.'

Rob pauses halfway through lifting pint to beard-smothered lips. 'Why don't we? Not a fanzine, but we could start a website about the music scene in Sheffield.'

'Great idea. Except that I don't know how to make a website. And nor do you.'

'No, but Danny does, he's into all that geeky stuff. I'll ask him to do it. We can write about the bands we see, about the local music scene, all that shit.'

'You're serious? You and me as music journalists?'

'Yeah, why not? It's just words. With your – how did Seth describe it? – "naïve schoolboy enthusiasm", and my wit and sophistication, we'll definitely get some readers. More than four, anyway.'

'But music journalism is your ambition,' I say, trying to give myself time to think this through. Can I do this? Can I really put all those random thoughts down as actual words?

'No reason we can't both do it,' Rob says, warming to the idea visibly. 'The world will always need music writers. Anyway, you've been to loads more gigs than me recently, you're the expert these days.'

'You really think so?'

'Of course. You'll need to be a bit more judgemental, of course; you can't just like everything, no one wants to read that. But the potential's there, my friend. You were a Bon

Jovi-loving pup when I first met you, and now I need you to keep me up to date. I'd not even heard of Muse until you told me about them.'

'You're on,' I say. 'Let's do it.'

I go to the bar this time for two more pints and two celebratory shots of tequila. I slam mine down in relief: my career is finally sorted.

'Do you agree with Seth?' I ask. 'Is Britpop really over?'

Rob empties half his pint, then brings his glass down with an authoritative thud. '"Britpop" doesn't mean anything. It's a label, a name for a diverse collection of British guitar bands that happened to be popular at the same time. It was an easy way of making people identify with contemporary music, a trick the media have always used: punk, glam, grunge, Madchester. But while some of the bands of the Nineties may continue, whatever Britpop represented, especially the whole notion of "Cool Britannia", died when Noel had tea and cakes with Blair and his cronies. That was the point when the establishment stole it, packaged it and tried to sell us the very thing we created.'

I've always dismissed Rob's intellectual posturing as pretension. I was wrong; he is, like most people, just much cleverer than me.

'That's profound, mate. When did you come up with that?'

'I didn't. I read it in *NME* a few weeks back. Can't remember who wrote it, Stuart Maconie or someone. Passing other people's opinions off as your own is a key part of music journalism.'

'It still makes me sad, though,' I sigh. 'It was the soundtrack for our whole generation.'

'Bollocks,' replies Rob. 'What about Emma? She listens to folk music. Nor does Lou listen to Britpop, from what you've told me. Danny's into metal, he wouldn't know his Space

263

from his Supernaturals. Even Andy spends as much time listening to classical music as he does to Garbage. The only people who'll miss it are people like us, who like white, mostly male guitar bands. Anyway, even if they split up, we can still listen to their CDs. My dad's been listening to the Doors for thirty odd years now, and they're all dead. I think they are, anyway. I promise you, my friend, in twenty years' time, we'll be sitting together, drinking beer, listening to Pulp B-sides and slagging off Menswear. Now stop being so fucking morbid, it's the last day of term. Let's get drunk.'

We pass the afternoon reminiscing about the bands we've seen – the good, the bad and the average – the beers we've quaffed, the rocks he's climbed, the goals I've scored, and the girls and boys we've loved and lost. By six, Rob is too drunk to continue, those three early pints costing him dearly in the final reckoning. He sets off home, but I head in the other direction, through parks scented with the smoke from a hundred disposable barbecues, and towards the Student's Union for that final rite of student passage: the end-of-year Leavers' Ball.

* * *

I opt for a tactical piss before entering the congested dance floor. But even the toilets are rammed; I battle my way to the front, wait for a free urinal, and wriggle in carefully. I glance to either side to check my elbows are sufficiently tucked in and there won't be any awkward nudging. That pastel-blue shirt looks familiar, though …

Jonathan.

Five thousand students are here tonight, and I end up slashing next to him. I stare at the wall, desperate to get it over with as quickly as possible, but nothing happens. There are more than ten pints of fluid inside me; surely the pressure on my bladder should be doing something? Jonathan, of course, is gushing like a hosepipe; he can even piss better than me. We stand side by side, penises in hand.

There's no dignified way out; I have to say something.

'Hi, Jonathan.'

'Chris. How's the ankle?'

'Better, thanks. So, our last night as students, eh?'

He doesn't reply. It doesn't really need further comment, to be fair.

'Any plans for next year?' I ask, willing my bladder to stop messing about.

'I've got a job with the Labour Party. A junior position, to start with. You?'

'I'm staying in Sheffield. For now. I'm going to be a music journalist.'

'Right.' He's the first person I've told about my new career and he doesn't sound overly impressed. Which is annoying, as impressing people is the whole point of being a music journalist. Jonathan zips up while I give up, following him to sinks hidden beneath a carpet of soggy turquoise paper towels.

'Shall we get a beer? Just, y'know, to show there's no hard feelings?'

'There are. Plenty. You slept with my girlfriend.'

'Oh, right. I meant about my ankle, actually.' So he does know. That explains why he broke up with Lou. And broke my ankle. 'How did you know?'

'Gloria told me. Lou's mother. She rang me as soon as you left. She thought I had a right to know.'

This seems a very low act. Ratting on your own daughter? I didn't think mothers did that sort of thing. Mrs Banks really does have issues with infidelity. 'I guess that explains your tackle in Kenya.'

'No, that was an accident. You signed a form confirming it, remember?'

'True.' He's careful, making sure nothing can be pinned on him. Like a true politician: the Labour Party are lucky to have him. 'We didn't sleep together, if that helps,' I say as we barge our way out of the toilets.

'Not really. But it was a long time ago. Good luck with the music writing.'

He moves off through the crowd, and I head to the bar, needing one more beer to tap the urinary keg and free me up for an evening of bad dancing, excessive drinking and bidding farewell to my student days.

* * *

But by ten pm, I've had my fill of cheesy hits and greasy floors. When S Club 7 segue into B*Witched, it's time to call it a night. Before tackling Crookesmoor's legendary hills, I find a spot on the grass banks outside the Union and watch as lights flicker on across Sheffield. There are half a million people out there and, not counting students, I've met about four. Including a milkman. Will I meet more as a non-student? Or will the city lose its allure? I've already been here for three years. It seemed like an eternity at the start, an unending expanse of opportunity and hope, yet what do I have to show for it? An average degree, an extensive CD collection and a modest string of failed romances.

But it's my city now, and will be for another year at least. I'll have to let my parents know. I'll call them tomorrow. Maybe the day after, there's a risk I might not feel all that well tomorrow. I close my eyes, hoping it might stop my head from spinning, or at least slow the revolutions down.

'Hello, sweetie. I wondered if I might see you here.'

Emma walks towards me, trampling the flowerbeds as she comes, before flopping down with the grace of a new-born flamingo. She has glitter all over her face and the tightest top

I've ever seen her in; no flowery skirts or Bohemian knitwear tonight. I forgot how lovely she is.

How did I forget how lovely she is?

'God, I'm really drunk,' she giggles, toppling over on the grass.

'Try lying down, it helps.'

She shuffles herself next to me and we gaze at the sky together. Tonight must be a special night; every single star is shooting. They're definitely all moving.

'How's the play coming along?'

'We're performing at the Edinburgh Fringe this summer! Isn't that incredible? We've even got a title. "Heaven Knows I'm Miserable Now". Like the Smiths song. Rob thought of it.'

'Rob's been helping you?' A pang of jealousy shoots through me. 'Why didn't you ask me?'

'You weren't talking to me, remember, sweetie?'

'Oh yeah.' Damn you, silent treatment.

'You can still help if you like. We need someone to sell tickets. We've hired a flat in Leith and there's a room spare. You could come up for the whole summer if you like, see a bit of Scotland. What do you think?'

'What about Angus?'

'We broke up. It turns out he thought the open relationship agreement was hypothetical. He didn't take it very well when I told him about you. His mum told me never to call him again.'

Suddenly I'm sober. This new information needs urgent processing. Partly the superb news that Angus is the dick I've always taken him to be. But more importantly I have an invitation to spend the summer messing about at the Edinburgh Festival with actors and my playwright ex-girlfriend. This sounds like the ideal preparation for a career as a music journalist. I'm about to accept, but Emma is still jabbering away

'It's strange, isn't it? Angus and I were together for years and now he won't even speak to me. Don't you think it's odd how quickly we can go from sex to silence?'

I recall how crushed I was by that very transition in the first year, when Martina cast me aside so ruthlessly. OK, that was only one night (one hour, to be honest), while Angus and Emma were together for years, but Emma is the first person to share this view. Are we soulmates? I've heard about soulmates without ever knowing exactly what they are. But people who have the same ideas about sex must count, surely?

I roll onto one shoulder and treat Emma to my deepest most meaningful gaze. She giggles, then kisses me.

Then burps.

'I need to go back inside,' she says, sitting up. 'I'm supposed to be getting the next round in for the girls. I only came out to get some fresh air, then I saw you.'

'I'm sorry I didn't come round, after the party,' I blurt worried that she'll forget about inviting me to Scotland. 'I wanted to. But I didn't know what to say. Pathetic, isn't it?'

'Aye, a wee bit. But I didn't come to see you either. Rob said you were back with that Louise girl, then you weren't, and I wasn't sure what was going on.' She leans over to pick up one of the flyers for the night's event, which are living up to their name by fluttering all over campus. She writes on the back of one and hands it over.

'That's my mobile phone number. I finally cracked and bought one. Call me if you decide to come up to Scotland, I can meet you at the station. And enjoy your last night as a student, sweetie. It's a funny feeling, isn't it? Three years, and now it's all over.'

'The times they are a-changing,' I reply. It's one of her favourite songs.

'Aye. And it's nearly the end of the century. Just like Blur predicted,' she says.

I once told her it's in my top three Blur songs, and she's remembered. I'm touched. I'm even prepared to overlook the fact she got the title wrong. I fold up the paper and slip it into my pocket, then help her to her feet.

'You'll like Scotland, Chris. I promise. Maybe things will be a wee bit less confusing this time.'

I watch her walk slowly back towards the Student's Union, squashing another row of pansies as she goes. The fresh air is making me feel better.

'Who was that?'

I spin round to see Lou picking her way through the flowerbed, far more sure-footedly than Emma. 'Just someone on Rob's course.'

'She wouldn't be called Emma, would she?' Lou enquires, sitting down on the grass.

I considered telling a lie, but she always sees through them. 'Er, yeah, she might be.'

'She's very pretty. Are you two back together?'

'Not sure. We haven't spoken for months, but she just asked if I want to get back together this summer.' Did she? Or did she ask me to spend my summer working for her? 'I think she did. It's not always easy to tell what she means.'

'It looked like she's keen on you.' Lou shuffles herself next to me, then kicks my leg. 'Are you going to go?'

'I don't know,' I confess. 'It might be awkward, spending the summer with my ex. But what do I know? I'm clueless around females.'

She doesn't correct me.

'Speaking of exes, guess who I had a piss next to earlier?' I continue.

'Enlighten me.'

'Jonathan. He knew about our trip to Grindleford all along – and it was your mum who told him.'

'I know. We had a big fight about it.'

'Bit sneaky, isn't it? Your own mum grassing you up?'

'I told you, she has a thing about infidelity. I wasn't surprised,' Lou says, lying back on the grass. 'She likes you, though, even if she didn't approve of what happened. She blamed it all on me, not you.'

'I thought you might call me,' I say, after a pause. 'After we went for dinner.'

'I was concentrating on my exams. I wanted to get a place at Oxford. Which worked, because they've offered me one.'

'Congratulations,' I say, trying to sound genuine. Oxford isn't far from London, where Jonathan will be. Which makes it inevitable that they will–

'I've turned it down. I've accepted a place on a teacher training course in Sheffield. I think I simply needed to know that Oxford would accept me. Can you understand that?'

'Nope.'

She pulls her knees to her chest; the evening breeze is cool, even though it's June. I sit up to put my arm round her but decide against it. Without looking, she reaches behind her for my arm and pulls it over her shoulders.

'I'm going to be in Sheffield too,' I say. 'I'm staying on with Rob and Andy.'

'What are you going to do?'

'I'm going to be a music journalist.'

It's an incredible thing, the ability to mock someone without speaking, without moving so much as a finger. But after a year of spending time with Louise Banks, I know all the signs: the slight twitch in the muscles beneath her shoulders; the flicker at the corner of her mouth.

'A music journalist. Writing about Blur and Pulp and those hairy twins.'

'They're not twins, Noel's older. And not just them, up and coming bands as well, like Doves and Elbow and Gomez. It's Rob's idea, we're going to set up a website together.' I can feel her shoulders shaking beneath my arm. 'Why are you laughing?'

'I'm laughing, Christopher, at how ridiculously simple your life is. I have spent three years working exceptionally hard to get into Oxford, and spent the last three weeks agonising about what to do after they belatedly offer me a place. You, meanwhile, on your last day at university, decide to take up a hopelessly unrealistic career because your housemate suggests it. I can't decide if you're boyishly charming or emotionally immature.'

'I'm the first one,' I mumble. 'Boyishly charming.'

'I hope so, Chris. I really do,' Lou says, placing her head on my shoulder. 'Listen: if you decide not to go to Scotland, you can come and visit me. My mum's away on a cruise – definitely this time, I got a postcard from Corsica this morning – and I'm driving back home tomorrow. This is my mobile phone number.'

She reaches into her bag and takes out a neatly folded flyer for the Leavers' Ball, then writes her name and number on it.

'Call me when you've decided. I can pick you up at the station.'

'You don't trust me to find my way through a small village?'

'Not entirely,' she says, removing my arm gently and rising. 'And Chris? I won't make this offer again. So decide quickly.'

She leaves without another word, without so much as a glance back.

Cool. Very cool.

He's On The Phone

One shoe is still on when I wake; the other foot is sockless. I lift my head from the sofa cushion to reveal a large patch of drool. The clock on the video player blinks two forty-three. It's light outside, so it must be the afternoon. I have no idea when, or even how, I got home, but even trying to remember is painful. Slowly, carefully, I return my head to the moist cushion. Of all the headaches I've known in my short life, this is on a new level; it pounds furiously against all sides of my skull, threatening to break through and shatter it into a thousand sorry pieces.

But any hangover this bad must have a good night behind it. And the two pieces of paper, each with a phone number on, are evidence of that.

One from Lou, one from Emma.

Lou and Emma.

Emma and Lou.

I've spent three years at university trying to get girls to like me, and on my last night I manage it twice. Becoming a music journalist is already paying off. Nothing has been sealed yet, of course, but for once in my life the decision is mine to make.

Lou or Emma?

Emma or Lou?

Maybe Emma *and* Lou?

Hmm, probably too ambitious, that one.

One path offers a summer of actors, artists and luvvies in Edinburgh; theatre, culture, maybe some folk bands; lochs, whisky, mountains. And, at the centre of it all, Emma.

Wonderful, green-eyed, flowery-skirted Emma, with her love of words and impressive film collection. She's cute, kitschy, quirky; big-hearted, loving and kind.

Maybe too loving? She's already shown that monogamy isn't her thing; just because Angus is out of the way doesn't mean there won't be others.

The other path takes me to the Peak District, a summer of lazy walks, meals in country pubs, and a cosy house with a remarkable cheese collection. And Lou. Tall, slender, graceful Lou, with her long legs and short temper. The girl I longed for, waited for, fought for (kind of). Laughing with me one minute, scolding me the next. But with the ghosts of Jonathan and Mike never far away, and a drug problem that might resurface. Plus a concerted lack of interest in music, football or snooker. And possibly me. It's a love that is half-requited at best.

This isn't a decision to be made in my current state. Booze seeps from every pore and my breath tangs with the promise of vomit. Last night's excesses need expunging, one way or another. I haul myself upright and, once the room stops spinning sufficiently for me to locate the door, make my way up the stairs and to the bathroom.

Half an hour later, I emerge with an empty stomach and slightly clearer head, still exhausted but feeling infinitely better. I sit on the top stair and look once more at my two flyers. Normally I would ask someone to decide for me, but there's no sign of Rob or Andy. Besides, the days of letting other people dictate my life are over.

I'm twenty-one. I'm an adult. It's time to make decisions in a considered, thoughtful manner.

I carefully fold each into a plane and, ensuring exactly the same amount of force is applied to each – fairness is paramount – launch them down the stairs.

Shuffling carefully down each step, I stop by the first plane, four stairs up from the bottom. Beyond is the winner, which made it all the way to the hallway. I unfold it and read the name. I knew, deep down, who I wanted it to be. It seems that fate and amateur aerodynamics have backed me up. Which is a relief, as it means I don't have to reclimb the stairs and do it again.

I dial the number and wait for the voice. She picks up after three rings.

'Hello? Hi, it's Chris. I was just ringing to say hello. And to ask you about your invitation last night ...'

30

The Day We Caught The Train

She's waiting at the station, as promised. I wave as the train pulls lethargically into the platform. A few steps forward and she's right outside the carriage door.

We hug, then kiss awkwardly, each going for somewhere between the lips and a cheek, and end up bumping noses.

'How was the journey?'

'Oh, you know. I stared out the window mostly.'

We kiss again, less awkwardly this time.

'Welcome to Scotland.'

'Thanks. It's very hilly.'

'Aye, we do have a few wee hills. Come on, I'll show you round.'

Emma takes my hand and guides me skilfully through the maze of tourists on The Royal Mile. We make microscopic small talk – what I ate on the journey (two ham and pickle sandwiches, a Mars bar and a bag of roast beef Monster Munch), the old man who snored from Newcastle onwards, how rehearsals for her play are going – and Edinburgh castle looms ever closer as we walk.

'Do you want to go inside?' Emma asks.

The queue stretches halfway down the street.

'We can go another day,' I reply. 'Let's go to a pub instead.'

'OK, there's a good one on the Cowgate.'

It's even busier inside, but we manage to find a free seat in a window bay. Emma offers to go to the bar and I let her: in crowded pubs with overworked staff, it helps to be a pretty girl with large breasts. Soon enough, she returns with a pint for me and something with Coke for her. I wait for her to sit down before speaking.

'Emma, I'm going to try and make things work with Lou. I know you're fine with open relationships, and I would be too, but she won't be, trust me. So I don't think I can spend the summer here. I'm sorry. I came up to tell you face to face, it seemed like the right thing to do. I'm really sorry.'

Emma doesn't say anything, doesn't even react. I hope she heard; it took a four-hour train journey to build up the courage to say it, and I don't want to have to repeat it. The pub is noisy, but I'm certain it was loud enough. The couple next to us – American, if the size of their cameras is anything to go by – heard, judging by the sympathetic looks on their faces.

Eventually, Emma turns to look at me.

'Thank you, sweetie, I appreciate you telling me,' she says. 'How long are you going to stay?'

'I'm not sure. I bought a return, in case you wanted me to go back straight away.'

'I don't.'

'Good.'

I pick up a beermat and rip off one of the corners. The Americans' eyes flit between Emma and me. They look at her kindly; less so at me.

'Can I ask why?' Emma says.

I've been dreading this question more than any other. She is sweet and kind, and doesn't seem to find me annoying, like most people do. Or at least she hides it better. And she is so, so pretty. But Lou is just that little bit prettier. And I've wanted to be with Lou for longer, so it feels like more of an achievement. As justifications go, these are immature, pathetic and shallow. But if you've read this far, it should come as little surprise that I'm all those things.

'I looked into my heart, and searched my feelings, and I think that you and me, we connect more as friends, on an emotional level. I didn't want to risk losing that by basing things on the physical side of a relationship.'

Emma nods, slowly. 'That's bullshit, sweetie. But thank you for trying.'

She sips her drink through the straw. The American husband looks like he'll pummel me, if Emma only gives him the word. 'Does she know you're here?'

'Yeah, she does. She's OK with it.'

I try to fit the pieces back of the beermat back together on the window sill. This feels far worse than I thought it would.

'Was it her idea for you to come up and tell me?'

'It was, actually. She said I should do it in person.'

'I thought it didn't sound quite like you. You've got many qualities, sweetie, but courage isn't one of them.'

I'm desperate to ask what my many qualities are, but it doesn't seem like the right moment. The American lady looks like she wants to give Emma a big hug, and I almost hope she does, to save me from having to do it. I would welcome a hug myself.

'Why not stay for a couple of days?' Emma says, taking my hand. 'You said you've never been to Scotland, it'd be a shame not to see some of it. Once you've rung your wee girlfriend and checked it's alright, of course. There's loads of good music on in the pubs, I'll even show you the folkie ones. If you're still interested in folk music, and it wasn't just a ruse to sleep with me.'

'I am. It wasn't. Thank you, Emma.'

'So it's agreed. You have a wee holiday in Scotland, then I'll pack you off on the train back. Or I might take you to a pub in Leith Docks, tell them you're English and that you dumped me, and leave you there. I haven't decided yet.'

She squeezes my hand as she says it, though, which means it almost certainly won't happen.

'Why don't we go up to the castle and watch the sun set?' I suggest. 'You said it's a beautiful view from up there.'

'Aye, why not? But the view's better from Calton Hill.'

I last about an hour before hunger and boredom overpower me. I had literally no idea that the sun takes so long to set in Scotland. It's still loitering at ten pm. When my gurgles become too loud to hide anymore, Emma takes pity on me, even though I don't deserve it.

'Come on, I'll take you to the chippie,' she laughs.

'Can I have a deep-fried Mars Bar?'

'No, don't be such a tourist. I'll treat you to a macaroni pie, though.'

'A macaroni pie? That sounds disgusting.'

'They're delicious. Wait until you try one.'

With a flash of her fake green eyes which, despite everything, are still twinkling, Emma leads the way.

She's taken it pretty well. Much better than I would have done.

31

Come Back To What You Know

Lou doesn't wave or walk towards my door as the train pulls in, but remains on the platform bench. I go and sit next to her.

'How are you?' she asks.

'Fine, thanks. It's good to see you.'

'You saw me four days ago.'

'That's true. It's good anyway.'

We kiss briefly, then she moves ever-so-slightly away, arms folded.

'And? How did she take it?'

'Emma? She was fine about it. She even bought me dinner afterwards. Have you ever had a macaroni pie? They're delicious.'

'I can't say I have.'

'You should try it, loads of pasta and cheese and really thick– actually, it wasn't that delicious.' Lou's expression suggests that she doesn't need to know any more about my brief trip across the border.

'Is that all you've brought with you?' she asks, nodding at my small rucksack.

'Yeah, for now. I wasn't sure how long I'll be staying this time. I won't be certain of anything until I've been in every room to check your mum's not hiding somewhere.'

A smile finally cracks her face. 'Come on, let's go.'

We walk towards the village, hand in hand; she's not hiding me away in the car this time. But as we reach the turning to her former farmhouse, she slows to a halt.

'Chris, I have to ask, and I know it's hypocritical after Mike and everything, but ... did you sleep with her?'

'With Emma? Yeah, of course. Only a few times, though.'

She closes her eyes and sighs. 'Well, it's my fault I suppose. I knew it was a risk sending you up there.'

'What, in Scotland? No, we didn't have sex there, I meant in total.'

'Thank God.' Her shoulders drop about a foot, before that familiar mix of amusement and contempt reappears. 'You two only slept together a few times?'

'Um, yeah. Pretty much.'

'Weren't you together for months?'

'Yeah, but we did a lot of talking. Not talking: communicating. That's so much more important in a relationship than the physical side, don't you think?'

'No, I fucking don't. I expect us to be having sex several times a day. For the first few weeks at least. Was that her decision or yours?'

'Hers mostly.' I don't tell her about Angus. Admitting to being the odd one out in a love triangle isn't the alpha-male image I want to portray, not when we are – hopefully, finally – about to have sex. The increasing imminence of which has taken hold of my tongue once again.

We reach her house and I follow her into the kitchen. There is no sign of her snitching mother. Lou leans against the huge wooden table but I hesitate before joining her, then opt for the sink instead.

'Can I get some water?' I ask, trying to justify my move.

'Of course.'

I pour a glass and down it. Then pour another one.

'So, here we are. Just the two of us,' Lou says, twisting her hair and tilting her head to one side. Two obvious signs of flirting, straight out of my magazine top ten. 'There's no one around to distract us.'

'Uh-huh.'

'We can do whatever we want …'

This is the moment I've been waiting three long years for. She's the most stunning woman I've met, and I'm alone with her – and this time there's nothing to stop us. No disapproving mothers, no overbearing ex-boyfriends, no bare-footed, coffee-obsessed love rivals. There's nothing to stop me from unleashing the torrent of lust and adoration that has tormented me, day after day and night after night.

This is my moment.

My time.

So why am I still clutching hold of the sink like it's the last lifeboat on the Titanic?

'Should I kiss you?' I splutter, my knuckles white with the force of the grip.

'That would be nice.'

I prise my fingers from the porcelain and walk over. I put one hand softly behind her head, just like Emma taught me all those months ago, and kiss her firmly. Which seems to do the trick; things escalate swiftly into the reckless, fervent embrace I've been hoping for. Lou hoists herself onto the table and I lean over her, supporting her head as I ease her backwards. Reaching past her, I shove a neat stack of *Homes & Garden* onto the floor, then stretch a little further to push the large vase of flowers out of harm's way. Once the table top is clear, I try to climb onto her, but the table is a bit too high, especially with her on it, so I drag a chair round with my foot to get a leg-up and–

'No, I'm sorry, Chris, stop, stop, stop.'

'You have *got* to be kidding me. Seriously?'

'I'm so sorry, but not here,' she giggles. 'This is where Granny and Pops have Christmas dinner every year. I simply can't, not here, it wouldn't be right.'

'OK,' I say, backing off. 'Let's go upstairs.'

I take her hand and lead her to the kitchen door. But now fresh worries bubble up. Am I supposed to haul her urgently up to the bedroom, overcome with passion? Or should I be slow and sensual, allowing the tension to simmer up to boiling point? I'm unsure what I'm expected to do.

So I dawdle. I dawdle her to the bedroom. It's a new low in my sexual history.

'Are you OK?' she asks.

'Yes, I'm fine.'

'Because if you're not in a rush, can I tidy up the magazines? It was a very passionate gesture, but I can't bear the thought of them all over the floor.'

'I'll help,' I sigh dejectedly. We return to the kitchen and gather up the offending periodicals. Lou also takes the opportunity to rearrange the flowers in the vase.

'Tidying up as foreplay,' I say. 'I bet you've never had it so good.'

'Seduction at its finest, Christopher,' she says. Then puts her arms around me and hugs me.

'Shall we go for a walk or something?' I suggest. 'The moment's kind of passed, I'm guessing.'

'No. I've not had sex for nearly a year, let's get this over with, mister,' she says, leading the way this time. 'Meant in the nicest possible way, of course.'

I stop in the kitchen, chewing over what she's just said. 'So you and Mike never—'

'No, we didn't. God, is that still important to you?'

'Not really,' I lie.

'Good. Now get upstairs and take your clothes off.'

Surprisingly, the tidying up removed much of my awkwardness. I'm not recommending it as a fool-proof technique for all occasions, but on this one it does the trick. We go to her room and undress quickly before sliding under the duvet. The first go is a little inelegant, and over a bit too quickly. The second time takes a bit longer as I force myself to drag it out, even if it requires a bit of acting on my part. After that, everything clicks into place. During the course of the night, we do everything I've ever wanted to do, plus a few things I didn't even know about (despite all those years of studying 'Position of the Fortnight' in *More!*). By the time the morning light seeps in, I'm exhausted and almost relieved when she finally rolls off me.

'Wow.' Lou lies next to me, very red in the face.

'Was that OK?'

'Very OK. Three in a row. I've never had that before.'

'Three? All real ones?'

'Uh-huh.'

'And you've never had that before? Not even with–?'

'No.'

This is fantastic news. When it comes to sex, I've always assumed that my enthusiasm and energy just about compensate for the lack of any real talent. A bit like Menswear. If I can work out exactly what I've done right, I'll be fine in the future. Lou steps out of the bed and pulls on my discarded T-shirt.

'I need a drink. Do you want something?'

'Tea would be nice.'

'Tea. Of course.' She grins at me again – she's very smiley at the moment – and heads downstairs.

I take the opportunity to check out her room. There's a book about child wizards by her bed, but the rest are neatly stacked on shelves, each one exactly the same distance in from the edge; I don't even need to check if they are in alphabetical order. One wall is covered with pictures of her and various friends. I scan them quickly to check that there are none of Jonathan, but he's been erased. Opposite are framed certificates celebrating musical and sporting achievements, some arty photos of birds and, high above the door, a sepia-tinged poster of Leonard Cohen. He stares down at me, moody and disapproving, his image jarring with the rest of the room, out of place among the neatness and order.

Why is he here?

I don't remember Lou ever mentioning that she listens to him. Why did she put a poster of him up in her room? I'm not overly familiar with his work, but it isn't much like dance music or Robbie Williams, from what I heard when listening to ...

Jonathan.

At the start of the year he told me Leonard Cohen is one of his favourite artists.

He lent me Leonard Cohen CDs in Mombasa.

Of course it was Jonathan. His presence lingers in her bedroom like the ghost of ... of ... of her better-looking, cleverer ex-boyfriend.

Lou's footsteps beat out on the wooden staircase and I reposition myself to be staring disconsolately out of the window when she enters.

'What's up with you?'

'Nothing,' I sigh.

'Then pour the tea, I need to go to the bathroom.'

'I didn't know you liked Leonard Cohen,' I bark as she's halfway towards the door.

'I don't, not especially.'

'You've got a poster of him on your wall. I guess I know why.'

'Chris, I have no idea what you're talking about. Either start making sense or shut up.'

'Don't you think it's a bit out of order, having a poster from Jonathan still on your wall?'

She fixes me with a stare; even now, there are new ones coming out of her repertoire. 'That was a present from Daddy I've had it for about ten years. I don't much like it, but I keep it up there because he gave it to me. Mummy doesn't want any photos of him in the house. And Jonathan only started listening to Leonard Cohen on Daddy's recommendation last summer. They were chatting about music and Daddy lent him a CD. That's all there is to it.'

'Oh. Well, I didn't know that.'

'Why would you? But that's not the point. Jonathan and I were together for over two years. You need to accept that and move on. I'm not sure I can tiptoe around your feelings for the whole summer.'

She doesn't look like she's willing to tiptoe at all, let alone for a whole summer.

'I'll try,' I reply, trying to strike a balance between sounding bruised and not caring.

'Good. Now eat your toast before it goes cold.'

We eat our toast and I drain the teapot, then Lou has a shower. I wait until she's downstairs, then hunt down a towel to do the same. After two years of washing under the feeble trickle emitted by the useless, rusting contraption in my student house, I luxuriate in the steaming jets. As the water blasts down, the tensions and stresses of the last few months float away down the drain. Lou's right; I need to forget about Jonathan and focus on my many reasons to be cheerful.

Lou Banks is my girlfriend. I'm a music journalist. Jonathan is just a wannabe politician. And music is much cooler than politics, which is why Blair and his cronies were so keen to latch onto it, not the other way around. You never see musicians trying to be political.

Apart from Billy Bragg, of course.

And Chumbawamba.

The Levellers, too.

And Bob Dylan of course, although that's going back a bit. Punk was quite political too, I suppose. And the Manics can be very opinionated when they want to be.

OK, so there *is* a bit of crossover both ways, but the point is still valid; I have a much more exciting career ahead of me. Refreshed and revived, I head downstairs, hoping that the toast was merely the first course of breakfast. But Lou is by the door, putting on her jacket.

'Where are you going?' I ask.

'Meadowhall. I'm meeting Maria to do some shopping.'

'But it's our first proper day together. As a couple.' I try not to sound too dejected, but it's hard.

'Don't be silly, we've been dancing around each other all year, Chris. I've already said I'll meet her.'

'Shall I come?'

'No, you need to start working on articles for your website, if you're going to be a proper journalist. Make the most of the peace and quiet. And don't break anything or go into Mummy's room.'

She kisses me and leaves. I wait to hear the car pull away, then make myself some coffee before going back upstairs to explore Lou's mum's room.

* * *

Leonard Cohen was the first sign. My assumption, her reaction, my reaction to her reaction.

Her choosing to spend our first (official) day together shopping was another.

And there are several more over the next few days. We never talk, not properly. Emma was right; talking *is* important. Not as important as she thinks, perhaps; there's no need to analyse every last feeling to within an inch of its life. But Lou and I rarely talk about anything. There's occasional chatter about people we both know from Sheffield; the odd aside about what's on TV; a brief discussion about what we're having for dinner. But mostly we live independent lives in the same house. We don't get any closer, just eat together and have sex (which gets even more imaginative after I find Lou's mum's collection of soft-core books on the subject).

It's not her fault, not all of it. I get on her nerves, don't give her enough space. Then when she does want us to hang out, I'm not always keen. I still get things badly wrong, like the night she tells me we're going to meet her friends in the pub, but I've already planned to watch the England game (an important European Championships qualifier, away in Bulgaria). She demands to know which is more important, her or football. I say her, of course I do, but I pause before answering. Apparently you're not supposed to pause.

It's the T-shirt that strikes the decisive blow, though. Or rather, my belated and ungrateful response to the T-shirt that Lou kindly buys for me. I'm not sure exactly how long you can leave a 'thank you' before it stops sounding genuine, but two hours is definitely the wrong side of the cut-off.

'Take it back if you don't like it,' Lou says, not looking up from her book.

'I didn't say I didn't like it.'

'You didn't need to.' She's sitting in the armchair next to the conservatory, the furthest seat away from me on the sofa.

'I like it, honestly. It's just a Beautiful South T-shirt isn't really something I can wear at T in the Park.'

'They're on the line-up. I checked.'

288

She's right, they are. Third on the bill, after Blur and the Stereophonics. I like the Beautiful South, and I know she's made a real effort to find out who's playing without me knowing. That's part of the problem; I have no good reason to be annoyed, and any attempt to explain it makes me sound ungrateful and petty. Both of which I am.

'It's just …'

'It's just what, Chris? Explain it to me,' she snaps, finally looking up from her book.

It's just that I told you that this festival is all about Blur. I told you so many times. I even went back to Sheffield and got the pin board to show you.

It's just that I can't take myself seriously as a music writer in a Beautiful South T-shirt, because no one else will.

It's just that Emma would never make that mistake. She would know, instinctively, which T-shirt to get me. Not necessarily Blur; she'd have picked out a band she thought I might like, a folky one I don't know. She would have asked me afterwards how they were, and listened to the answer, however long and rambling it was.

'It's a bit small, that's all. I prefer my T-shirts looser.'

It's the best I can come up with.

'Leave it here, I'll change it for a bigger one.'

'Thanks.'

'And I'll change it for another band. Blur, is that the right one?'

It is. But it's already too late.

I leave the next day.

She doesn't seem too upset about it.

32

If…

We sit in a pub just outside Waverley station.

'You're absolutely sure about this?'

'I am.'

'Because sometimes, Chris, you spend ages thinking about something, and still make the wrong decision. And this is potentially the biggest decision of your life.'

'I've thought about it. A lot. It's the right thing to do.'

I'm halfway through my pint, but Rob has barely touched his. 'I dunno, Chris. I want to agree with you, but you've wanted this for three years. It's all you've talked about for most of them. And you're going give up on it, just like that?'

'My mind is made up.'

'I'm not going to try and change it, then.'

We clink glasses. Still he doesn't drink, though. I've rarely seen him this troubled.

'But it's *Blur*, Chris. Fucking Blur. Headlining the Saturday night of a festival. Your last big fish, the hole in the middle of your pin board. This might be the last concert they ever play, if those rumours are true.'

'This is more important,' I say, as bravely as I can.

'Really? There's thousands of girls out there, but there's only one Blur. And you're going to miss them to watch a fucking play?'

'It's not just any play, it's Emma's play.'

'Go tomorrow. Go next week. They're performing it all summer.'

'No, I want to be there for her opening night.'

Even as I say it, I'm wavering. Surely going tomorrow would still count as a romantic gesture? I could pretend I got the dates wrong, that I thought they were starting a day later.

No: it has to be tonight. The sacrifice is part of it, and I'll make damn sure she realises I've missed Blur for her.

'Well, Chris, I'm proud of you. My little hick mate from the country is finally growing up.'

'Thanks mate. And I'm sorry to waste the ticket.'

'It's not wasted. I've already called Andy, he's picking me up here. I knew you wouldn't change your mind, you daft twat. Still, it's your loss. In a few hours, Andy and I will be getting high in a field together while you're watching some atrocious student play about angels.'

'She's worth it.'

'Yeah, maybe. I just hope you're not too late. What if she's already fucking her leading man?'

This thought has crossed my mind. I don't deserve a second chance with Emma, and the whole gamble is heavily reliant on her being exceedingly forgiving and/or forgetful. That's why I'm planning to buy some flowers, just in case. Something posh, like roses.

'She's not like that.'

'No, you're right. Except when she was cheating on her boyfriend with you. But I'm sure that was a one-off.'

'Will you tell me what they're like?' I beg, panicking suddenly with the enormity of it all, of what I'm going to miss. Blur, I mean. I need all the details, not just the running order. Make sure you tell me everything.'

'I'm not going to watch Blur,' Rob says, draining the rest of his pint. 'I'm going to see Mogwai in the King Tut's tent. They're a much more interesting band than Blur, far more experimental. Now drink up, we've got time for a couple more before Andy gets here. Your round.'

Questions for reading groups

1. In the story, Chris manages to sleep with two girls who are far too good for him. Have you ever punched above your weight? How did you achieve it? How did it make you feel?

2. Many people think *Definitely Maybe* is the best Britpop album ever, while others say *Different Class* or *Parklife* or *Urban Hymns*. They are wrong, of course; the right answer is *The Sun Is Often Out*. Why do you think so many people are misguided in this matter? What role does the media play in leading us to incorrect conclusions?

3. This book contains several references to masturbation. Which other classic texts do you think might have been improved with a few jokes on this theme? *Jane Eyre*? *Hard Times*?

4. Who had the stupidest haircut in the Britpop era? Who wore the daftest clothes? Try to think beyond Nicky Wire when answering.

5. Do you know anyone who likes Bon Jovi? Do you think it is acceptable to like Bon Jovi? What do you think liking Bon Jovi says about a person?

Artwork
Cover design by Cybermouse MultiMedia (www.cybermouse-multimedia.com).

Acknowledgements

Thanks to everyone who helped with this book, especially Penny, Mark, Gordon, Hannah, Mike, Paul, Clara and Ailis, and AJ for sharing his knowledge of 90s music. Special thanks to Bill Allerton of Cybermouse Multimedia for his editorial inputs and insights.

Thanks to the Twitter Britpop community for their support, especially: @BritsPieces, @Chantal_Patton, @ComoCollective, @DedeArneaux, @dinkyanna, @grass_greener, @Is_Dave_there, @jeremypopscene, @Kelly__Wood, @losingmyedge79, @official_RobH, @quiveen, @SteHolywell, @stuiekerr, @TalesFromITDept, @TheHixmeister, @thetweetofpaul, @wh1974, @wolvesmarc.

About the author
Tim Woods is one of the many writers living in Berlin. *Love In The Time Of Britpop* is his first novel. He supports Liverpool, Swindon Town, Lewes and Hannover 96, and drinks a lot of coffee. You can follow him on Twitter: @tim_woods77

You can read more of his writing, about music, mountains, the songs featured in this book and more, at:
https://timiswritingabout.wordpress.com

Lightning Source UK Ltd.
Milton Keynes UK
UKHW020816100321
380099UK00015B/1593

9 781789 267693